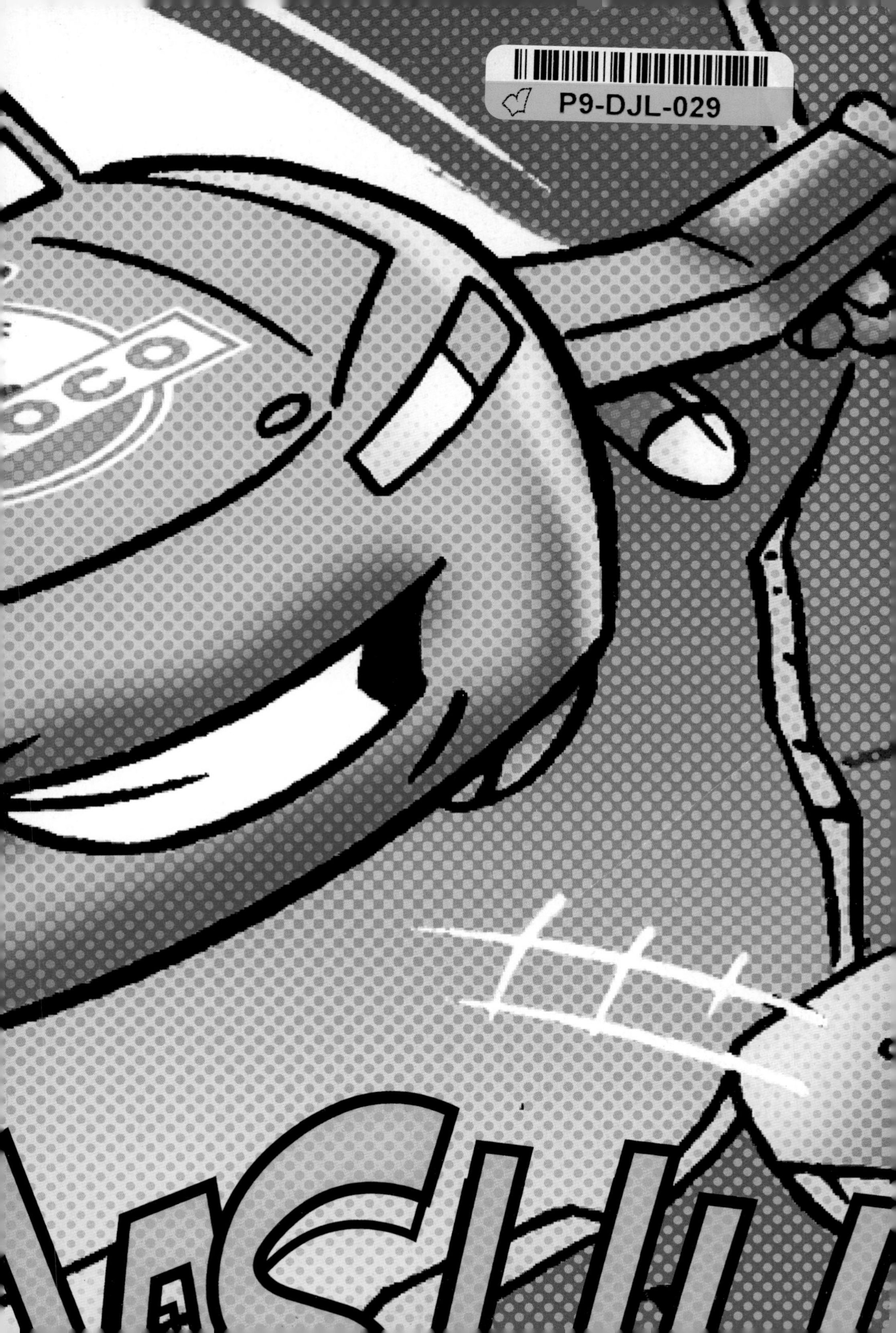

Radiator Springs

BOOM Kids!

ROSS RICHIE
chief executive officer

MARK WAID
editor-in-chief

ADAM FORTIER
vice president,
publishing

CHIP MOSHER
marketing director

MATT GAGNON
managing editor

JENNY CHRISTOPHER
sales director

WRITTEN BY:
ART & COLORS BY:

LETTERS:
COVER ARTIST:

DESIGNER:
EDITOR:

FIRST EDITION: NOVEMBER 2009

10 9 8 7 6 5 4 3 2 1
PRINTED BY WORLD COLOR PRESS, INC.,
ST-ROMUALD, QC., CANADA.

CARS – published by BOOM Kids!, a division of Boom Entertainment, Inc. All contents © 2009 Disney/Pixar, not including underlying vehicles owned by third parties; Dodge is a trademark of DaimlerChrysler Corporation; Plymouth Superbird is a trademark of Daimler-Chrysler Corporation; Petty marks used by permission of Petty Marketing LLC; Mack is a registered trademark of Mack Trucks, Inc.; Mazda Miata is a registered trademark of Mazda Motor Corporation; Cadillac Coupe de Ville is a registered trademark of General Motors. BOOM Kids! and the BOOM Kids! logo are trademarks of Boom Entertainment, Inc., registered in various countries and categories. All rights reserved.

Office of publication: 6310 San Vicente Blvd Ste 404, Los Angeles, CA 90048-5457.

A catalog record for this book is available from the Library of Congress and on our website at www.boom-kids.com on the Librarian Resource Page.

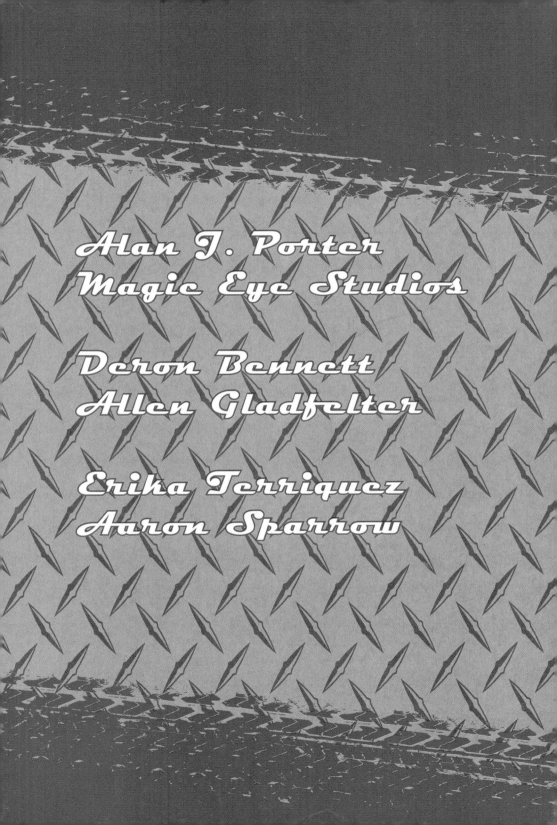

Alan J. Porter
Magic Eye Studios

Deron Bennett
Allen Gladfelter

Erika Terriquez
Aaron Sparrow

Chapter One

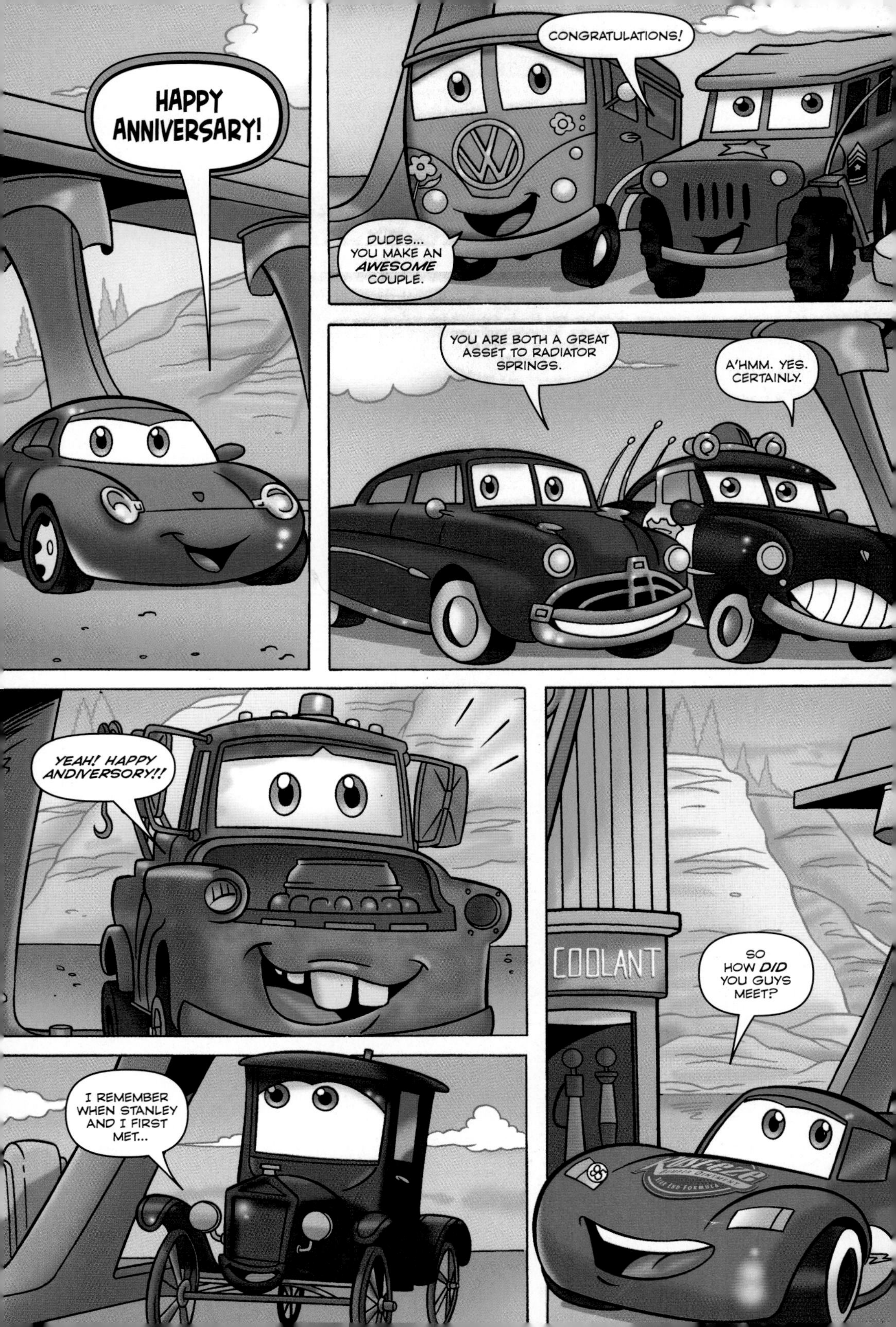
HAPPY ANNIVERSARY!
CONGRATULATIONS!
DUDES... YOU MAKE AN *AWESOME* COUPLE.
YOU ARE BOTH A GREAT ASSET TO RADIATOR SPRINGS.
A'HMM. YES. CERTAINLY.
YEAH! HAPPY ANDIVERSORY!!
COOLANT
SO HOW *DID* YOU GUYS MEET?
I REMEMBER WHEN STANLEY AND I FIRST MET...

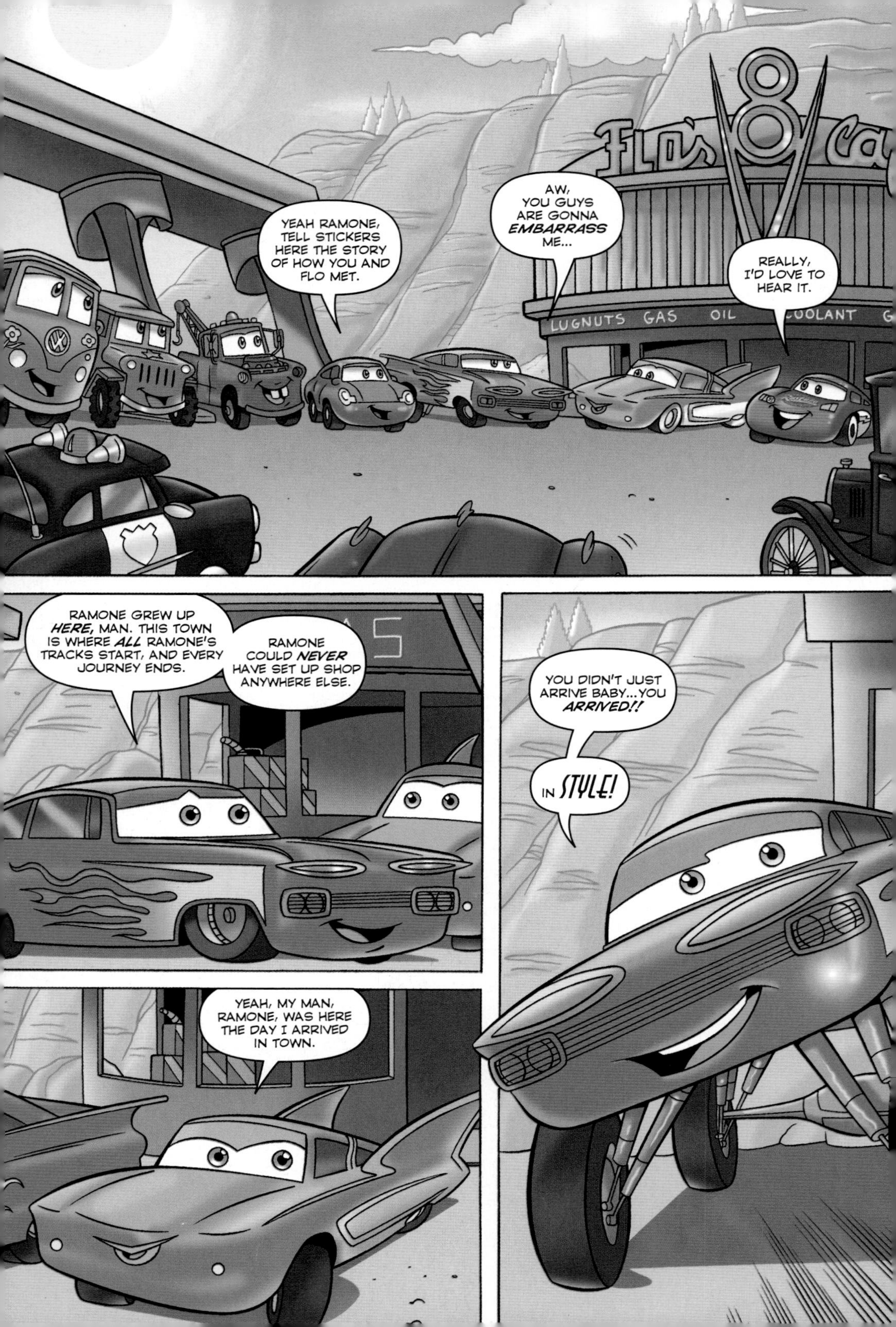
Flo's V8 Café
YEAH RAMONE, TELL STICKERS HERE THE STORY OF HOW YOU AND FLO MET.
AW, YOU GUYS ARE GONNA EMBARRASS ME...
REALLY, I'D LOVE TO HEAR IT.
LUGNUTS GAS OIL COOLANT
RAMONE GREW UP HERE, MAN. THIS TOWN IS WHERE ALL RAMONE'S TRACKS START, AND EVERY JOURNEY ENDS.
RAMONE COULD NEVER HAVE SET UP SHOP ANYWHERE ELSE.
YEAH, MY MAN, RAMONE, WAS HERE THE DAY I ARRIVED IN TOWN.
YOU DIDN'T JUST ARRIVE BABY...YOU ARRIVED!!
IN STYLE!

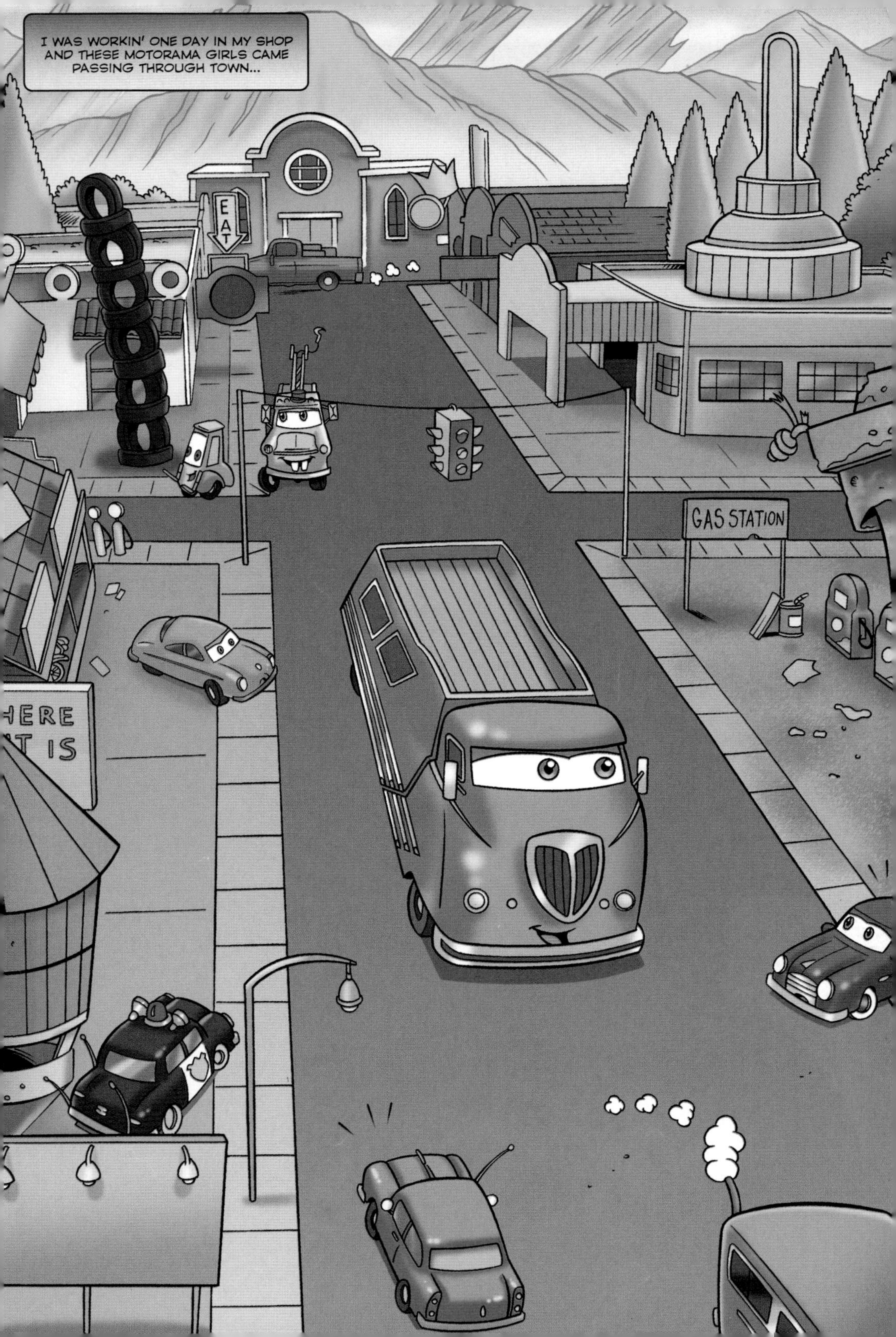
I WAS WORKIN' ONE DAY IN MY SHOP AND THESE MOTORAMA GIRLS CAME PASSING THROUGH TOWN...
EAT
GAS STATION
HERE
IT IS

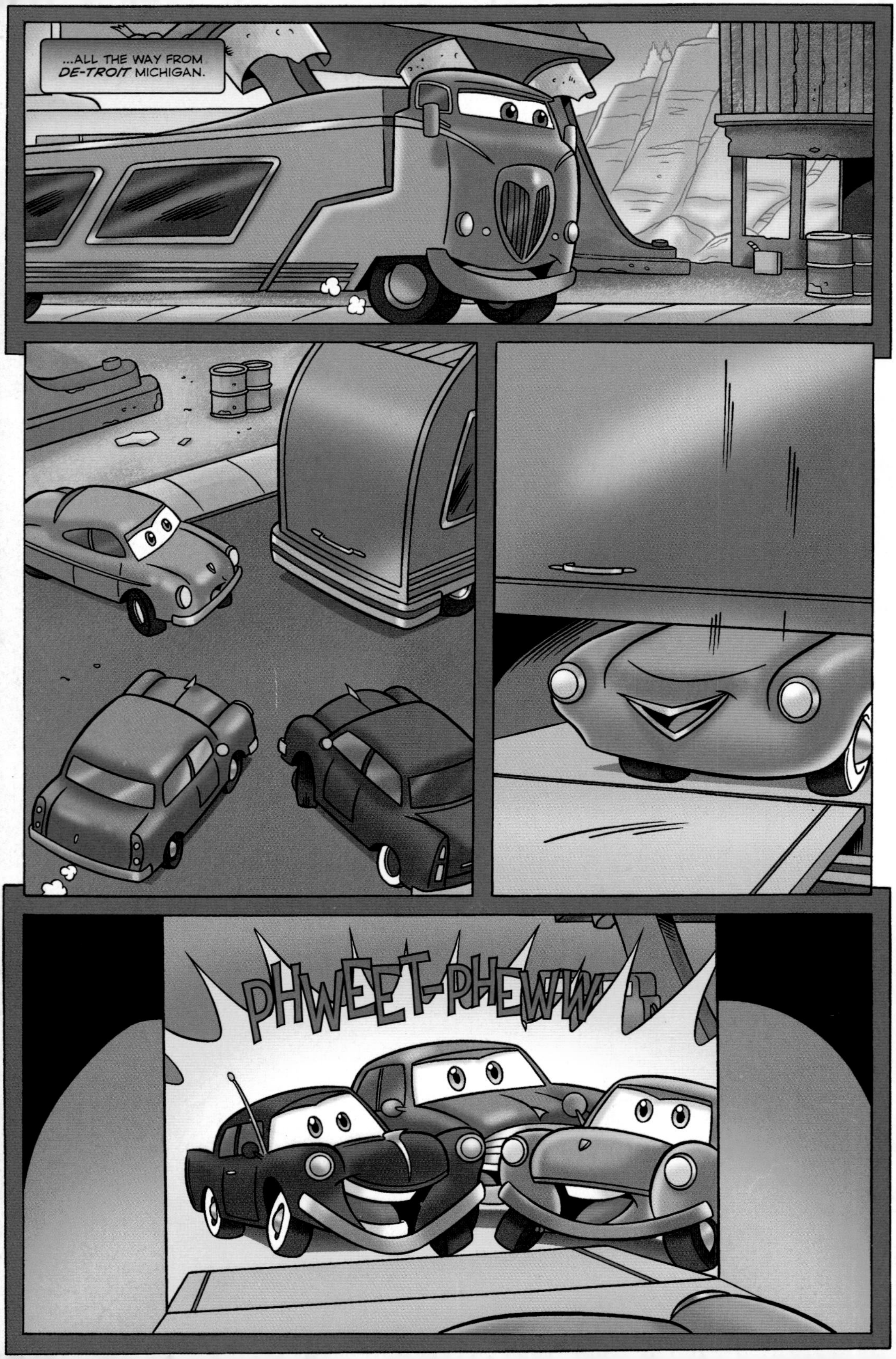
...ALL THE WAY FROM DE-TROIT MICHIGAN.
PHWEET-PHEWWW

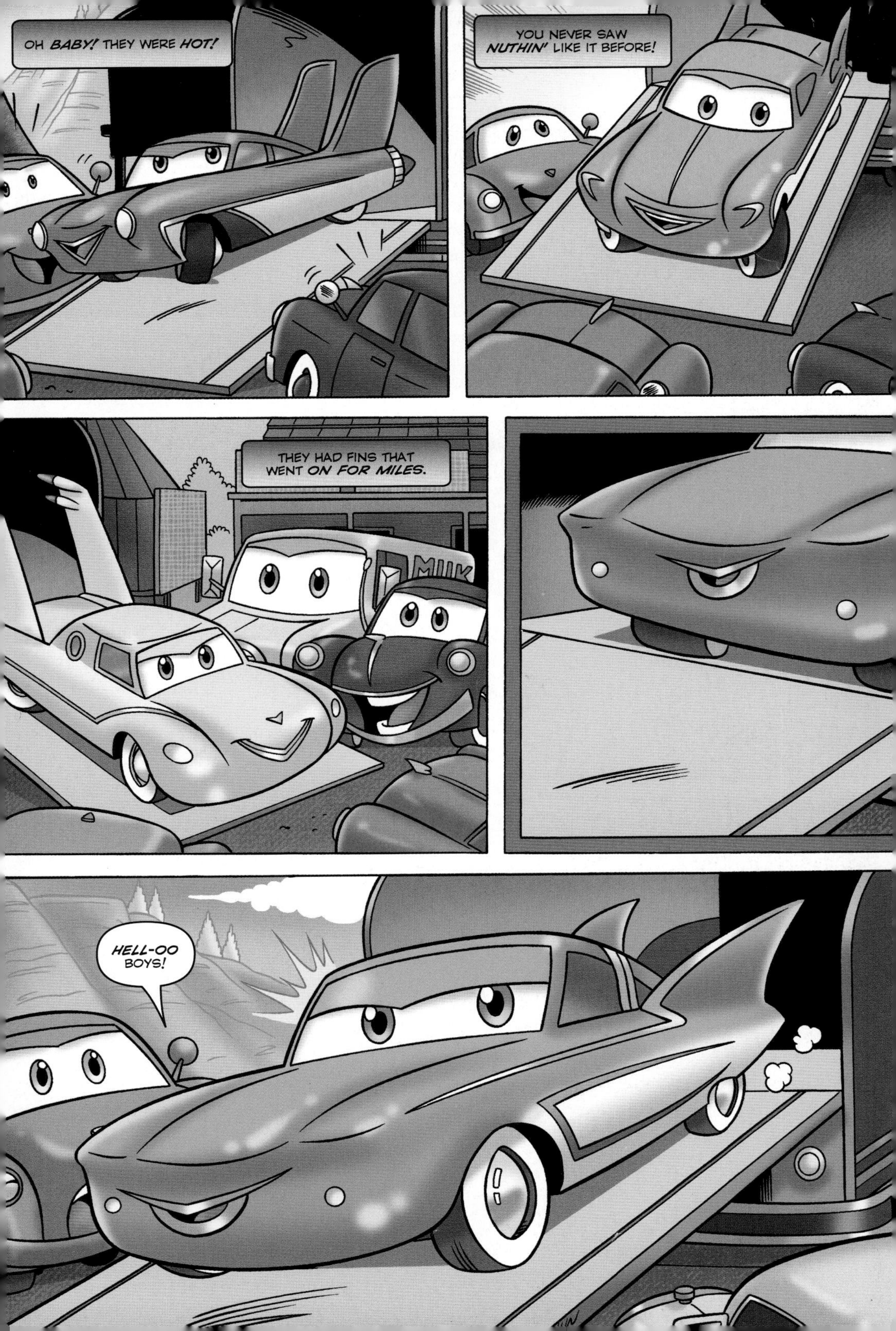
OH *BABY!* THEY WERE *HOT!*
YOU NEVER SAW *NUTHIN'* LIKE IT BEFORE!
THEY HAD FINS THAT WENT *ON FOR MILES.*
HELL-OO BOYS!

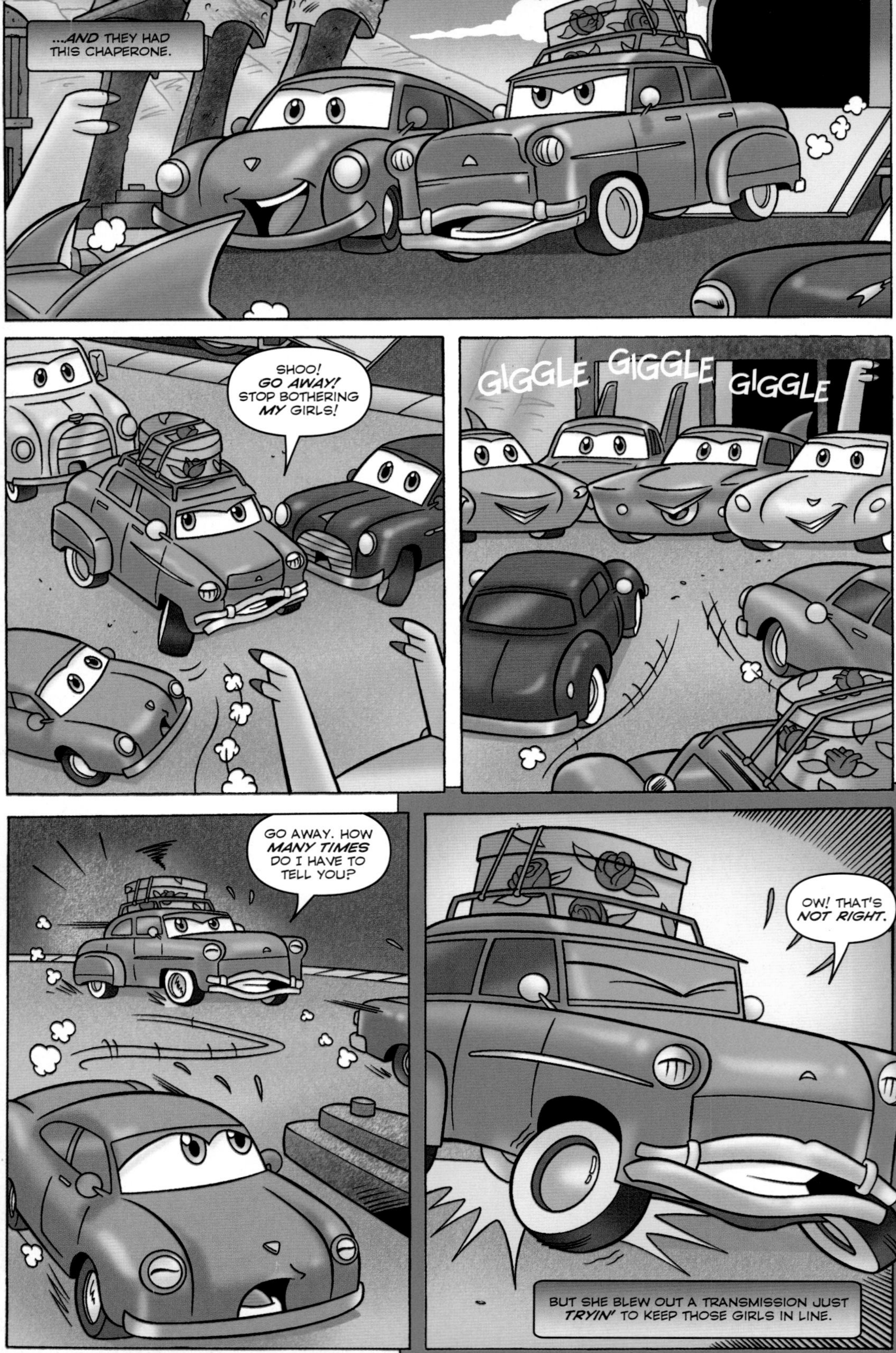
...AND THEY HAD THIS CHAPERONE.
SHOO! GO AWAY! STOP BOTHERING MY GIRLS!
GIGGLE GIGGLE GIGGLE
GO AWAY. HOW MANY TIMES DO I HAVE TO TELL YOU?
OW! THAT'S NOT RIGHT.
BUT SHE BLEW OUT A TRANSMISSION JUST TRYIN' TO KEEP THOSE GIRLS IN LINE.

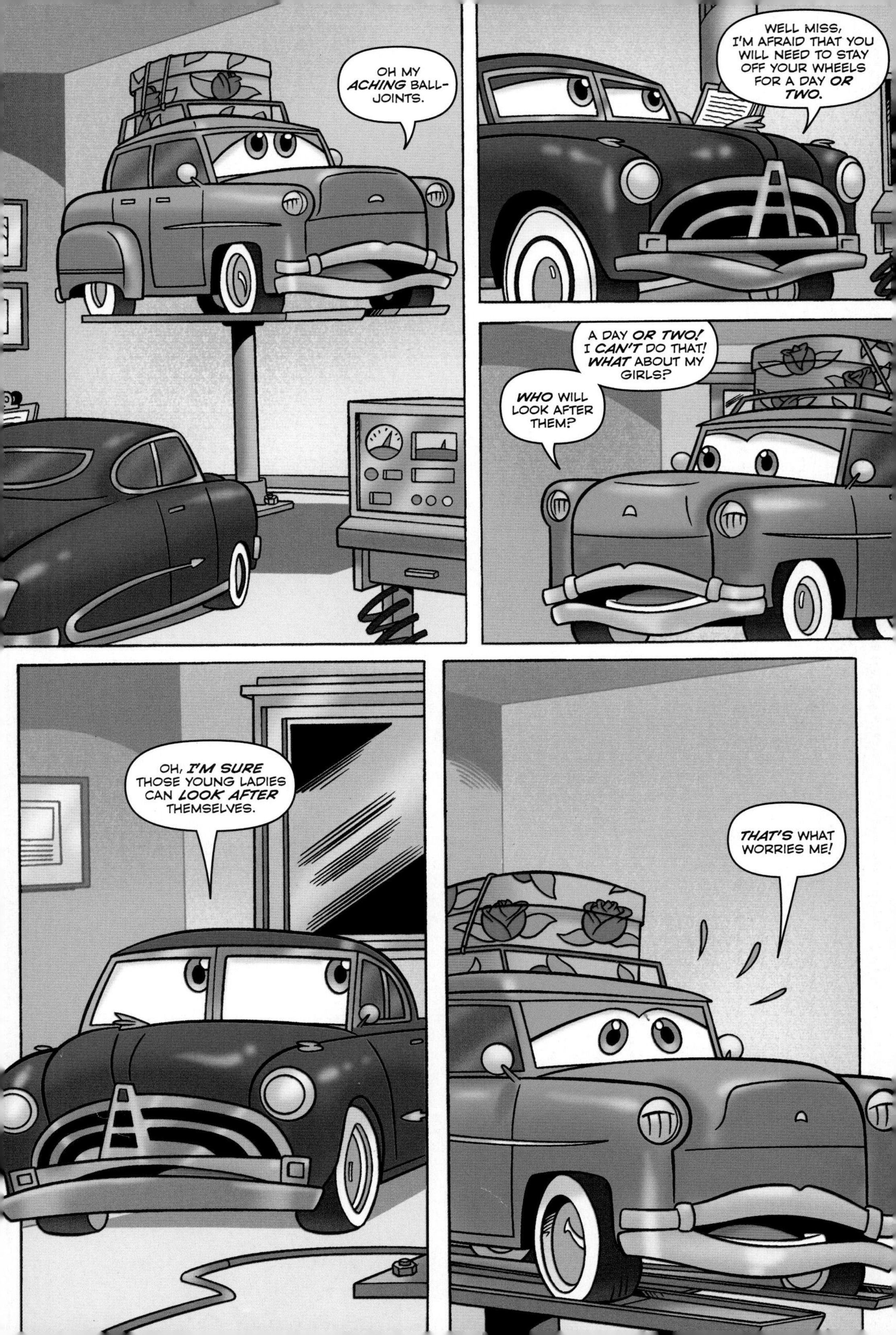
OH MY ACHING BALL-JOINTS.
WELL MISS, I'M AFRAID THAT YOU WILL NEED TO STAY OFF YOUR WHEELS FOR A DAY OR TWO.
A DAY OR TWO! I CAN'T DO THAT! WHAT ABOUT MY GIRLS?
WHO WILL LOOK AFTER THEM?
OH, I'M SURE THOSE YOUNG LADIES CAN LOOK AFTER THEMSELVES.
THAT'S WHAT WORRIES ME!

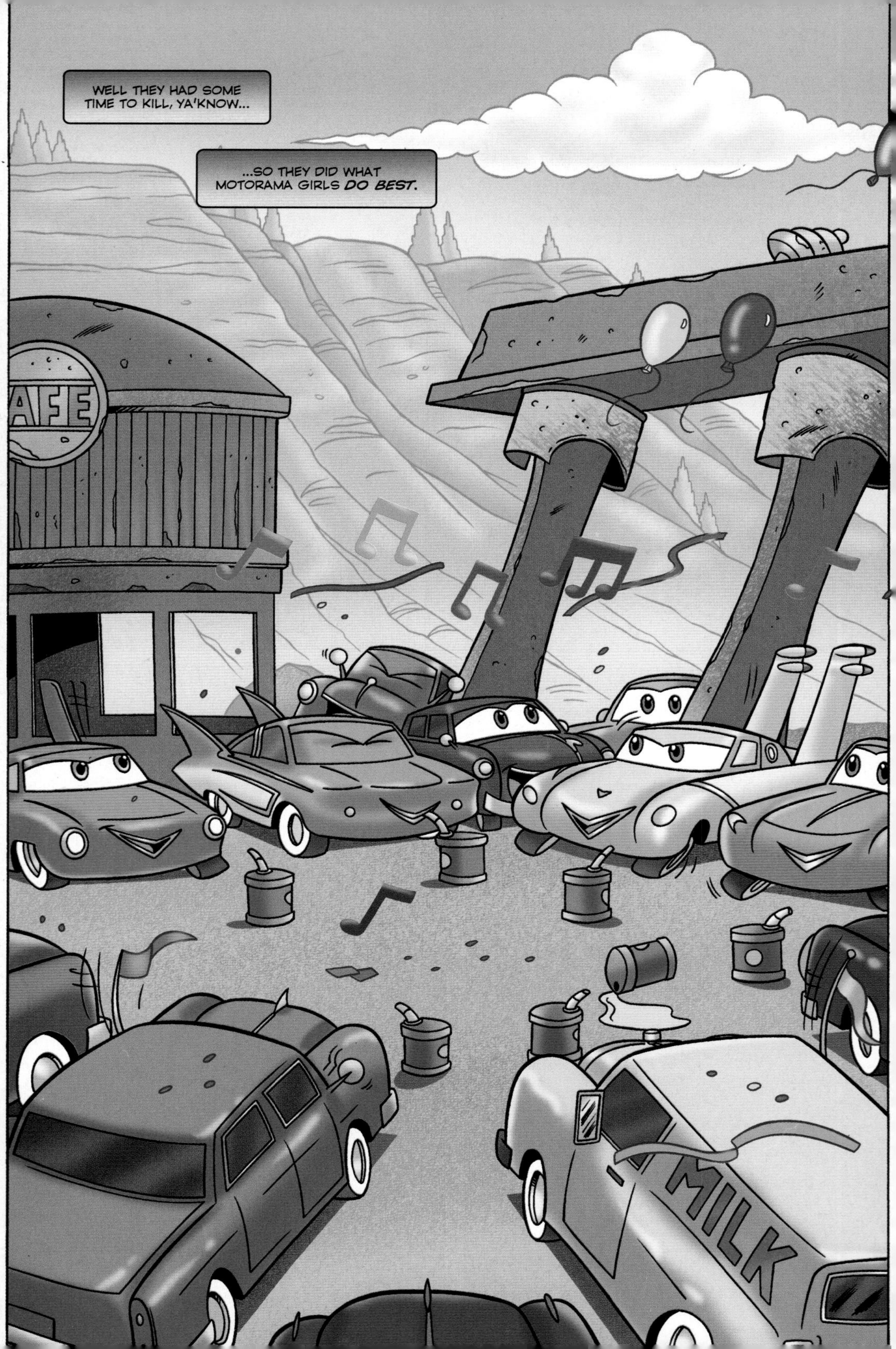
WELL THEY HAD SOME TIME TO KILL, YA'KNOW...
...SO THEY DID WHAT MOTORAMA GIRLS *DO BEST*.
AFE
MILK

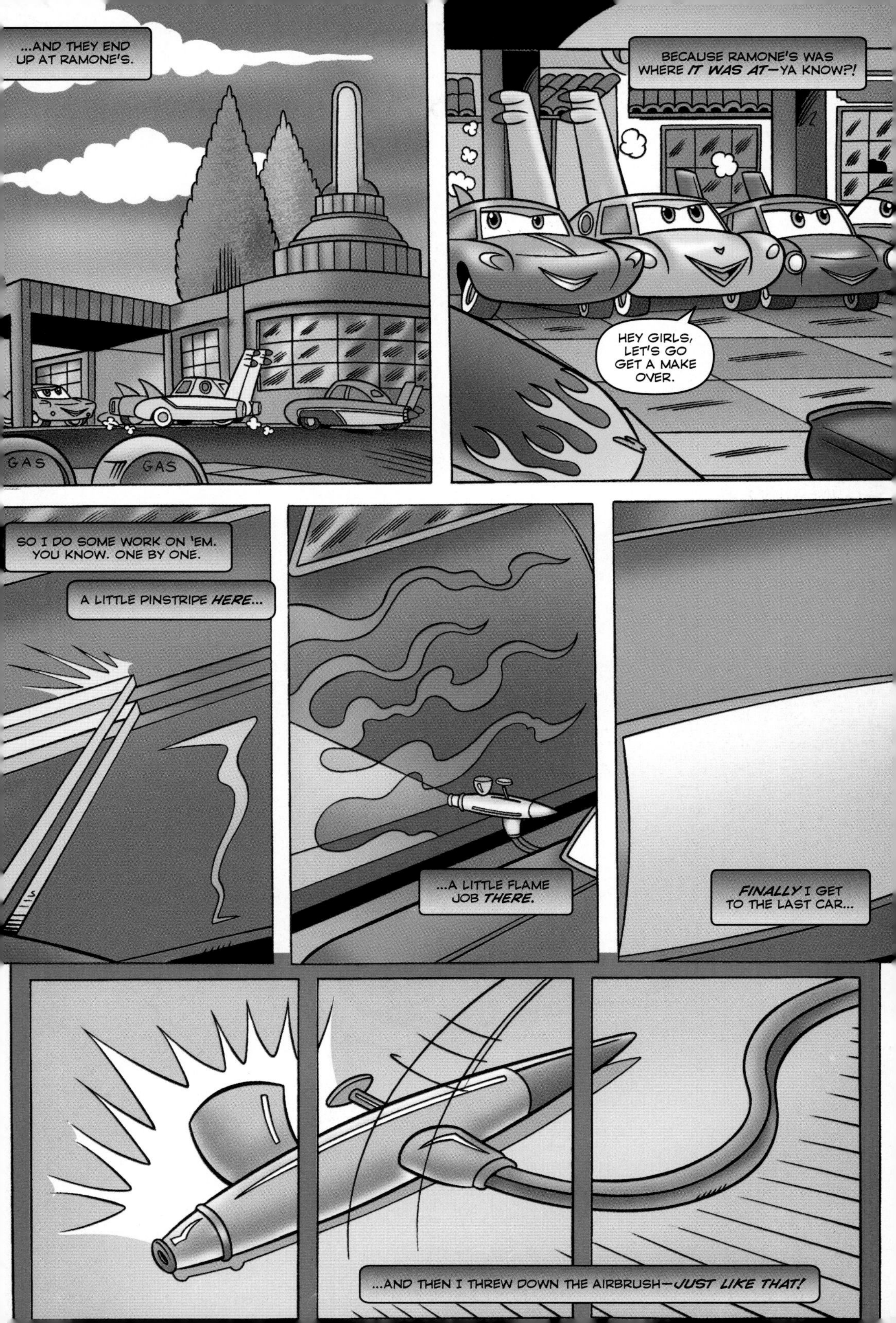
...AND THEY END UP AT RAMONE'S.
GAS
GAS
BECAUSE RAMONE'S WAS WHERE *IT WAS AT*—YA KNOW?!
HEY GIRLS, LET'S GO GET A MAKE OVER.
SO I DO SOME WORK ON 'EM. YOU KNOW. ONE BY ONE.
A LITTLE PINSTRIPE *HERE*...
...A LITTLE FLAME JOB *THERE*.
FINALLY I GET TO THE LAST CAR...
...AND THEN I THREW DOWN THE AIRBRUSH—*JUST LIKE THAT!*

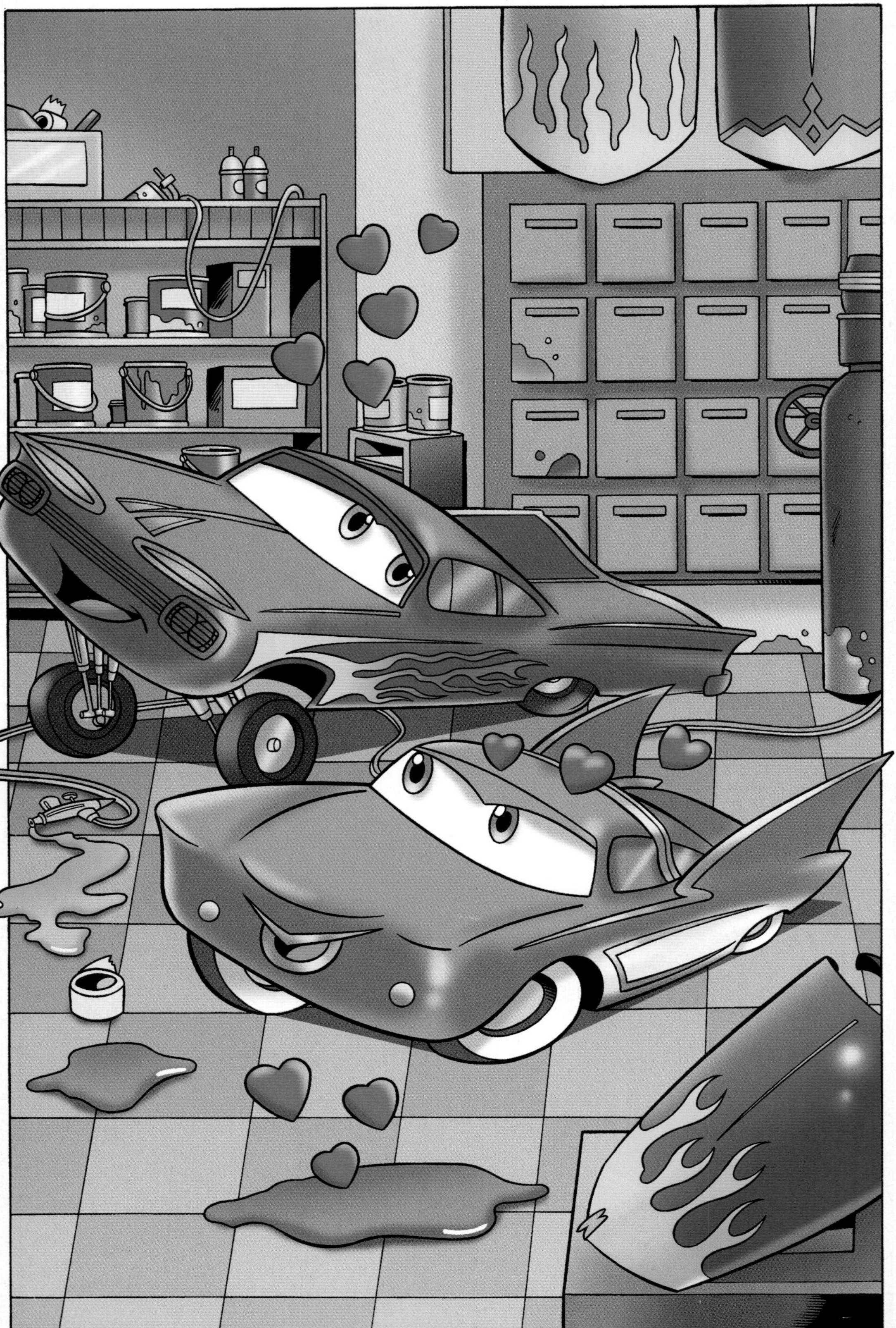

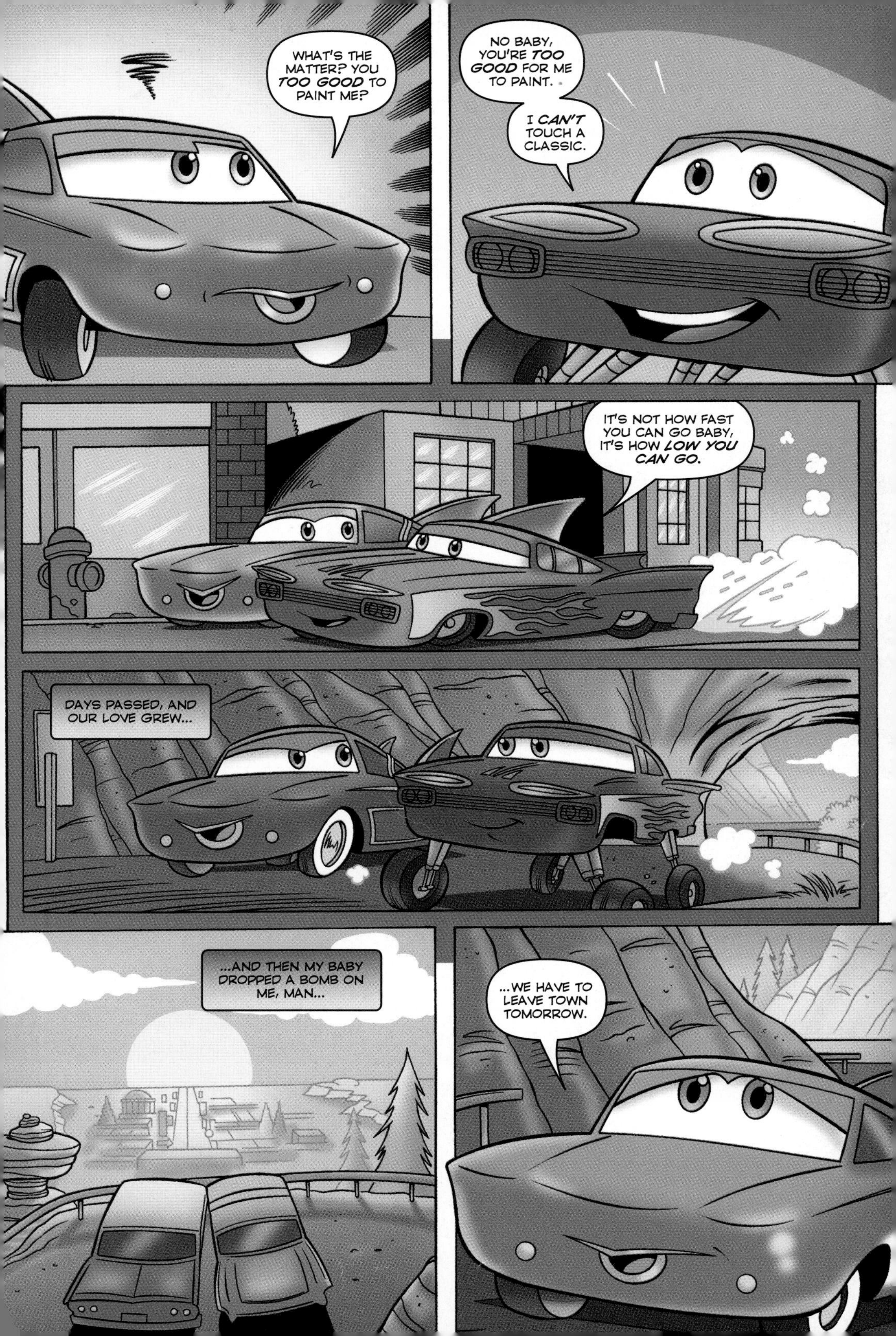
WHAT'S THE MATTER? YOU *TOO GOOD* TO PAINT ME?
NO BABY, YOU'RE *TOO GOOD* FOR ME TO PAINT.
I *CAN'T* TOUCH A CLASSIC.
IT'S NOT HOW FAST YOU CAN GO BABY, IT'S HOW *LOW YOU CAN GO.*
DAYS PASSED, AND OUR LOVE GREW...
...AND THEN MY BABY DROPPED A BOMB ON ME, MAN...
...WE HAVE TO LEAVE TOWN TOMORROW.

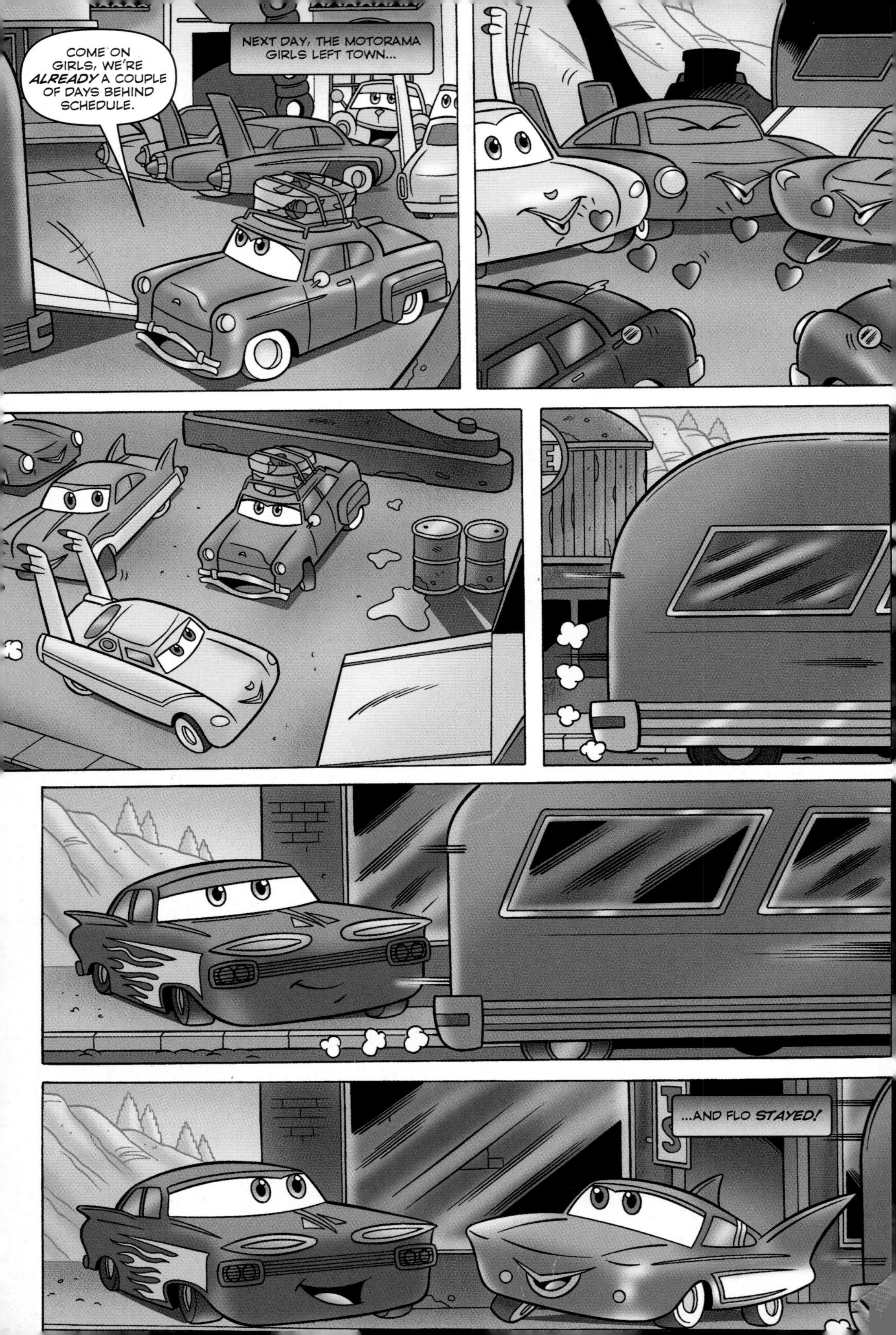
NEXT DAY, THE MOTORAMA GIRLS LEFT TOWN...
COME ON GIRLS, WE'RE *ALREADY* A COUPLE OF DAYS BEHIND SCHEDULE.
...AND FLO *STAYED!*

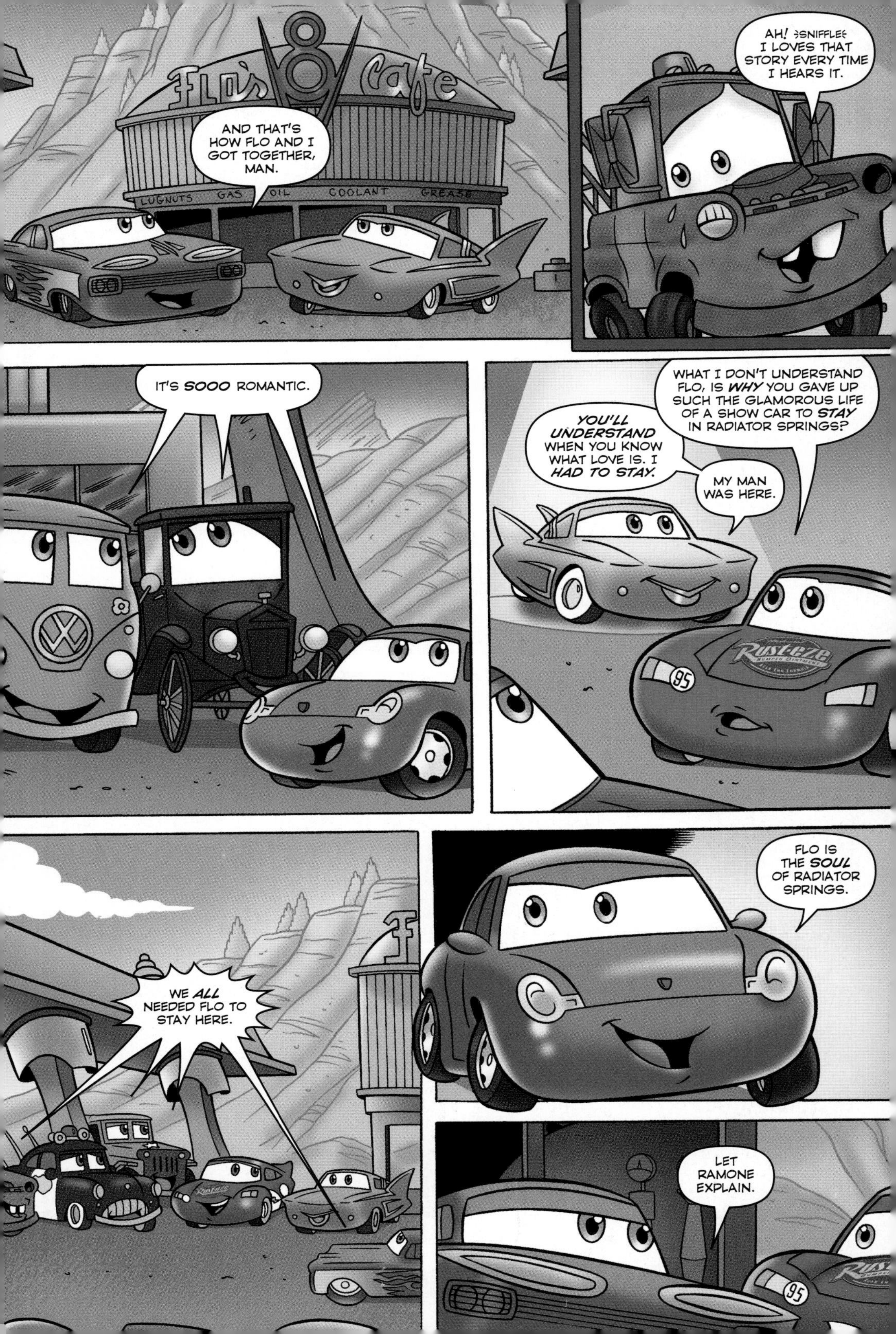
FLO'S V8 CAFE
AND THAT'S HOW FLO AND I GOT TOGETHER, MAN.
LUGNUTS GAS OIL COOLANT GREASE
AH! ≥SNIFFLE≤ I LOVES THAT STORY EVERY TIME I HEARS IT.
IT'S SOOO ROMANTIC.
WHAT I DON'T UNDERSTAND FLO, IS WHY YOU GAVE UP SUCH THE GLAMOROUS LIFE OF A SHOW CAR TO STAY IN RADIATOR SPRINGS?
YOU'LL UNDERSTAND WHEN YOU KNOW WHAT LOVE IS. I HAD TO STAY.
MY MAN WAS HERE.
RUST-EZE
95
WE ALL NEEDED FLO TO STAY HERE.
FLO IS THE SOUL OF RADIATOR SPRINGS.
LET RAMONE EXPLAIN.

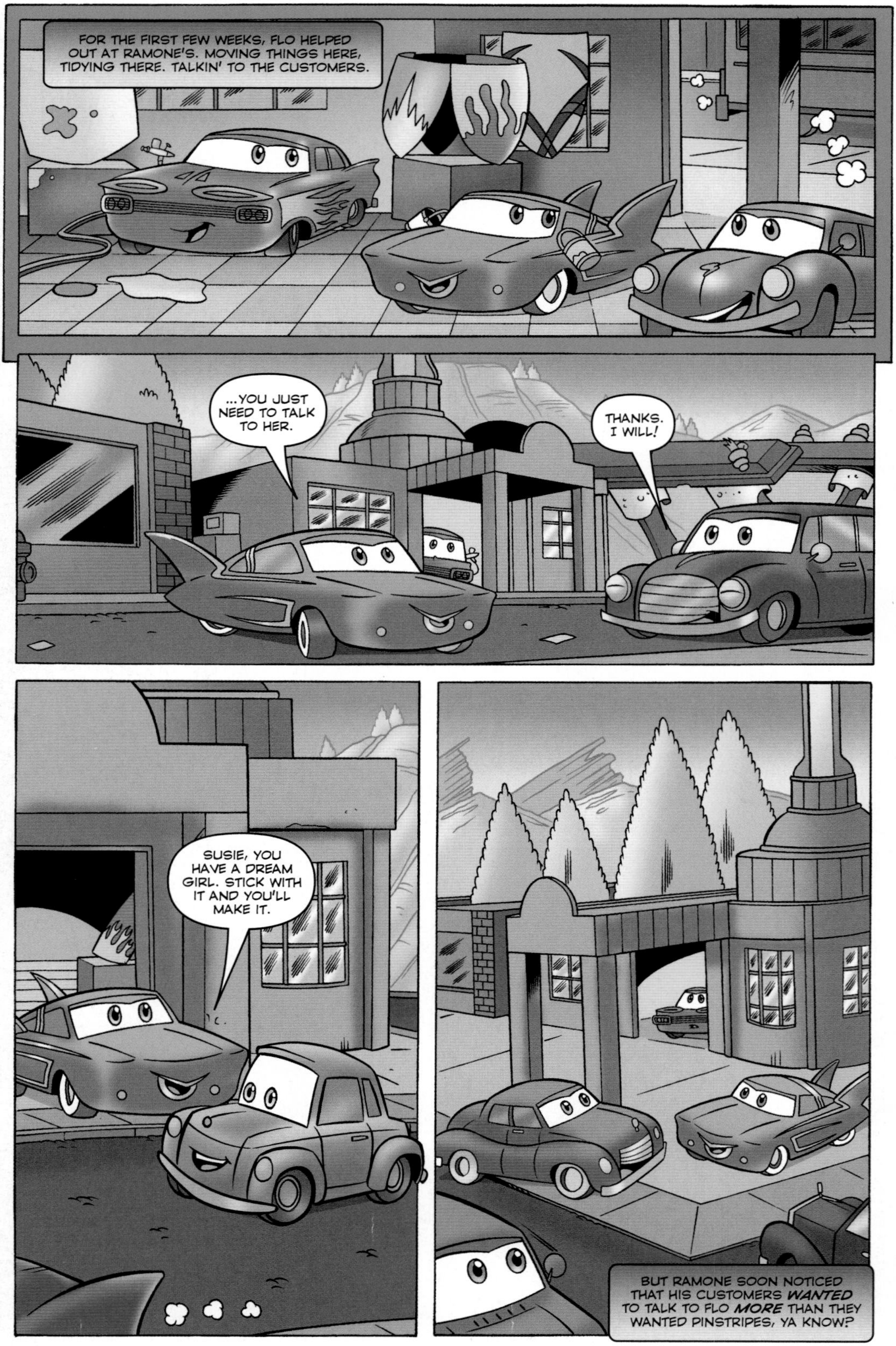
FOR THE FIRST FEW WEEKS, FLO HELPED OUT AT RAMONE'S. MOVING THINGS HERE, TIDYING THERE. TALKIN' TO THE CUSTOMERS.
...YOU JUST NEED TO TALK TO HER.
THANKS. I WILL!
SUSIE, YOU HAVE A DREAM GIRL. STICK WITH IT AND YOU'LL MAKE IT.
BUT RAMONE SOON NOTICED THAT HIS CUSTOMERS *WANTED* TO TALK TO FLO *MORE* THAN THEY WANTED PINSTRIPES, YA KNOW?

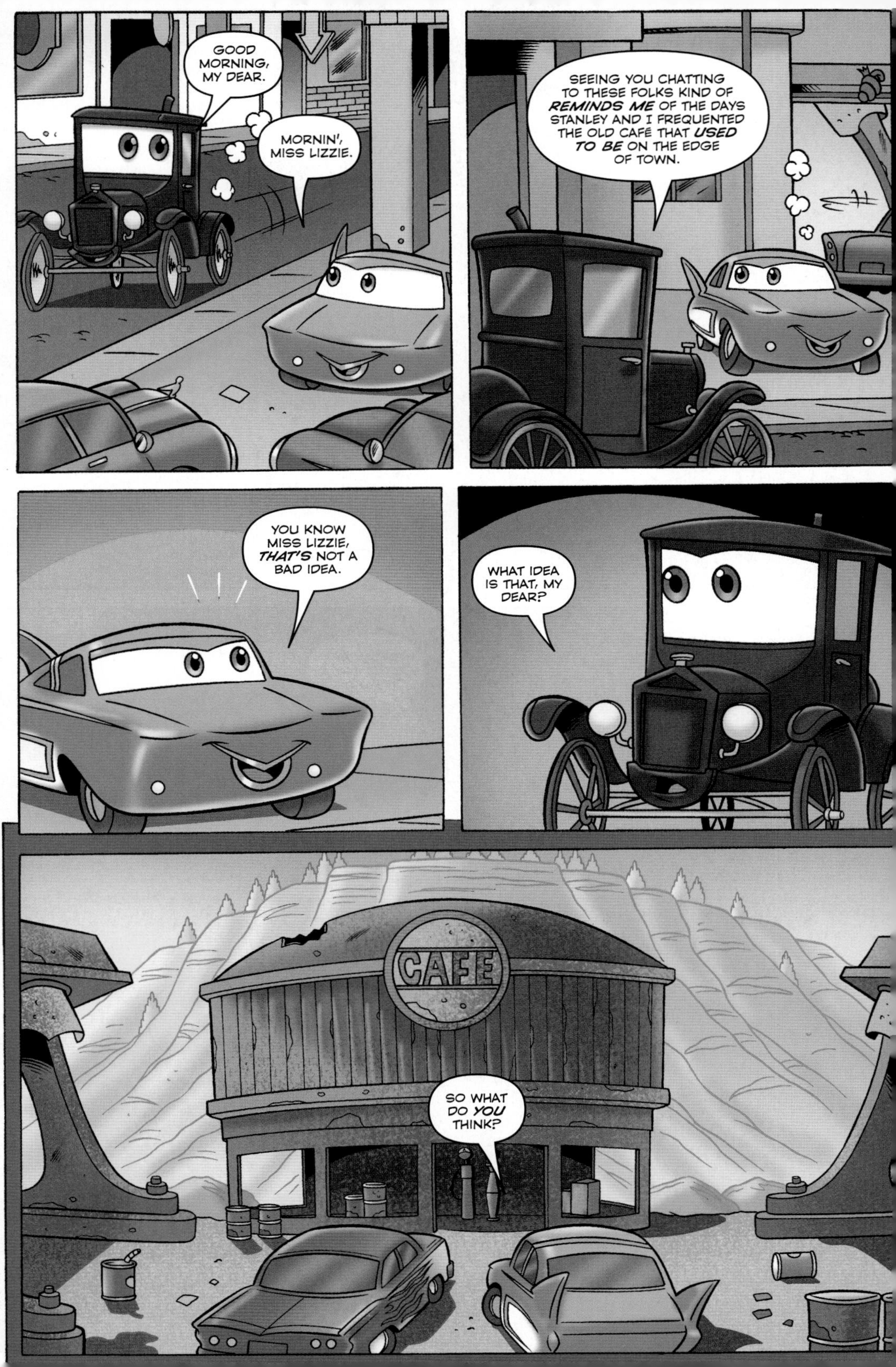
GOOD MORNING, MY DEAR.
MORNIN', MISS LIZZIE.
SEEING YOU CHATTING TO THESE FOLKS KIND OF *REMINDS ME* OF THE DAYS STANLEY AND I FREQUENTED THE OLD CAFÉ THAT *USED TO BE* ON THE EDGE OF TOWN.
YOU KNOW MISS LIZZIE, *THAT'S* NOT A BAD IDEA.
WHAT IDEA IS THAT, MY DEAR?
CAFE
SO WHAT DO *YOU* THINK?

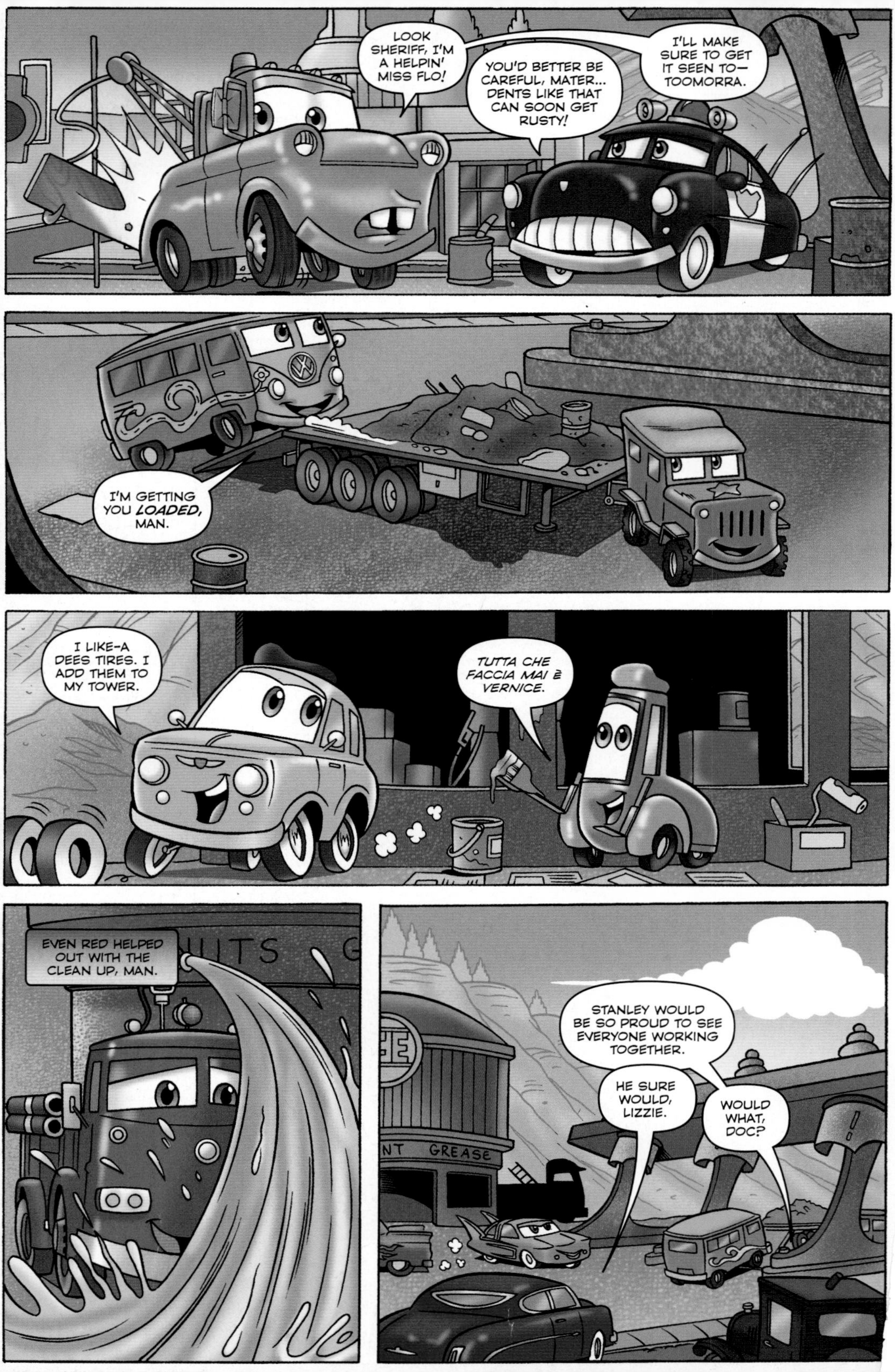

LOOK SHERIFF, I'M A HELPIN' MISS FLO!
YOU'D BETTER BE CAREFUL, MATER... DENTS LIKE THAT CAN SOON GET RUSTY!
I'LL MAKE SURE TO GET IT SEEN TO—TOOMORRA.
I'M GETTING YOU *LOADED,* MAN.
I LIKE-A DEES TIRES. I ADD THEM TO MY TOWER.
TUTTA CHE FACCIA MAI È VERNICE.
EVEN RED HELPED OUT WITH THE CLEAN UP, MAN.
STANLEY WOULD BE SO PROUD TO SEE EVERYONE WORKING TOGETHER.
HE SURE WOULD, LIZZIE.
WOULD WHAT, DOC?

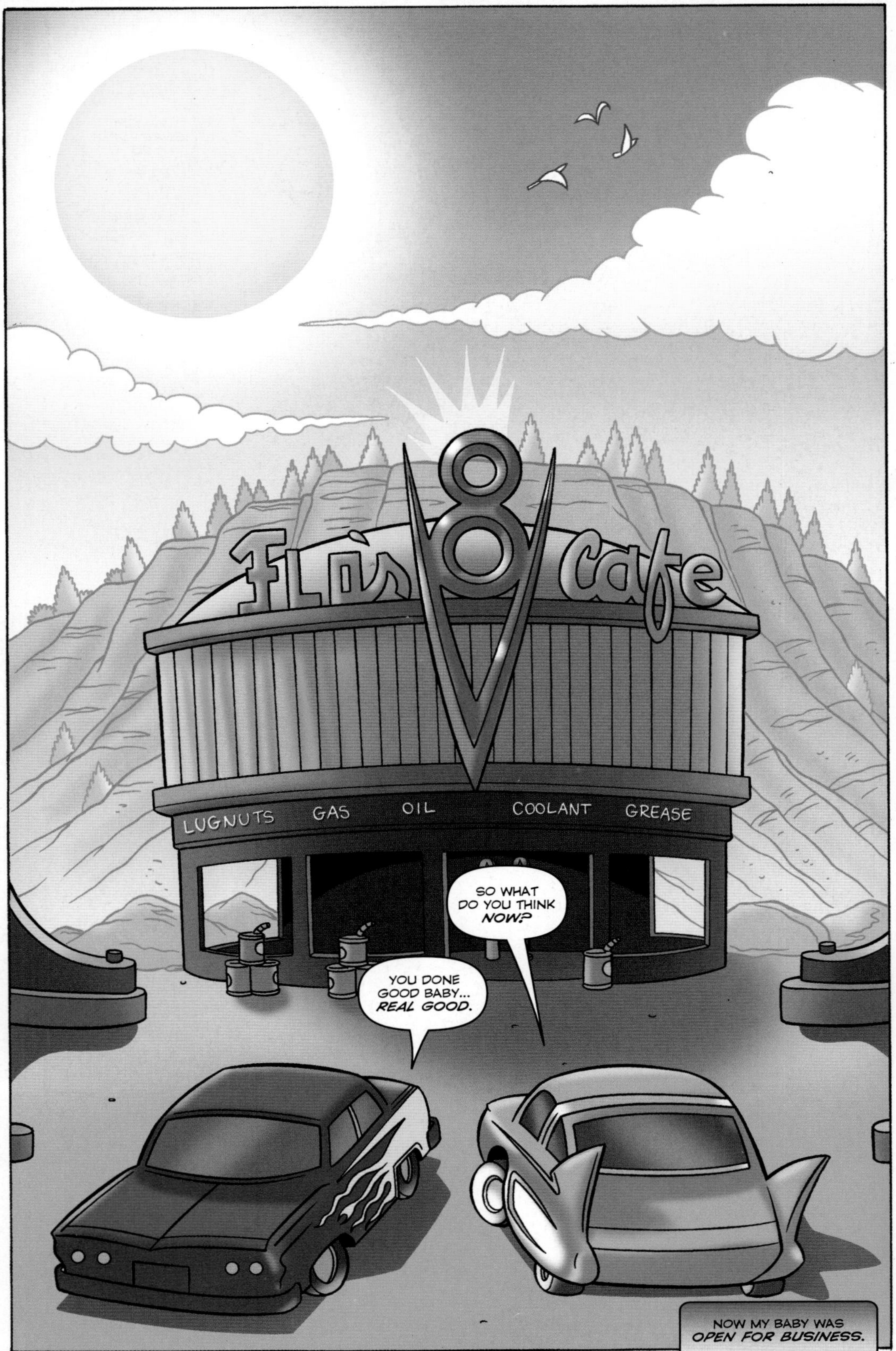
FLO'S V8 CAFE
LUGNUTS GAS OIL COOLANT GREASE
SO WHAT DO YOU THINK *NOW?*
YOU DONE GOOD BABY... *REAL GOOD.*
NOW MY BABY WAS *OPEN FOR BUSINESS.*

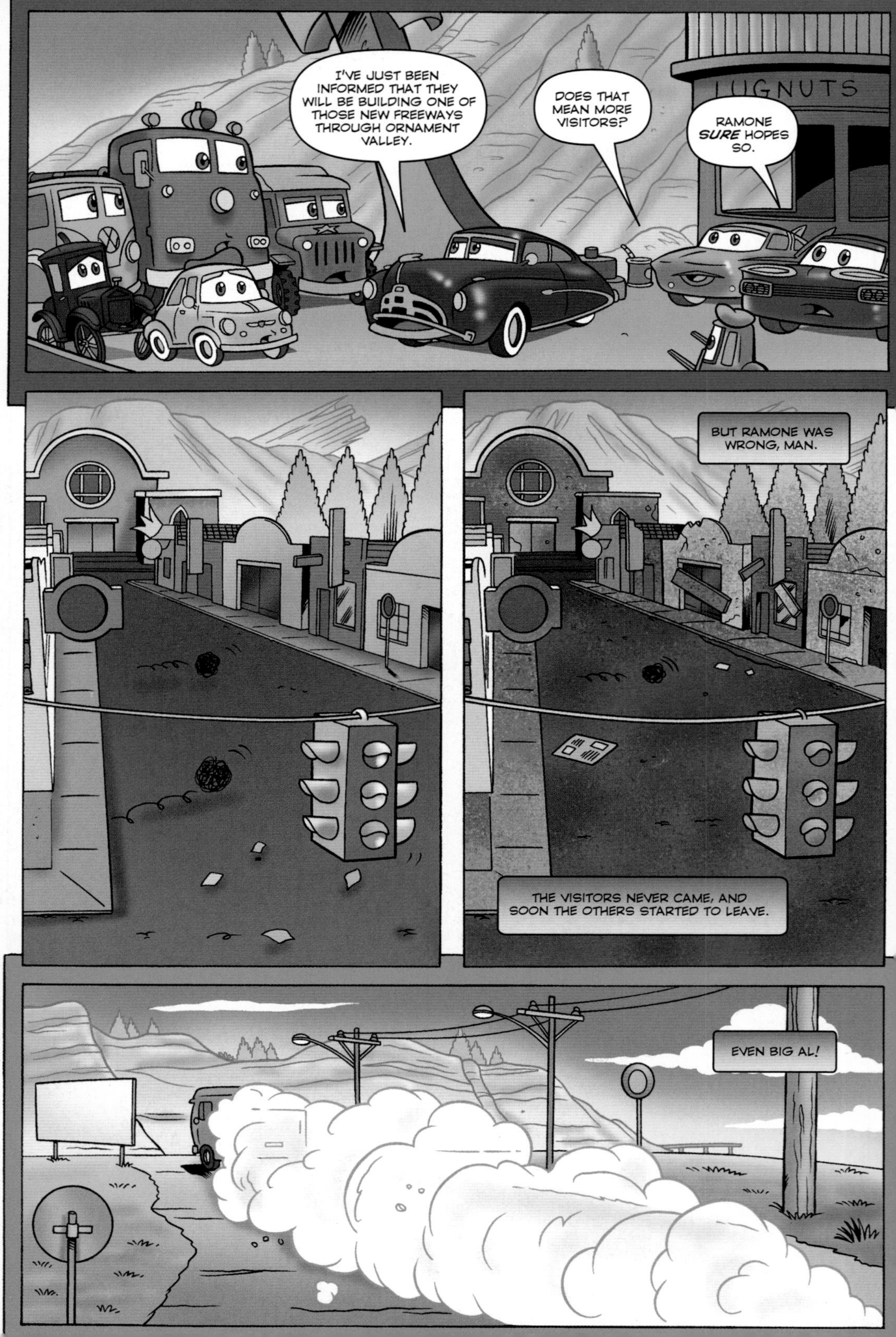
I'VE JUST BEEN INFORMED THAT THEY WILL BE BUILDING ONE OF THOSE NEW FREEWAYS THROUGH ORNAMENT VALLEY.
DOES THAT MEAN MORE VISITORS?
LUGNUTS
RAMONE SURE HOPES SO.
BUT RAMONE WAS WRONG, MAN.
THE VISITORS NEVER CAME, AND SOON THE OTHERS STARTED TO LEAVE.
EVEN BIG AL!

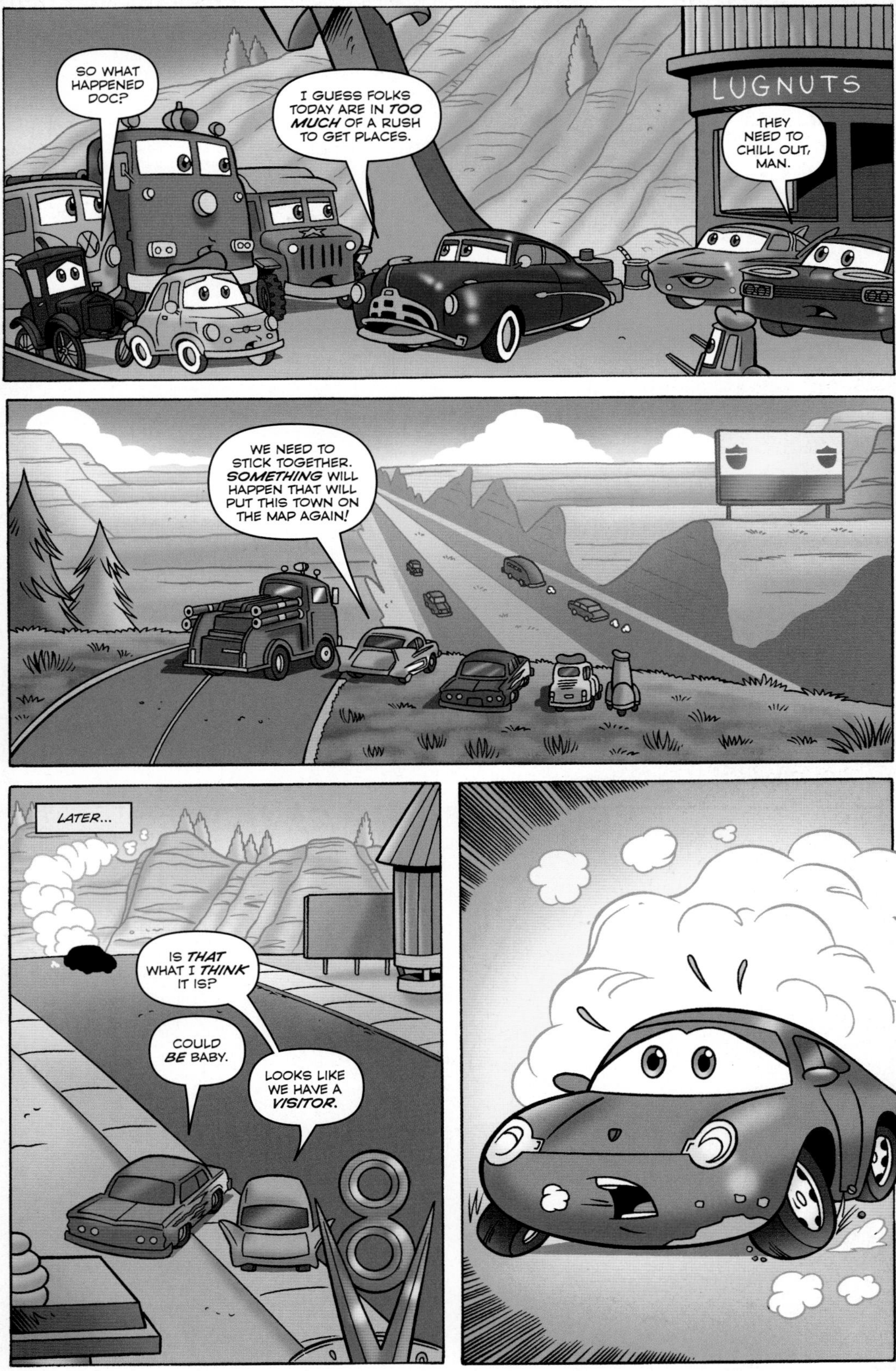
SO WHAT HAPPENED DOC?
I GUESS FOLKS TODAY ARE IN TOO MUCH OF A RUSH TO GET PLACES.
LUGNUTS
THEY NEED TO CHILL OUT, MAN.
WE NEED TO STICK TOGETHER. SOMETHING WILL HAPPEN THAT WILL PUT THIS TOWN ON THE MAP AGAIN!
LATER...
IS THAT WHAT I THINK IT IS?
COULD BE BABY.
LOOKS LIKE WE HAVE A VISITOR.

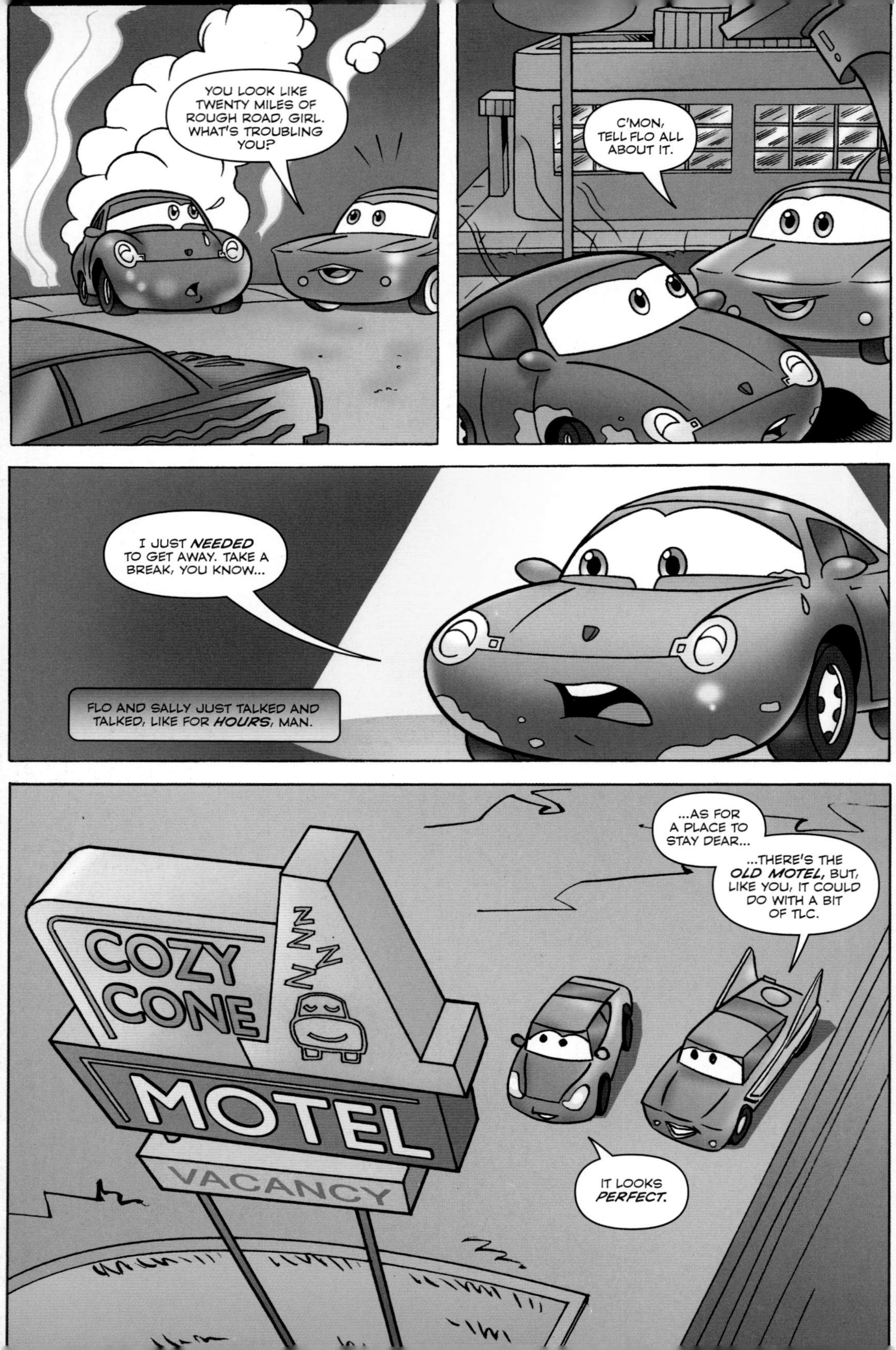
YOU LOOK LIKE TWENTY MILES OF ROUGH ROAD, GIRL. WHAT'S TROUBLING YOU?
C'MON, TELL FLO ALL ABOUT IT.
I JUST *NEEDED* TO GET AWAY. TAKE A BREAK, YOU KNOW...
FLO AND SALLY JUST TALKED AND TALKED, LIKE FOR *HOURS*, MAN.
COZY CONE
MOTEL
VACANCY
...AS FOR A PLACE TO STAY DEAR...
...THERE'S THE *OLD MOTEL*, BUT, LIKE YOU, IT COULD DO WITH A BIT OF TLC.
IT LOOKS *PERFECT*.

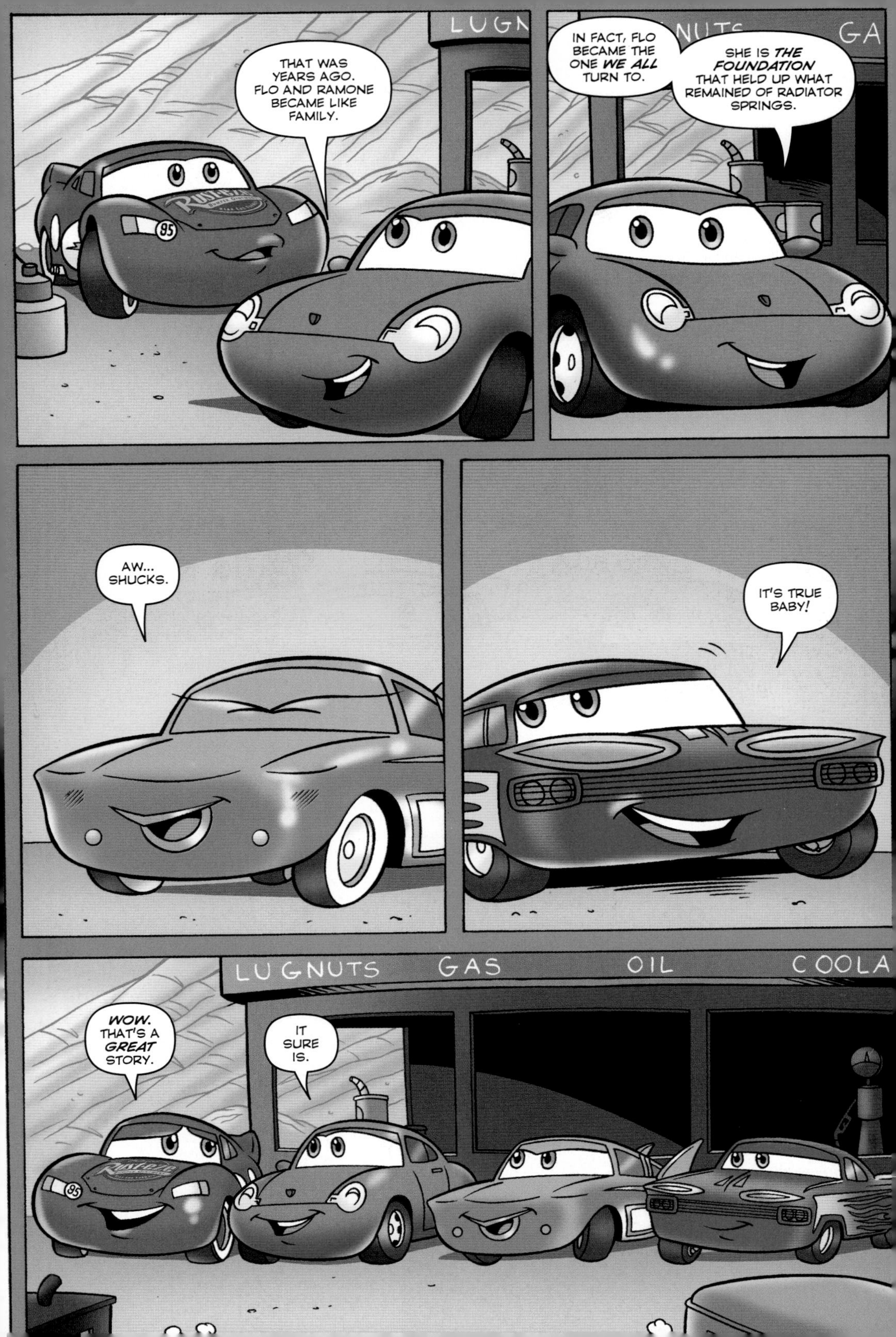
LUGN
THAT WAS YEARS AGO. FLO AND RAMONE BECAME LIKE FAMILY.
NUTS GA
IN FACT, FLO BECAME THE ONE *WE ALL* TURN TO.
SHE IS ***THE FOUNDATION*** THAT HELD UP WHAT REMAINED OF RADIATOR SPRINGS.
AW... SHUCKS.
IT'S TRUE BABY!
LUGNUTS GAS OIL COOLA
WOW. THAT'S A ***GREAT*** STORY.
IT SURE IS.

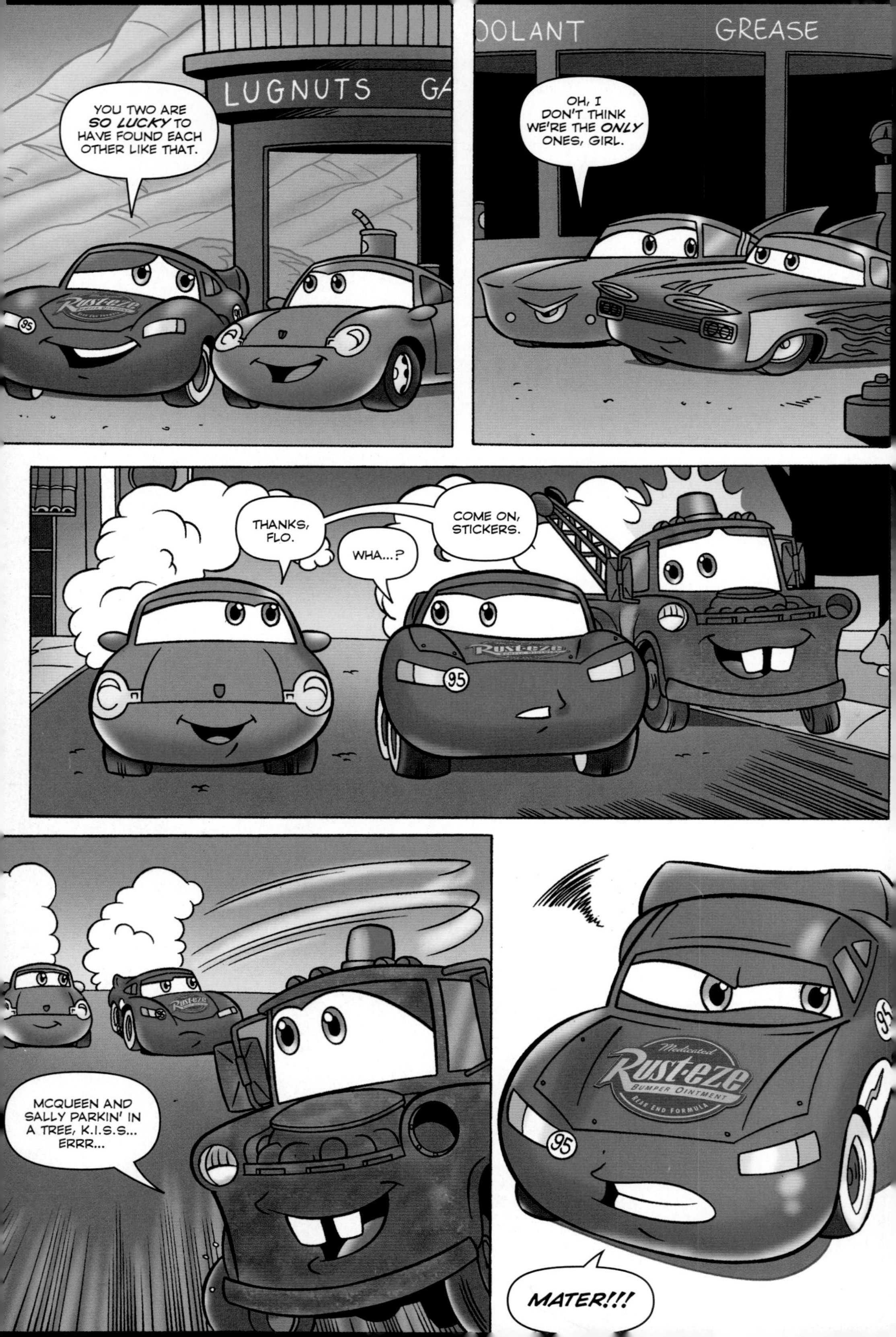
LUGNUTS
YOU TWO ARE SO LUCKY TO HAVE FOUND EACH OTHER LIKE THAT.
OOLANT
GREASE
OH, I DON'T THINK WE'RE THE ONLY ONES, GIRL.
THANKS, FLO.
COME ON, STICKERS.
WHA...?
MCQUEEN AND SALLY PARKIN' IN A TREE, K.I.S.S... ERRR...
MATER!!!

Chapter Two

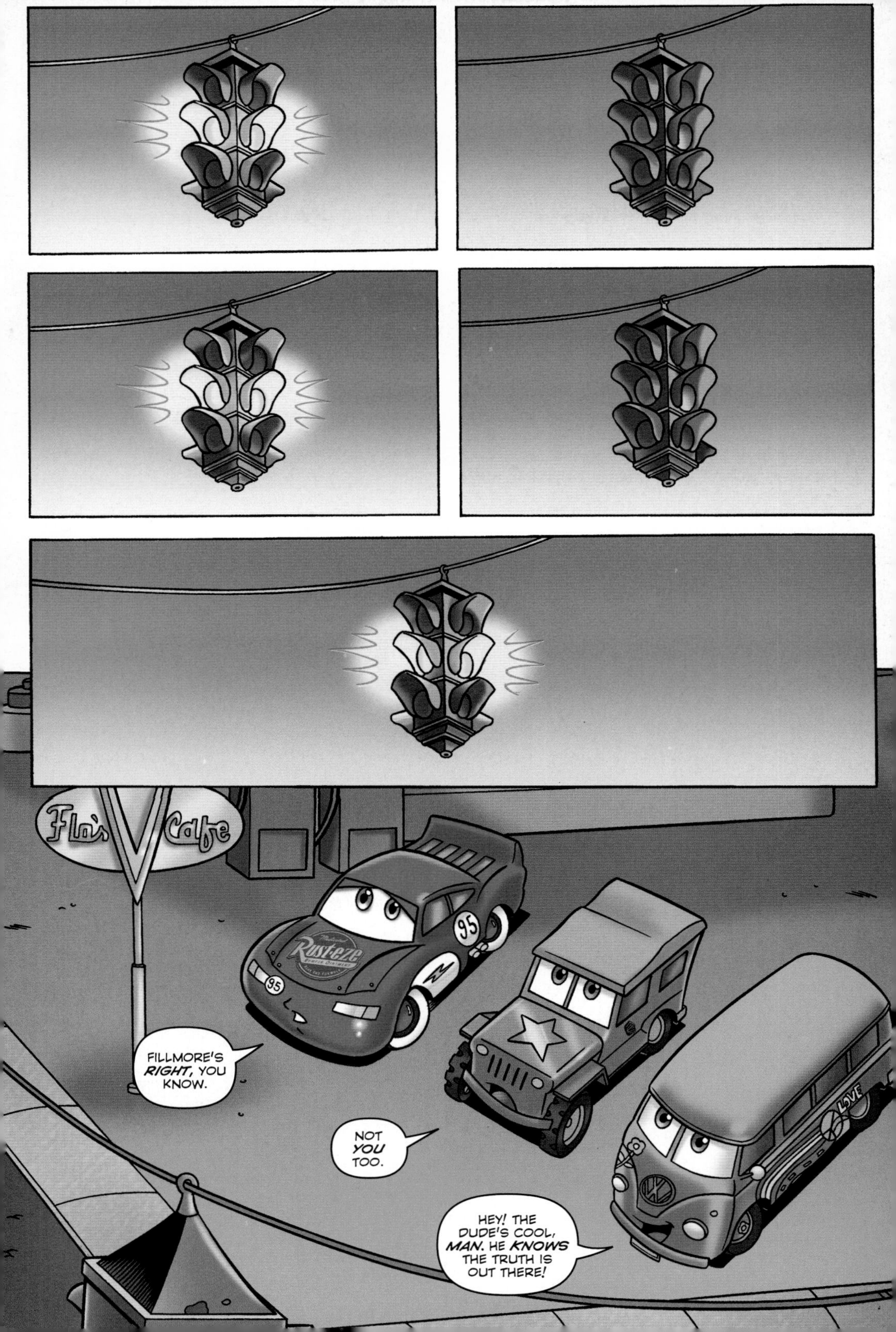
Flo's Cafe
Rust-eze
95
FILLMORE'S *RIGHT*, YOU KNOW.
NOT *YOU* TOO.
HEY! THE DUDE'S COOL, *MAN*. HE *KNOWS* THE TRUTH IS OUT THERE!
LOVE

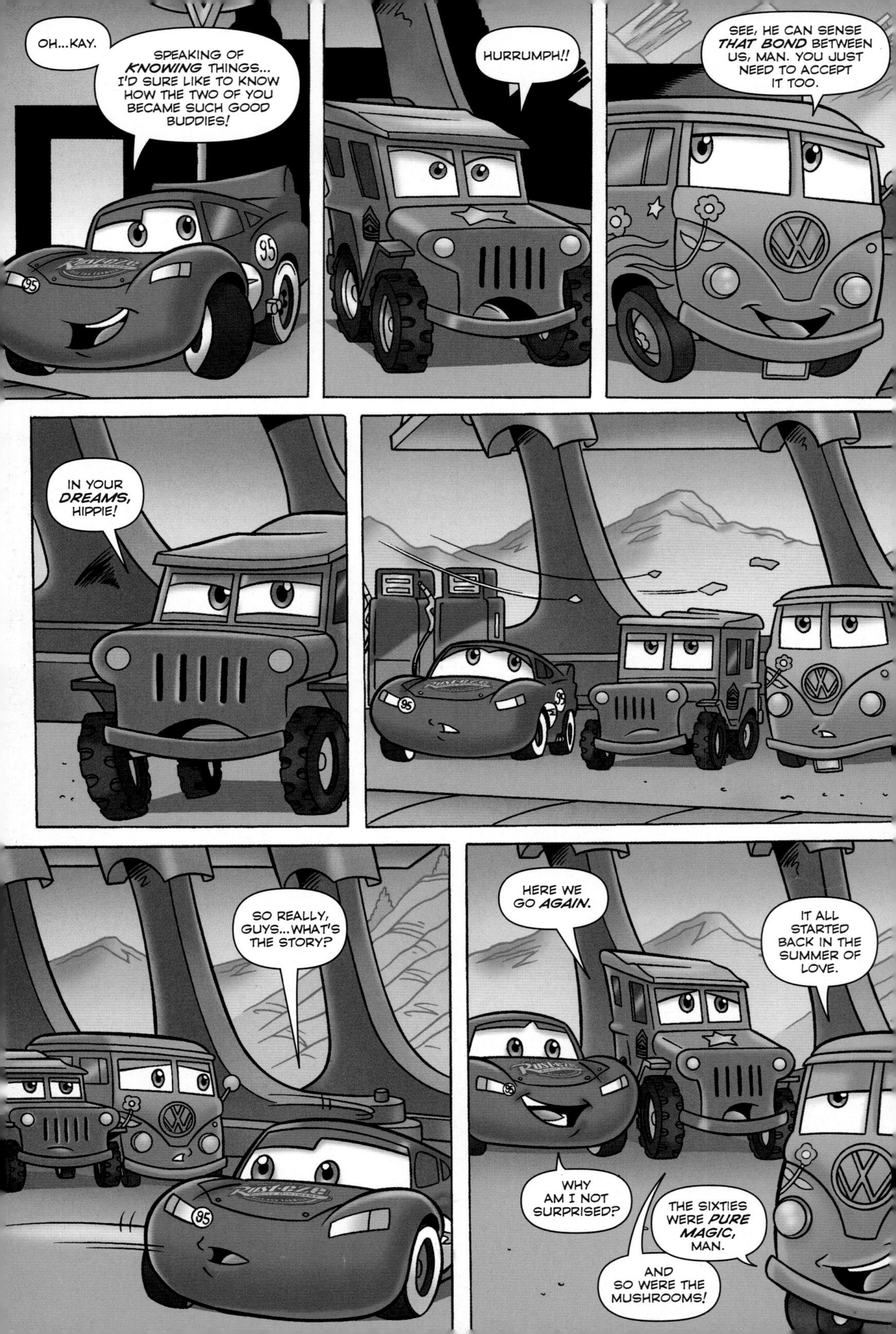
OH...KAY.
SPEAKING OF KNOWING THINGS... I'D SURE LIKE TO KNOW HOW THE TWO OF YOU BECAME SUCH GOOD BUDDIES!
HURRUMPH!!
SEE, HE CAN SENSE THAT BOND BETWEEN US, MAN. YOU JUST NEED TO ACCEPT IT TOO.
IN YOUR DREAMS, HIPPIE!
SO REALLY, GUYS...WHAT'S THE STORY?
HERE WE GO AGAIN.
IT ALL STARTED BACK IN THE SUMMER OF LOVE.
WHY AM I NOT SURPRISED?
THE SIXTIES WERE PURE MAGIC, MAN.
AND SO WERE THE MUSHROOMS!

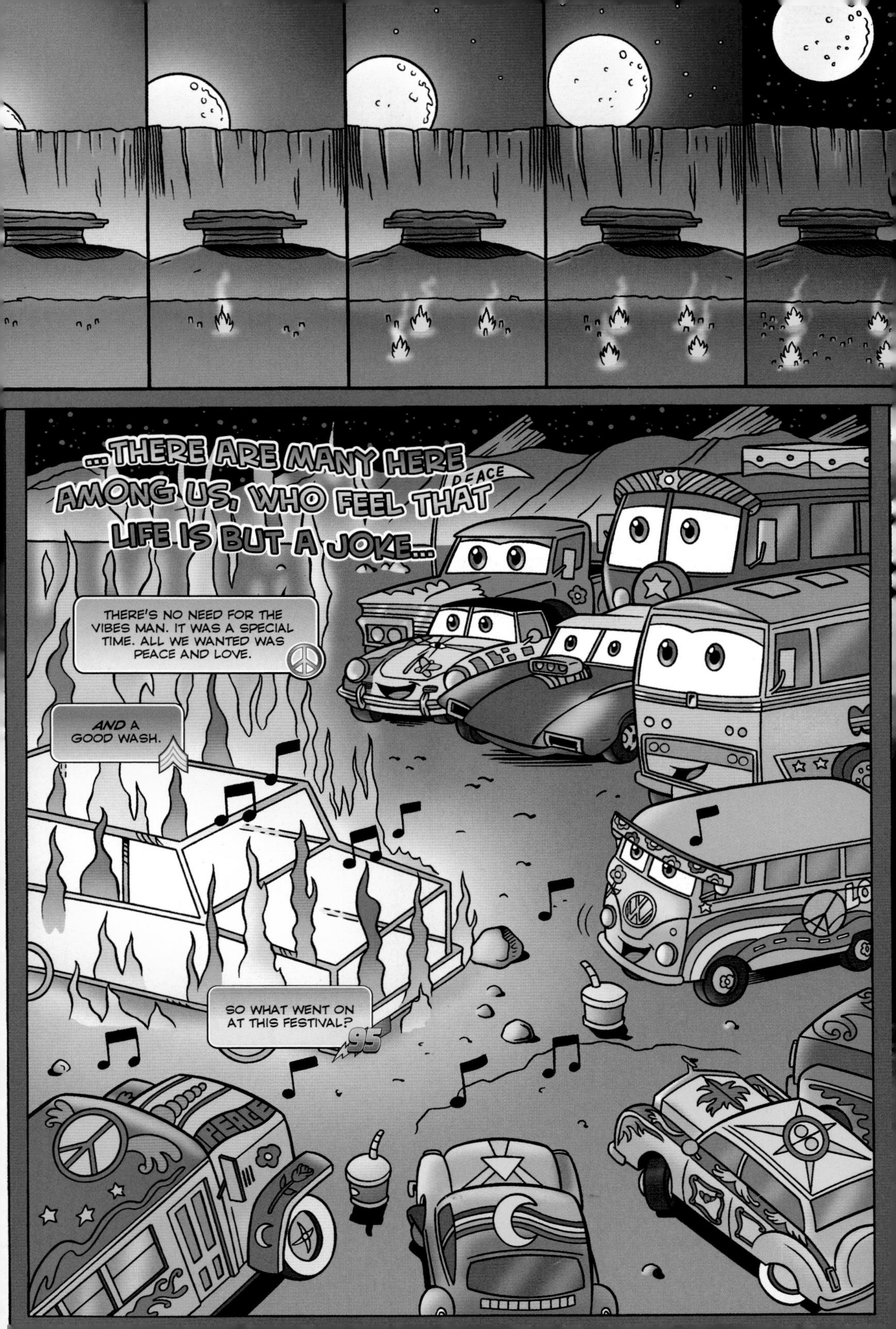
...THERE ARE MANY HERE AMONG US, WHO FEEL THAT LIFE IS BUT A JOKE...
THERE'S NO NEED FOR THE VIBES MAN. IT WAS A SPECIAL TIME. ALL WE WANTED WAS PEACE AND LOVE.
AND A GOOD WASH.
SO WHAT WENT ON AT THIS FESTIVAL?
PEACE

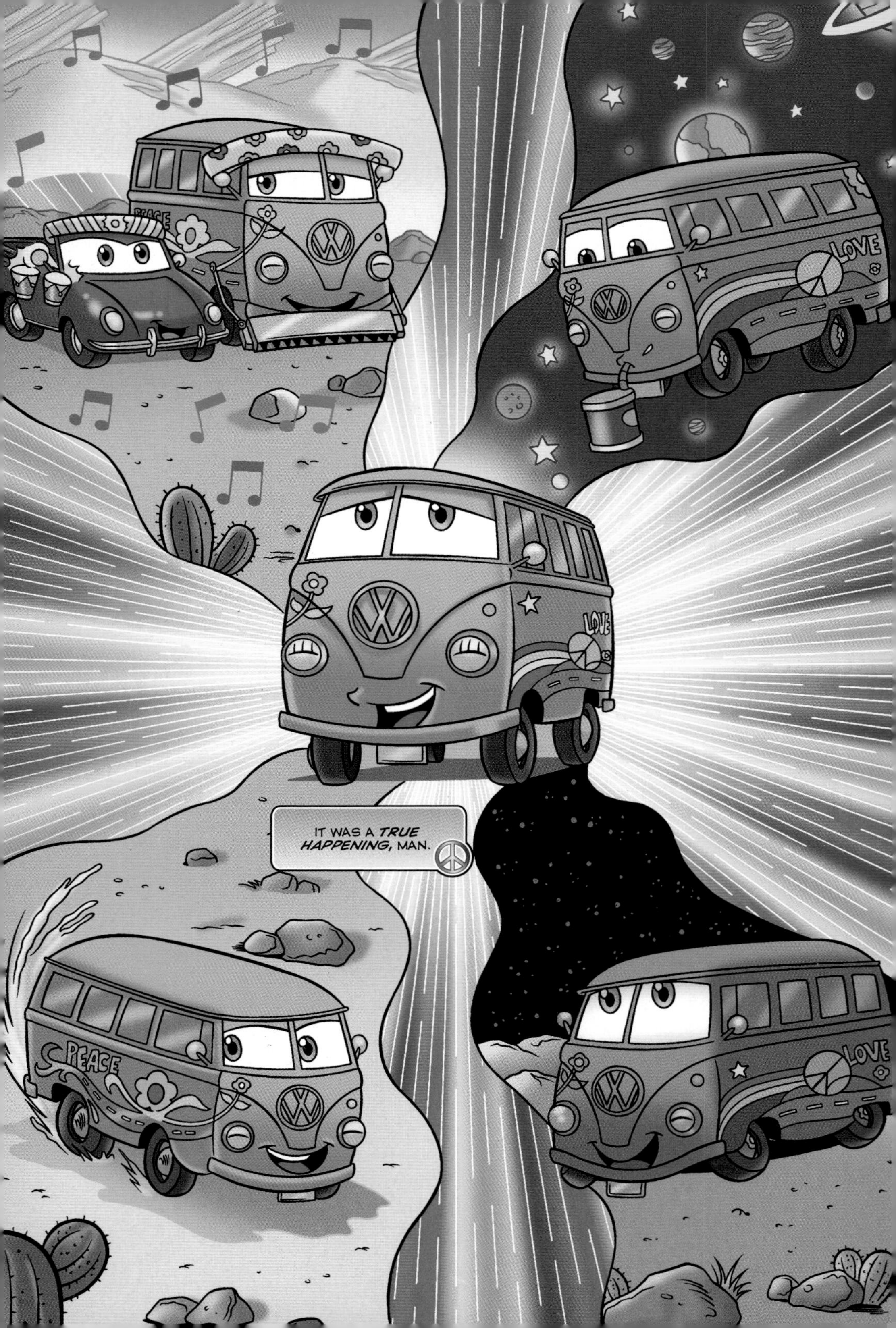
PEACE
LOVE
IT WAS A TRUE HAPPENING, MAN.
PEACE
LOVE

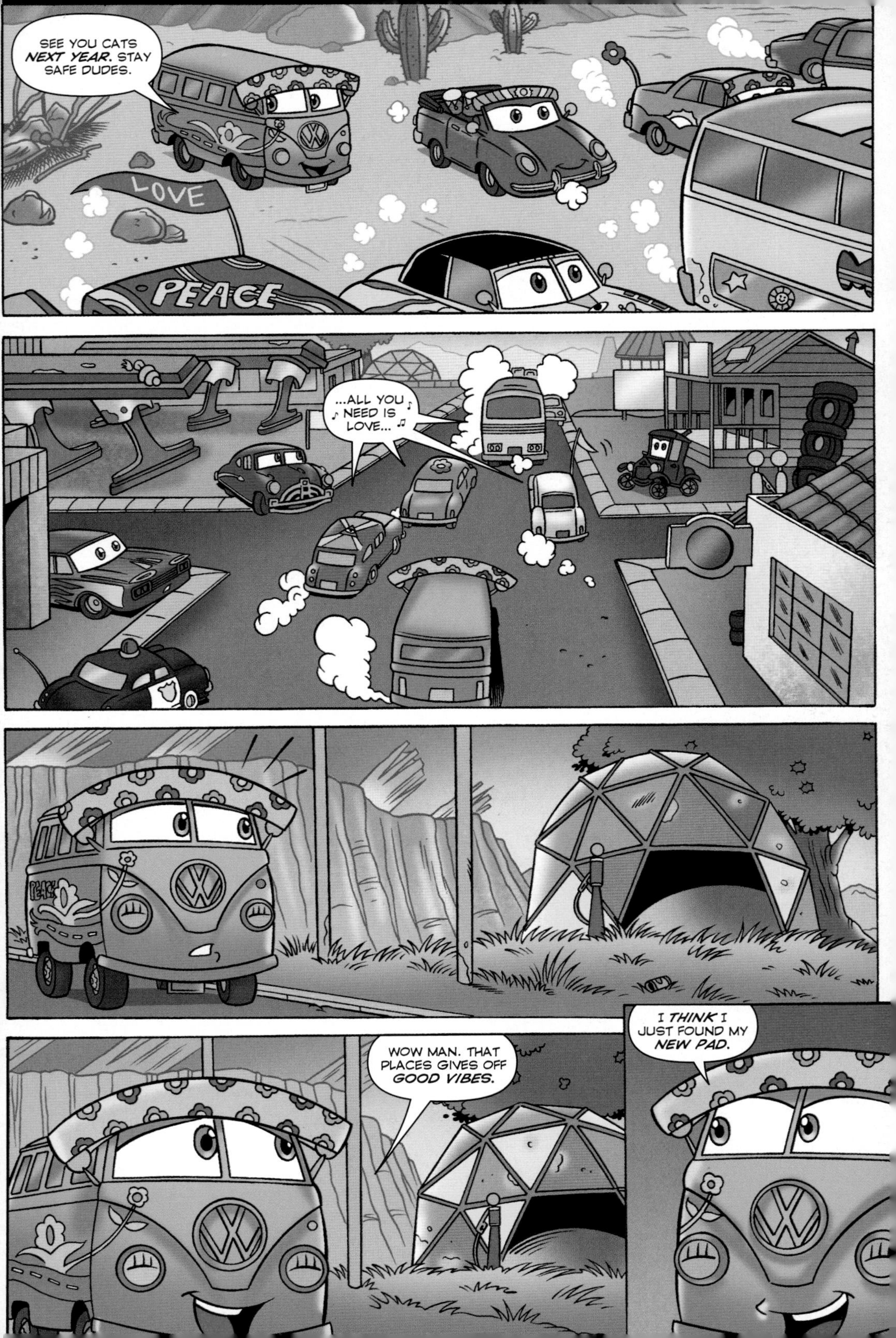

SEE YOU CATS NEXT YEAR. STAY SAFE DUDES.
LOVE
PEACE
...ALL YOU NEED IS LOVE...
WOW MAN. THAT PLACES GIVES OFF GOOD VIBES.
I THINK I JUST FOUND MY NEW PAD.

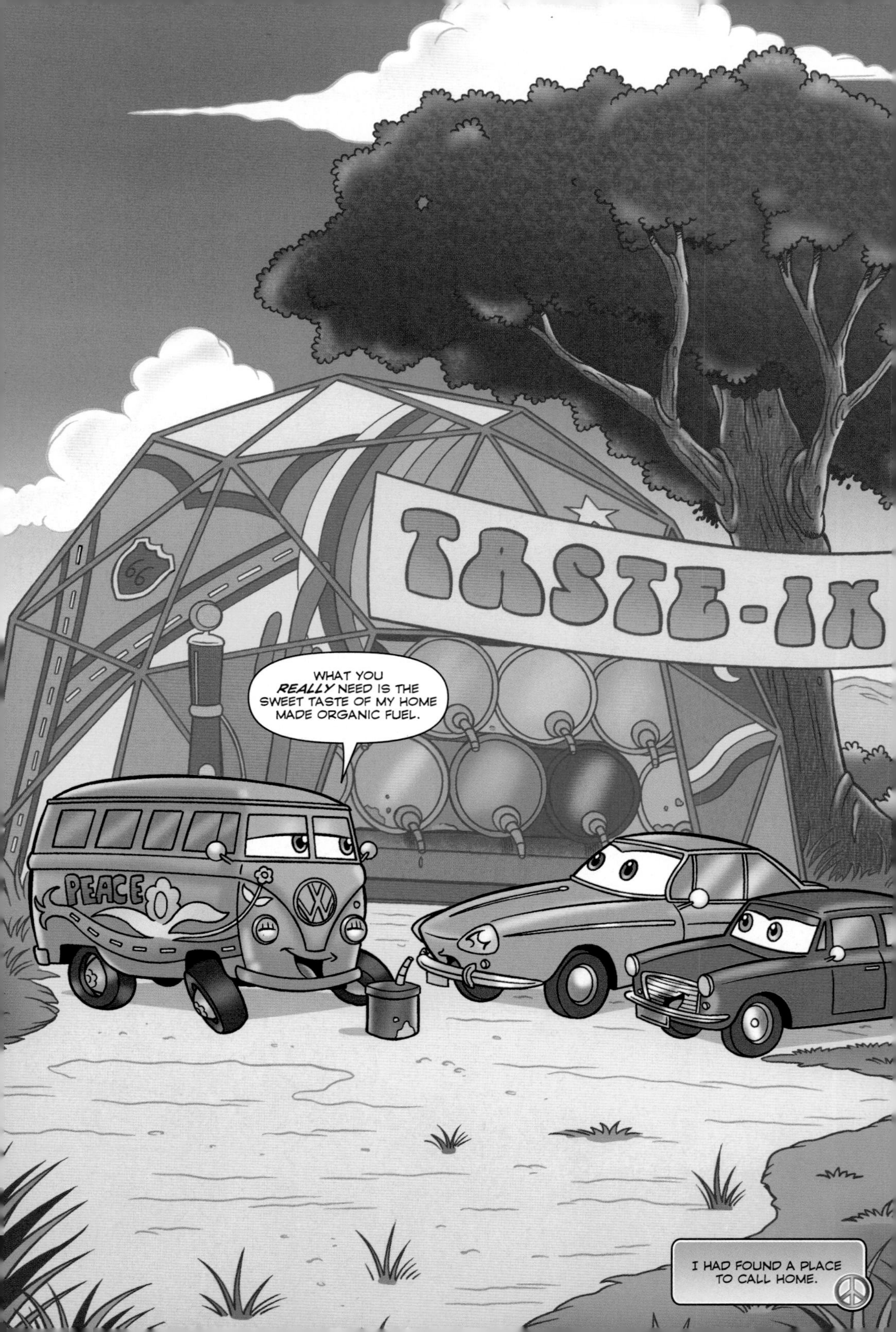
TASTE-IN
WHAT YOU REALLY NEED IS THE SWEET TASTE OF MY HOME MADE ORGANIC FUEL.
PEACE
I HAD FOUND A PLACE TO CALL HOME.

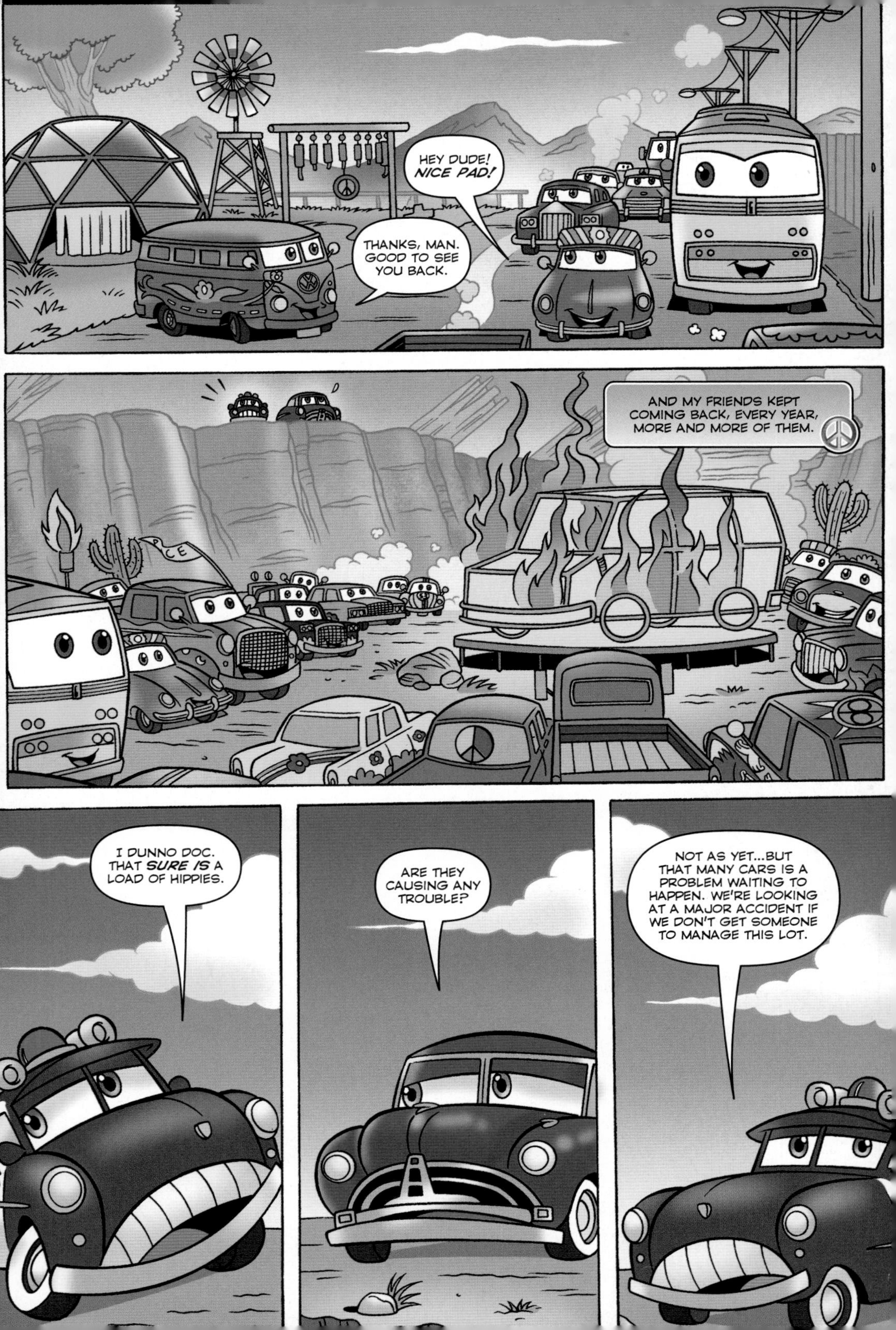
HEY DUDE! *NICE PAD!*
THANKS, MAN. GOOD TO SEE YOU BACK.
AND MY FRIENDS KEPT COMING BACK, EVERY YEAR, MORE AND MORE OF THEM.
I DUNNO DOC. THAT *SURE IS* A LOAD OF HIPPIES.
ARE THEY CAUSING ANY TROUBLE?
NOT AS YET...BUT THAT MANY CARS IS A PROBLEM WAITING TO HAPPEN. WE'RE LOOKING AT A MAJOR ACCIDENT IF WE DON'T GET SOMEONE TO MANAGE THIS LOT.

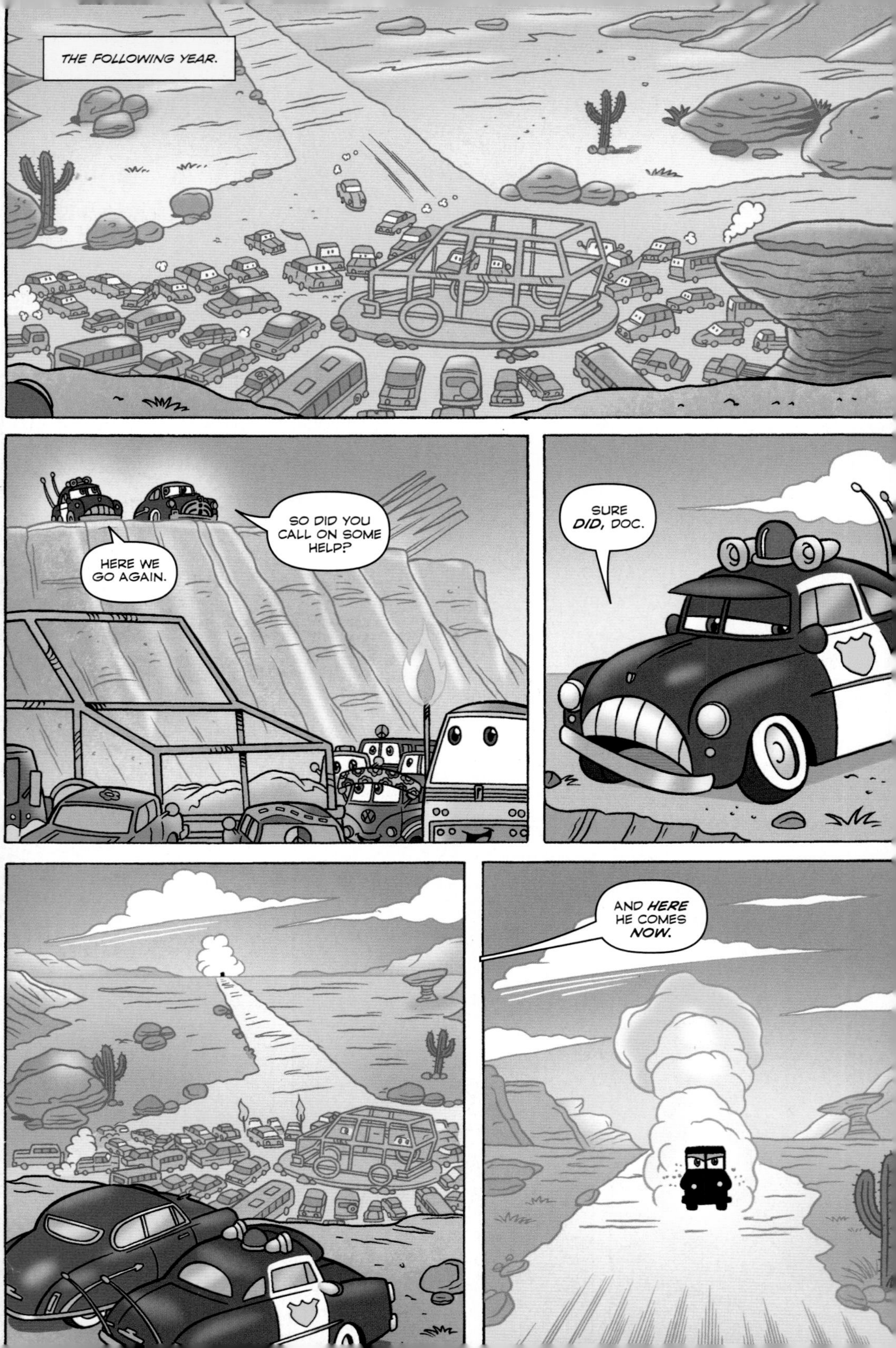
THE FOLLOWING YEAR.
HERE WE GO AGAIN.
SO DID YOU CALL ON SOME HELP?
SURE *DID*, DOC.
AND *HERE* HE COMES *NOW*.

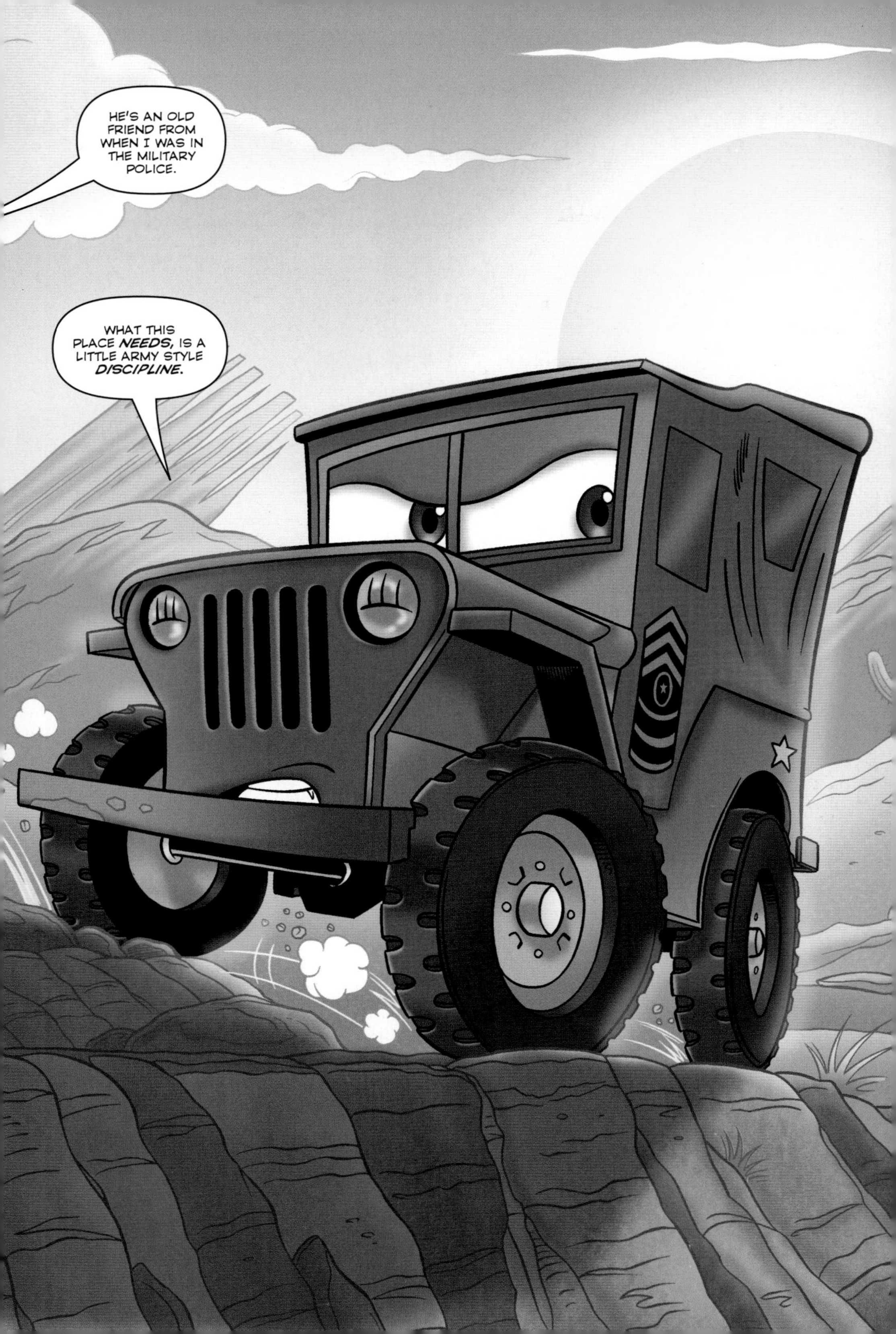
HE'S AN OLD FRIEND FROM WHEN I WAS IN THE MILITARY POLICE.
WHAT THIS PLACE **NEEDS**, IS A LITTLE ARMY STYLE **DISCIPLINE**.

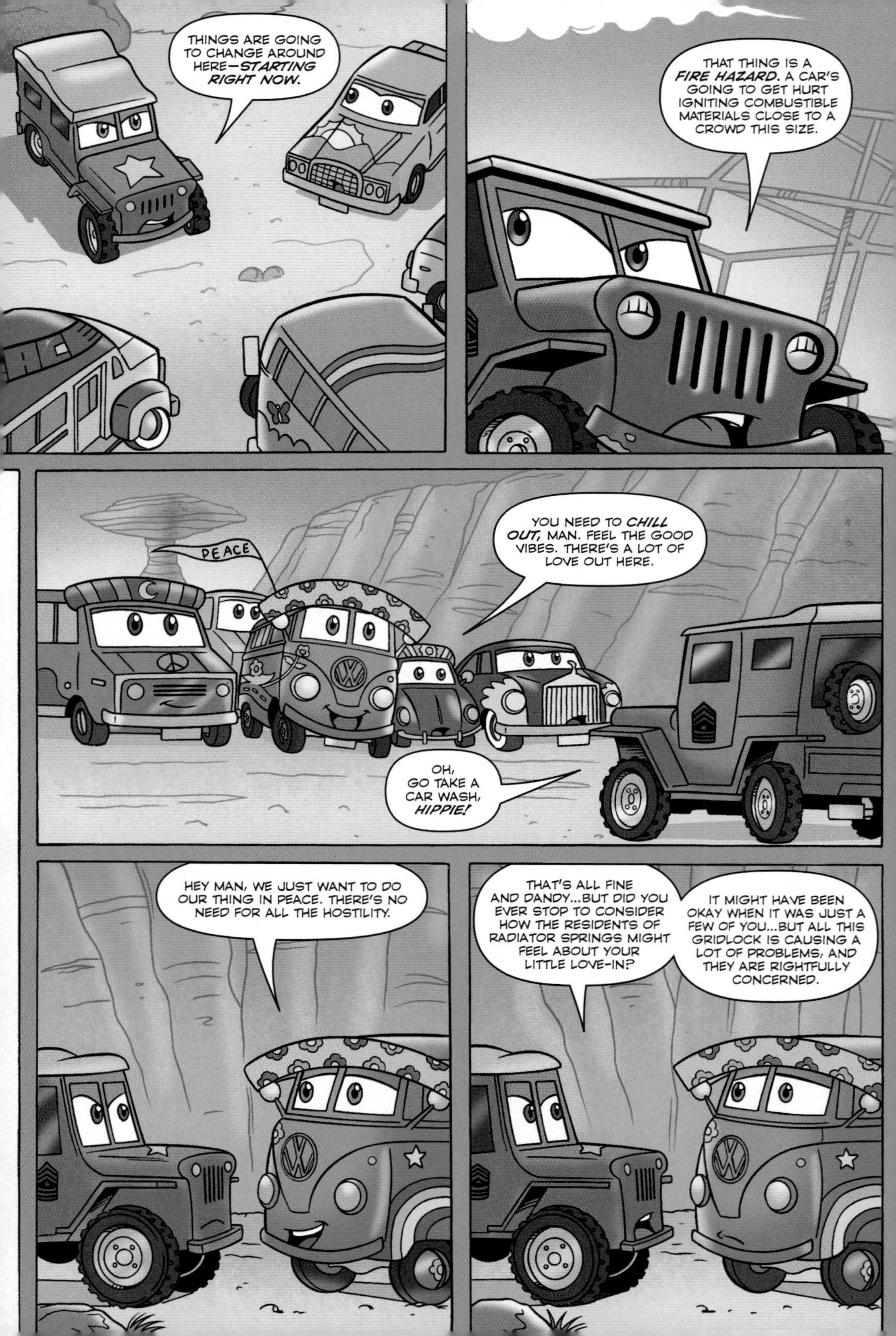
THINGS ARE GOING TO CHANGE AROUND HERE—*STARTING RIGHT NOW.*
THAT THING IS A *FIRE HAZARD.* A CAR'S GOING TO GET HURT IGNITING COMBUSTIBLE MATERIALS CLOSE TO A CROWD THIS SIZE.
PEACE
YOU NEED TO *CHILL OUT,* MAN. FEEL THE GOOD VIBES. THERE'S A LOT OF LOVE OUT HERE.
OH, GO TAKE A CAR WASH, *HIPPIE!*
HEY MAN, WE JUST WANT TO DO OUR THING IN PEACE. THERE'S NO NEED FOR ALL THE HOSTILITY.
THAT'S ALL FINE AND DANDY...BUT DID YOU EVER STOP TO CONSIDER HOW THE RESIDENTS OF RADIATOR SPRINGS MIGHT FEEL ABOUT YOUR LITTLE LOVE-IN?
IT MIGHT HAVE BEEN OKAY WHEN IT WAS JUST A FEW OF YOU...BUT ALL THIS GRIDLOCK IS CAUSING A LOT OF PROBLEMS, AND THEY ARE RIGHTFULLY CONCERNED.

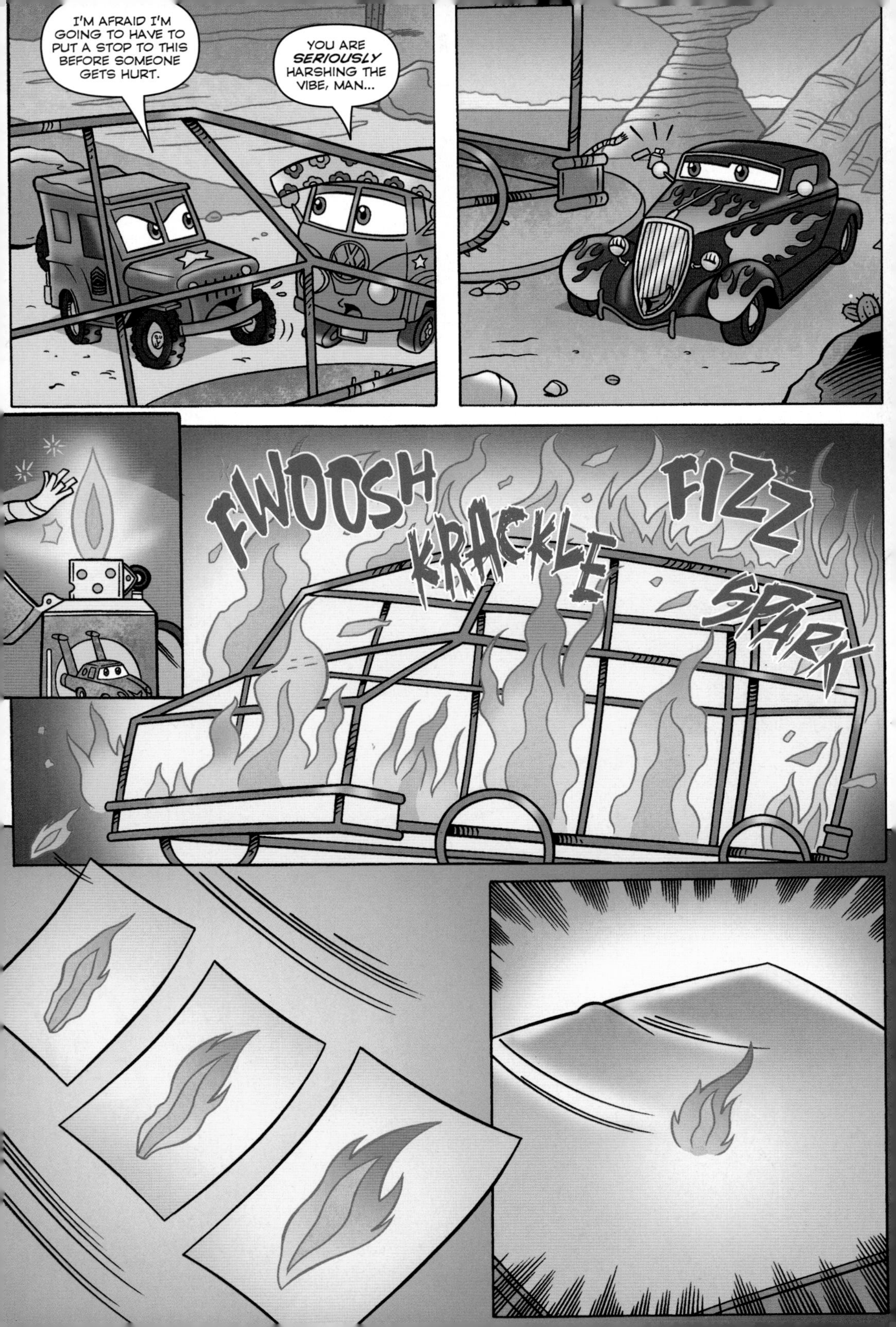

I'M AFRAID I'M GOING TO HAVE TO PUT A STOP TO THIS BEFORE SOMEONE GETS HURT.
YOU ARE *SERIOUSLY* HARSHING THE VIBE, MAN...
FWOOSH
KRACKLE
FIZZ
SPARK

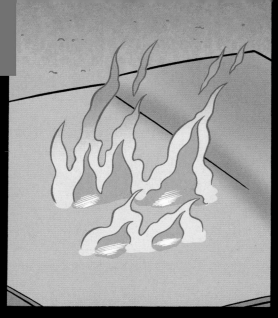

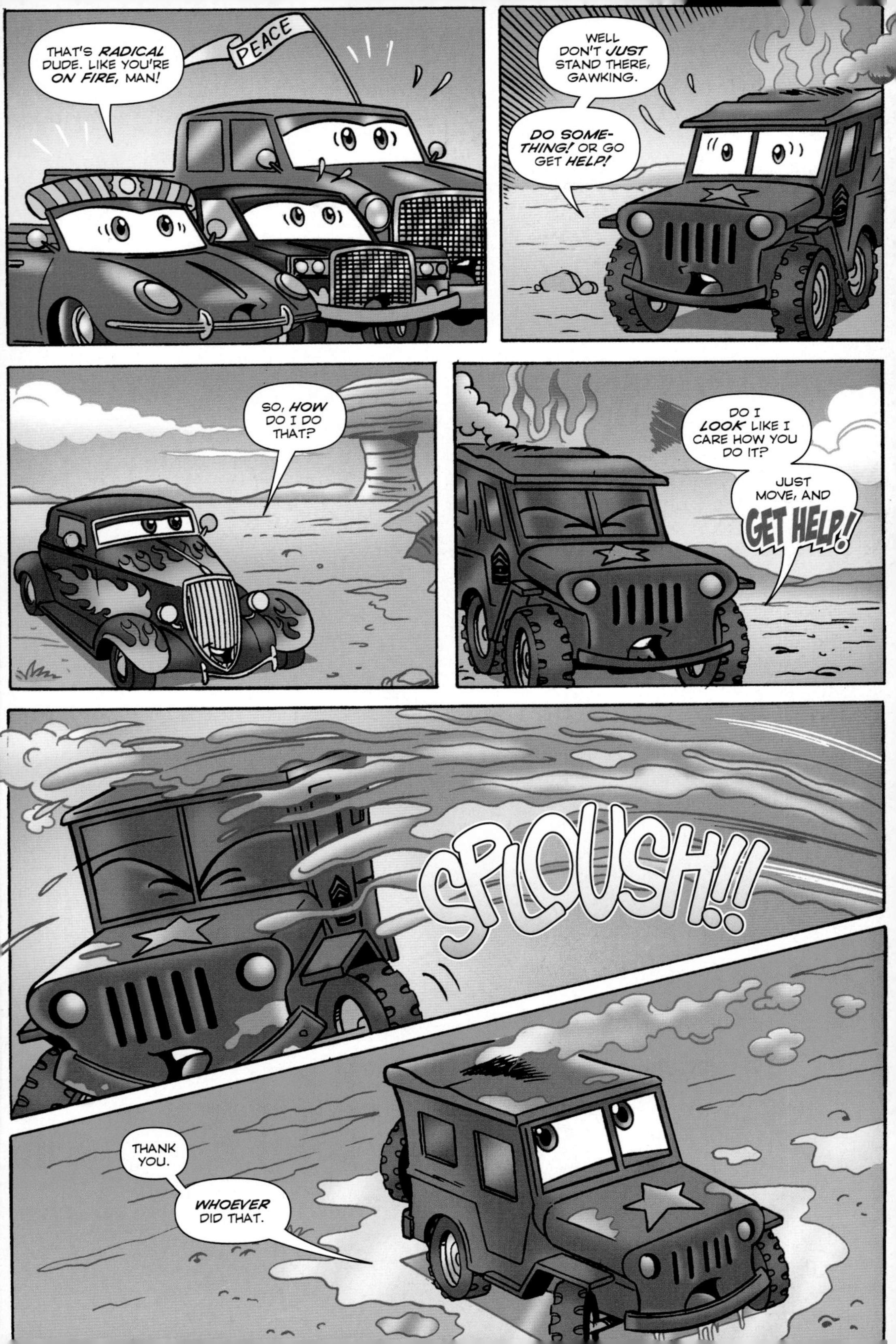
THAT'S RADICAL DUDE. LIKE YOU'RE ON FIRE, MAN!
PEACE
WELL DON'T JUST STAND THERE, GAWKING.
DO SOME-THING! OR GO GET HELP!
SO, HOW DO I DO THAT?
DO I LOOK LIKE I CARE HOW YOU DO IT?
JUST MOVE, AND GET HELP!
SPLOUSH!!
THANK YOU.
WHOEVER DID THAT.

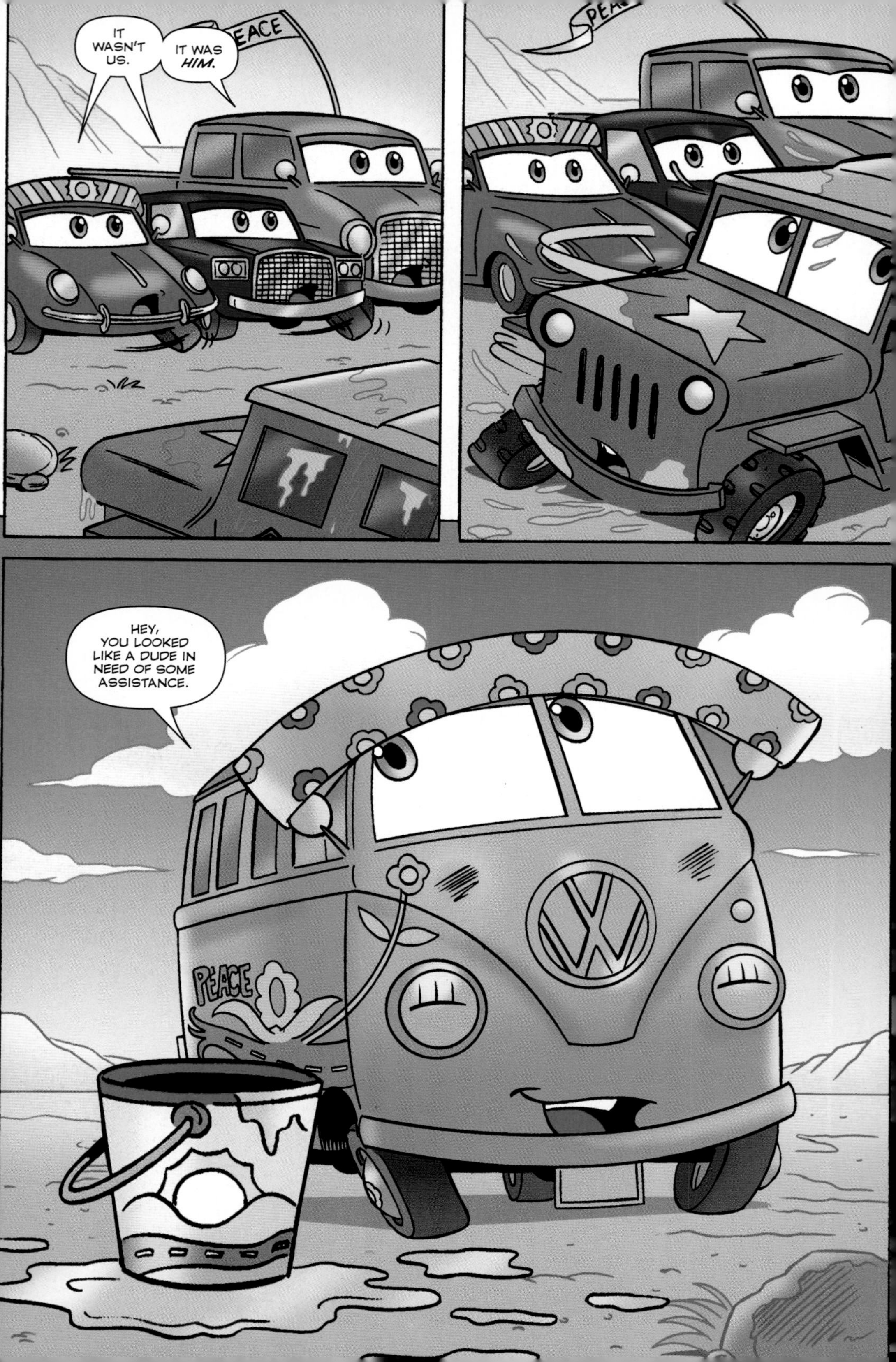
IT WASN'T US.
IT WAS *HIM.*
PEACE
HEY, YOU LOOKED LIKE A DUDE IN NEED OF SOME ASSISTANCE.
PEACE

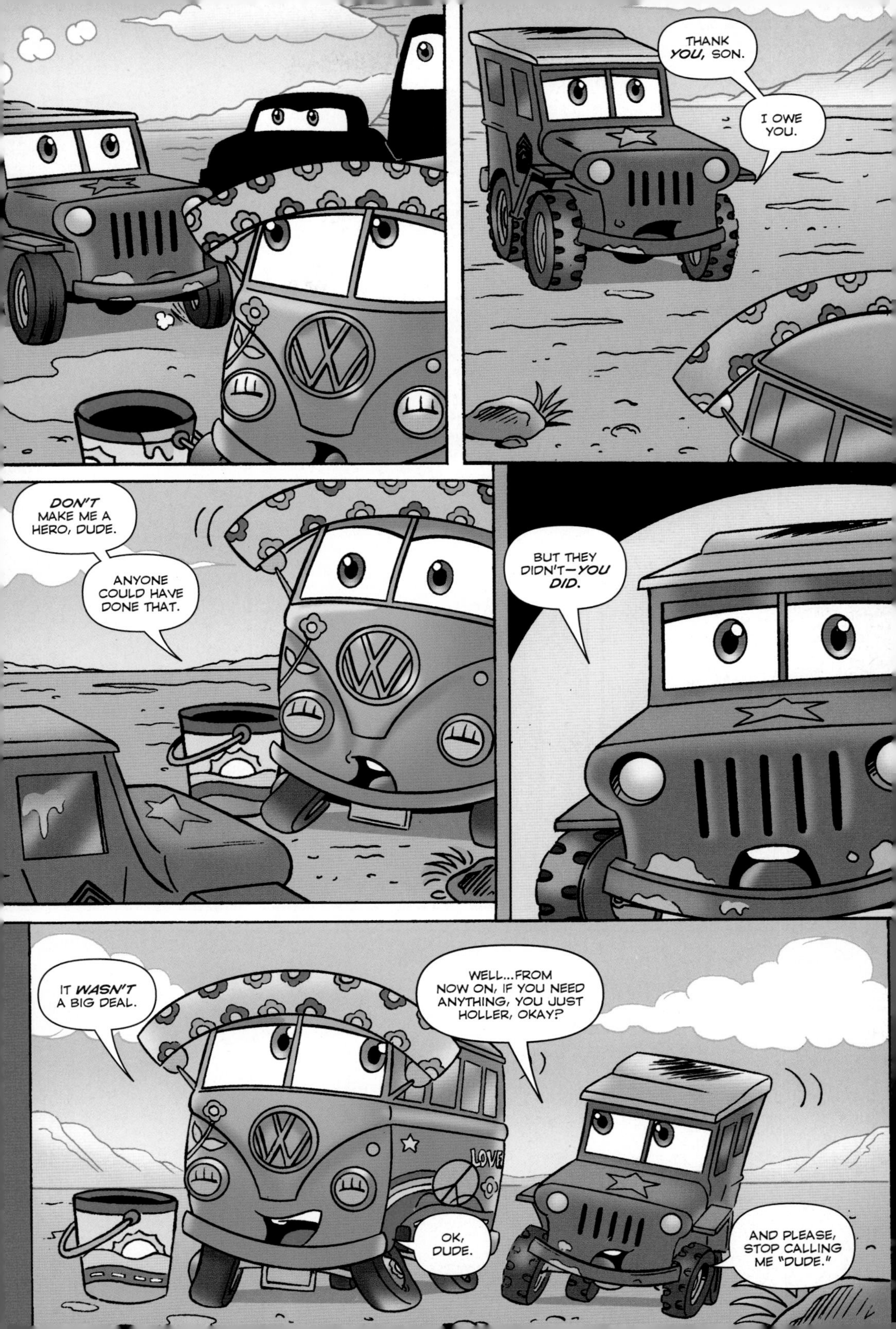
THANK *YOU*, SON.
I OWE YOU.
DON'T MAKE ME A HERO, DUDE.
ANYONE COULD HAVE DONE THAT.
BUT THEY DIDN'T—*YOU DID*.
IT *WASN'T* A BIG DEAL.
WELL...FROM NOW ON, IF YOU NEED ANYTHING, YOU JUST HOLLER, OKAY?
OK, DUDE.
AND PLEASE, STOP CALLING ME "DUDE."
LOVE

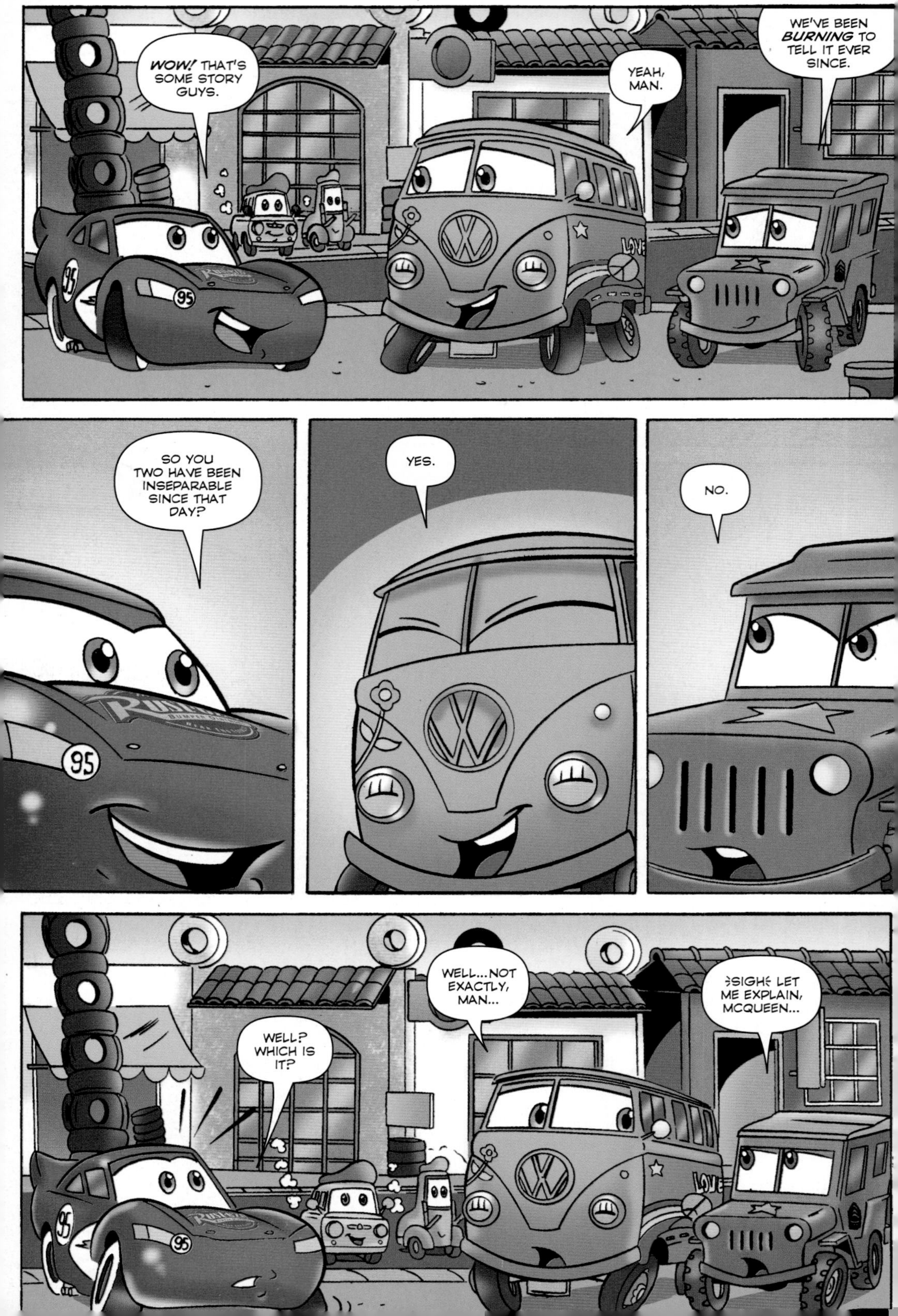
WOW! THAT'S SOME STORY GUYS.
YEAH, MAN.
WE'VE BEEN BURNING TO TELL IT EVER SINCE.
SO YOU TWO HAVE BEEN INSEPARABLE SINCE THAT DAY?
YES.
NO.
WELL? WHICH IS IT?
WELL...NOT EXACTLY, MAN...
SIGH LET ME EXPLAIN, MCQUEEN...

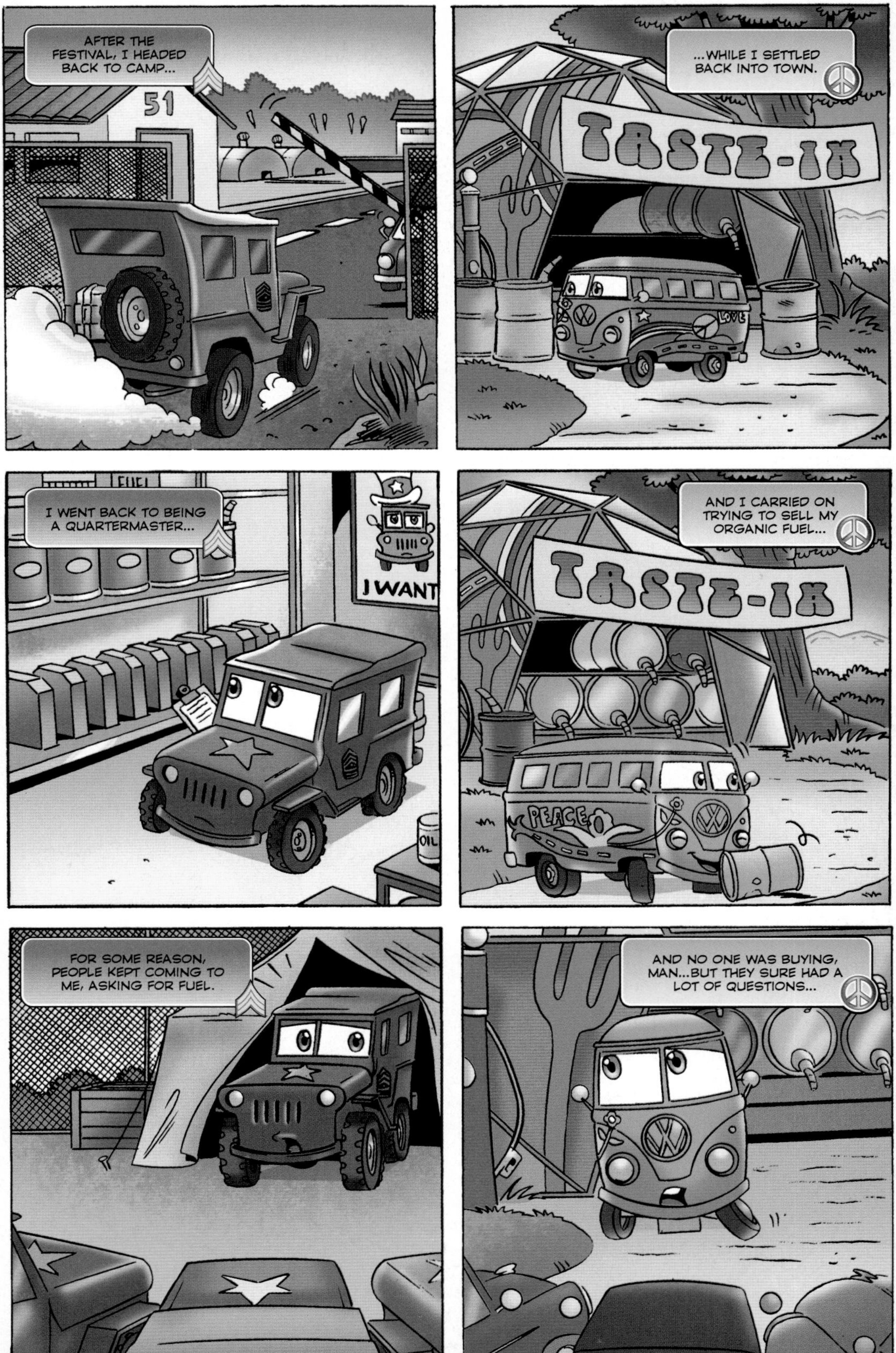
AFTER THE FESTIVAL, I HEADED BACK TO CAMP...
51
...WHILE I SETTLED BACK INTO TOWN.
TASTE-IN
LOVE
I WENT BACK TO BEING A QUARTERMASTER...
I WANT
OIL
AND I CARRIED ON TRYING TO SELL MY ORGANIC FUEL...
TASTE-IN
PEACE
FOR SOME REASON, PEOPLE KEPT COMING TO ME, ASKING FOR FUEL.
AND NO ONE WAS BUYING, MAN...BUT THEY SURE HAD A LOT OF QUESTIONS...

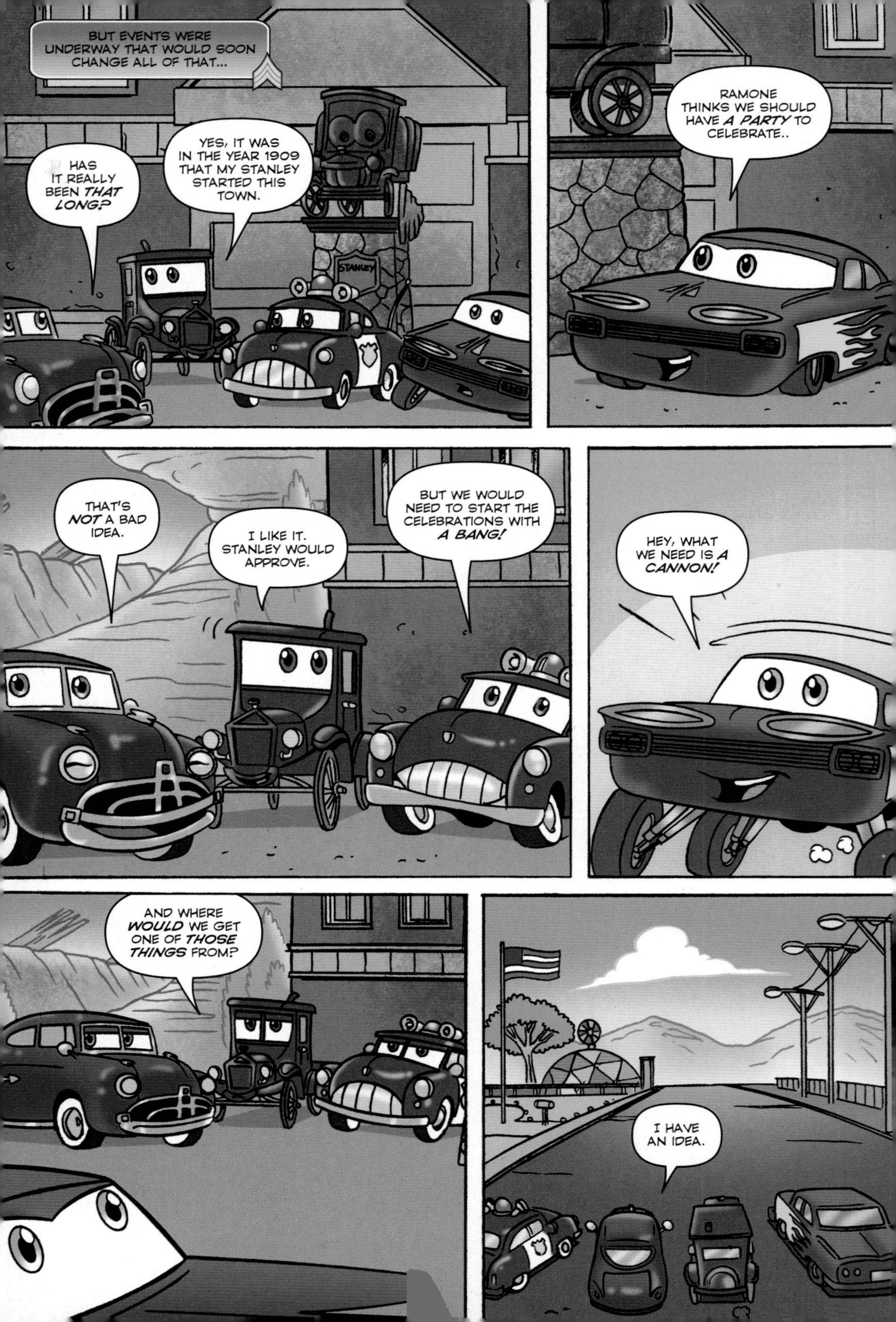
BUT EVENTS WERE UNDERWAY THAT WOULD SOON CHANGE ALL OF THAT...
HAS IT REALLY BEEN *THAT LONG?*
YES, IT WAS IN THE YEAR 1909 THAT MY STANLEY STARTED THIS TOWN.
STANLEY
RAMONE THINKS WE SHOULD HAVE *A PARTY* TO CELEBRATE..
THAT'S *NOT* A BAD IDEA.
I LIKE IT. STANLEY WOULD APPROVE.
BUT WE WOULD NEED TO START THE CELEBRATIONS WITH *A BANG!*
HEY, WHAT WE NEED IS *A CANNON!*
AND WHERE *WOULD* WE GET ONE OF *THOSE THINGS* FROM?
I HAVE AN IDEA.

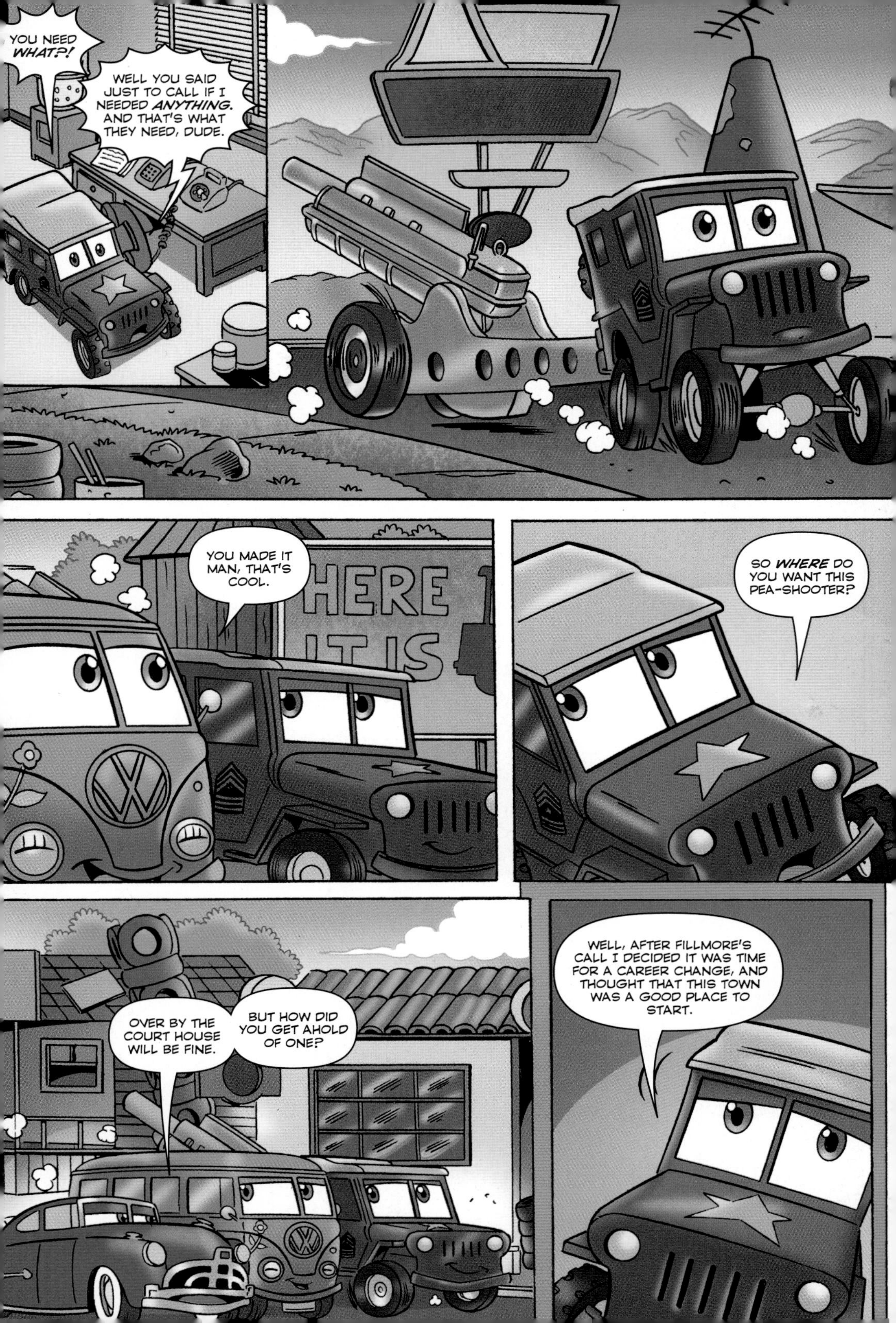

YOU NEED WHAT?!
WELL YOU SAID JUST TO CALL IF I NEEDED ANYTHING. AND THAT'S WHAT THEY NEED, DUDE.
YOU MADE IT MAN, THAT'S COOL.
HERE IT IS
SO WHERE DO YOU WANT THIS PEA-SHOOTER?
OVER BY THE COURT HOUSE WILL BE FINE.
BUT HOW DID YOU GET AHOLD OF ONE?
WELL, AFTER FILLMORE'S CALL I DECIDED IT WAS TIME FOR A CAREER CHANGE, AND THOUGHT THAT THIS TOWN WAS A GOOD PLACE TO START.

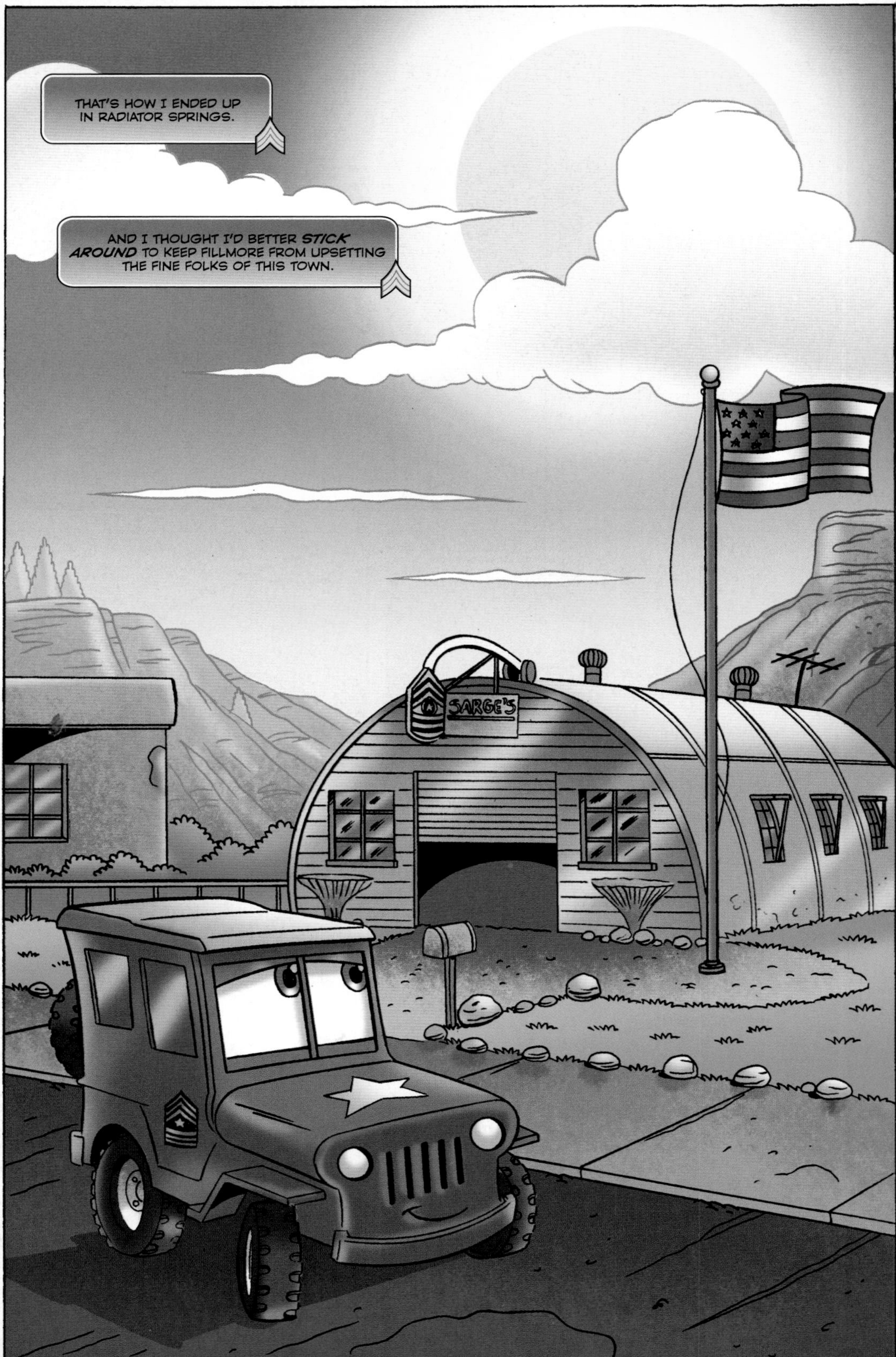

THAT'S HOW I ENDED UP IN RADIATOR SPRINGS.
AND I THOUGHT I'D BETTER *STICK AROUND* TO KEEP FILLMORE FROM UPSETTING THE FINE FOLKS OF THIS TOWN.
SARGE'S

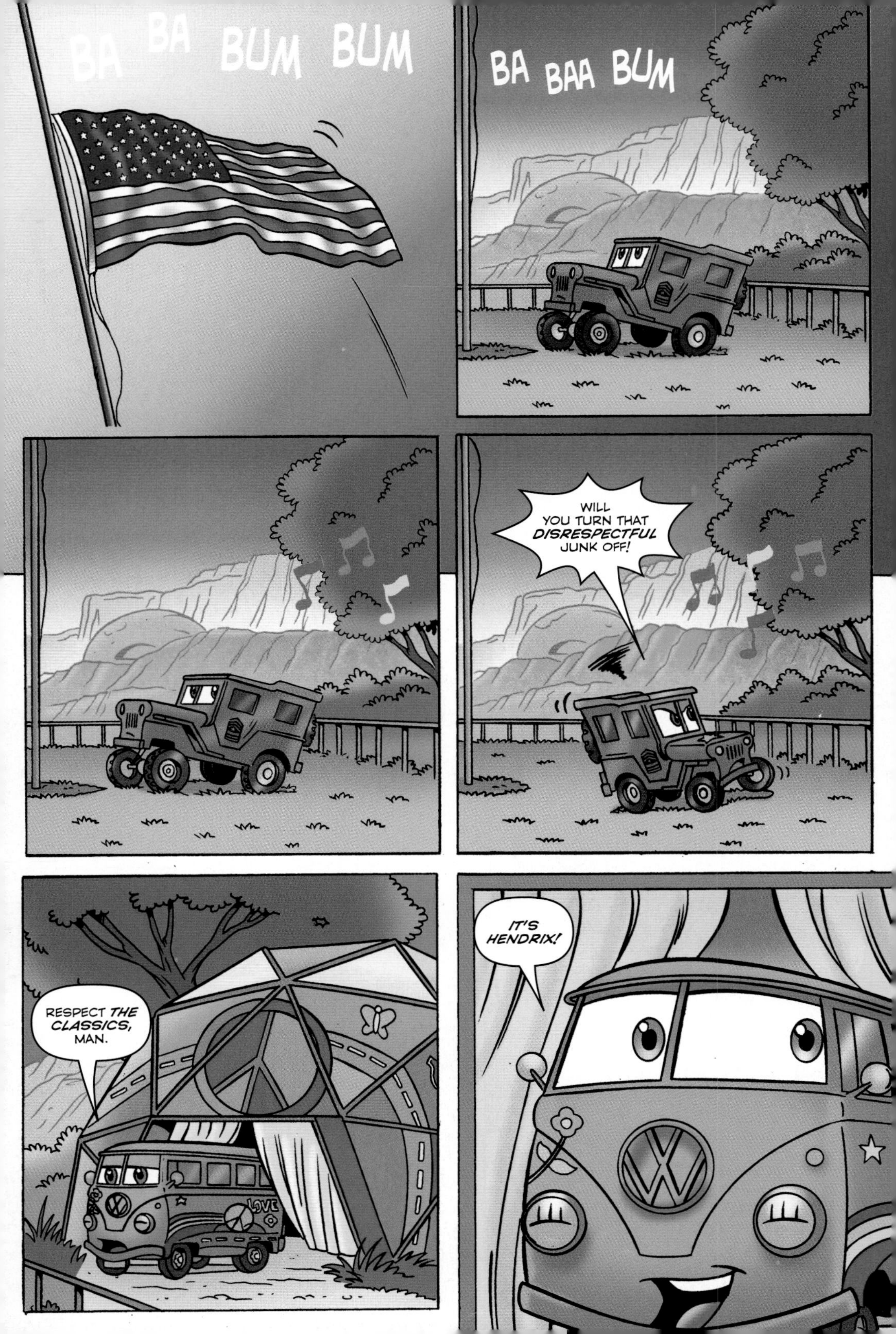
BA BA BUM BUM
BA BAA BUM
WILL YOU TURN THAT *DISRESPECTFUL* JUNK OFF!
RESPECT *THE CLASSICS,* MAN.
IT'S HENDRIX!

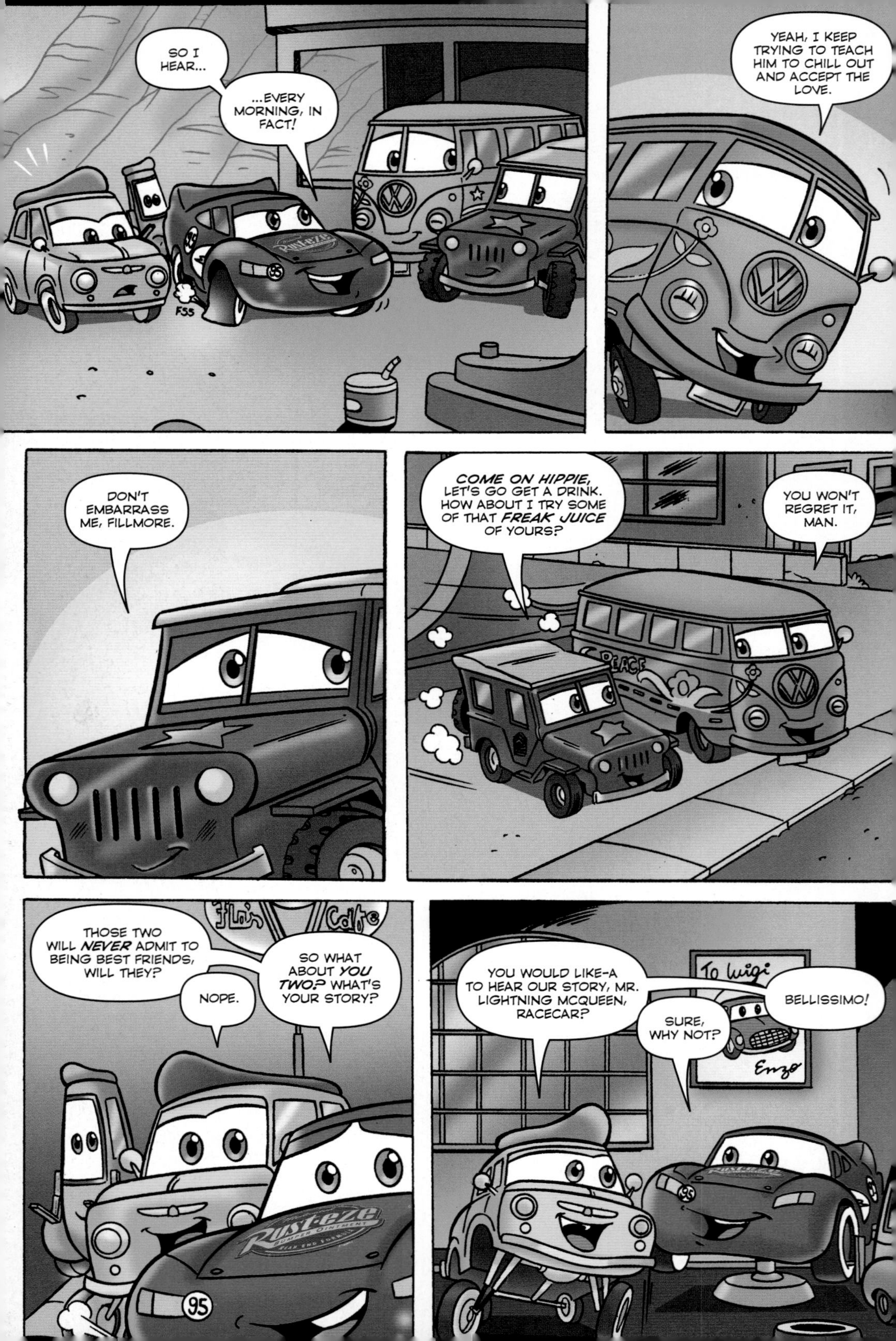
SO I HEAR...
...EVERY MORNING, IN FACT!
F55
YEAH, I KEEP TRYING TO TEACH HIM TO CHILL OUT AND ACCEPT THE LOVE.
DON'T EMBARRASS ME, FILLMORE.
COME ON HIPPIE, LET'S GO GET A DRINK. HOW ABOUT I TRY SOME OF THAT FREAK JUICE OF YOURS?
YOU WON'T REGRET IT, MAN.
PEACE
THOSE TWO WILL NEVER ADMIT TO BEING BEST FRIENDS, WILL THEY?
NOPE.
SO WHAT ABOUT YOU TWO? WHAT'S YOUR STORY?
Rust-eze
95
YOU WOULD LIKE-A TO HEAR OUR STORY, MR. LIGHTNING MCQUEEN, RACECAR?
SURE, WHY NOT?
BELLISSIMO!
To Luigi
Enzo

Chapter Three

OK, MR. RACECAR. IF YOU WANNA *HEAR OUR STORY*, YOU HAVE TO DO *ONE THING* FIRST.

WHAT'S THAT?

YOU HAVE TO LET ME FIXA THAT *FLAT TIRE*.

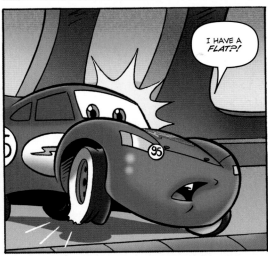

I HAVE A *FLAT?!*

PIT STOP!!

YOU GUYS *REALLY* LOVE TO FOLLOW RACING, DON'T YOU?

WE FOLLOW THE RACING *ALL OUR LIVES*.

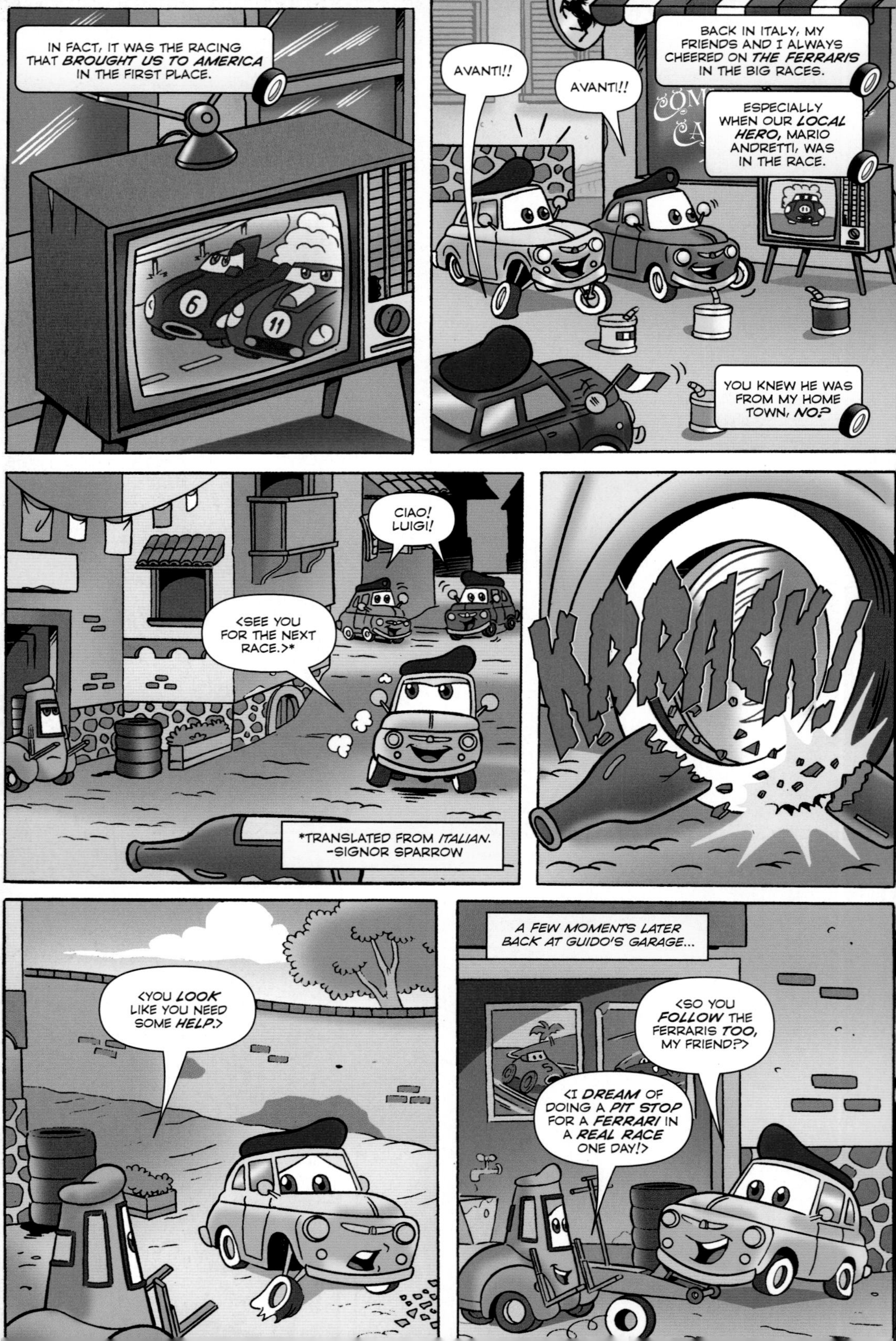

IN FACT, IT WAS THE RACING THAT *BROUGHT US TO AMERICA* IN THE FIRST PLACE.
AVANTI!!
AVANTI!!
BACK IN ITALY, MY FRIENDS AND I ALWAYS CHEERED ON *THE FERRARIS* IN THE BIG RACES.
ESPECIALLY WHEN OUR *LOCAL HERO,* MARIO ANDRETTI, WAS IN THE RACE.
YOU KNEW HE WAS FROM MY HOME TOWN, *NO?*
CIAO! LUIGI!
<SEE YOU FOR THE NEXT RACE.>*
*TRANSLATED FROM *ITALIAN*. -SIGNOR SPARROW
KRRACK!
<YOU *LOOK* LIKE YOU NEED SOME *HELP.*>
A FEW MOMENTS LATER BACK AT GUIDO'S GARAGE...
<SO YOU *FOLLOW* THE FERRARIS *TOO,* MY FRIEND?>
<I *DREAM* OF DOING A *PIT STOP* FOR A *FERRARI* IN A *REAL RACE* ONE DAY!>

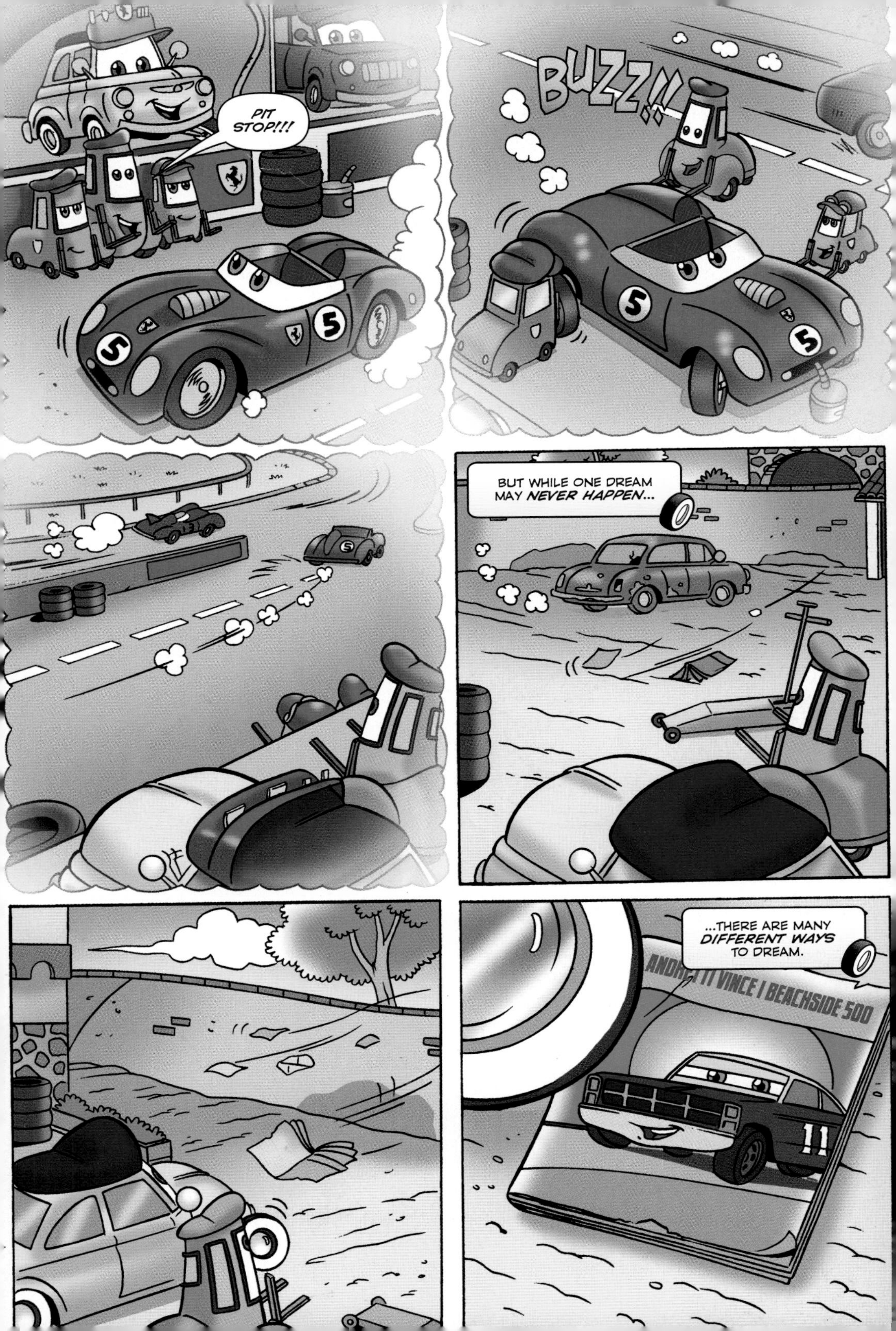
PIT STOP!!!
BUZZ!!
BUT WHILE ONE DREAM MAY *NEVER HAPPEN*...
...THERE ARE MANY *DIFFERENT WAYS* TO DREAM.
BEACHSIDE 500

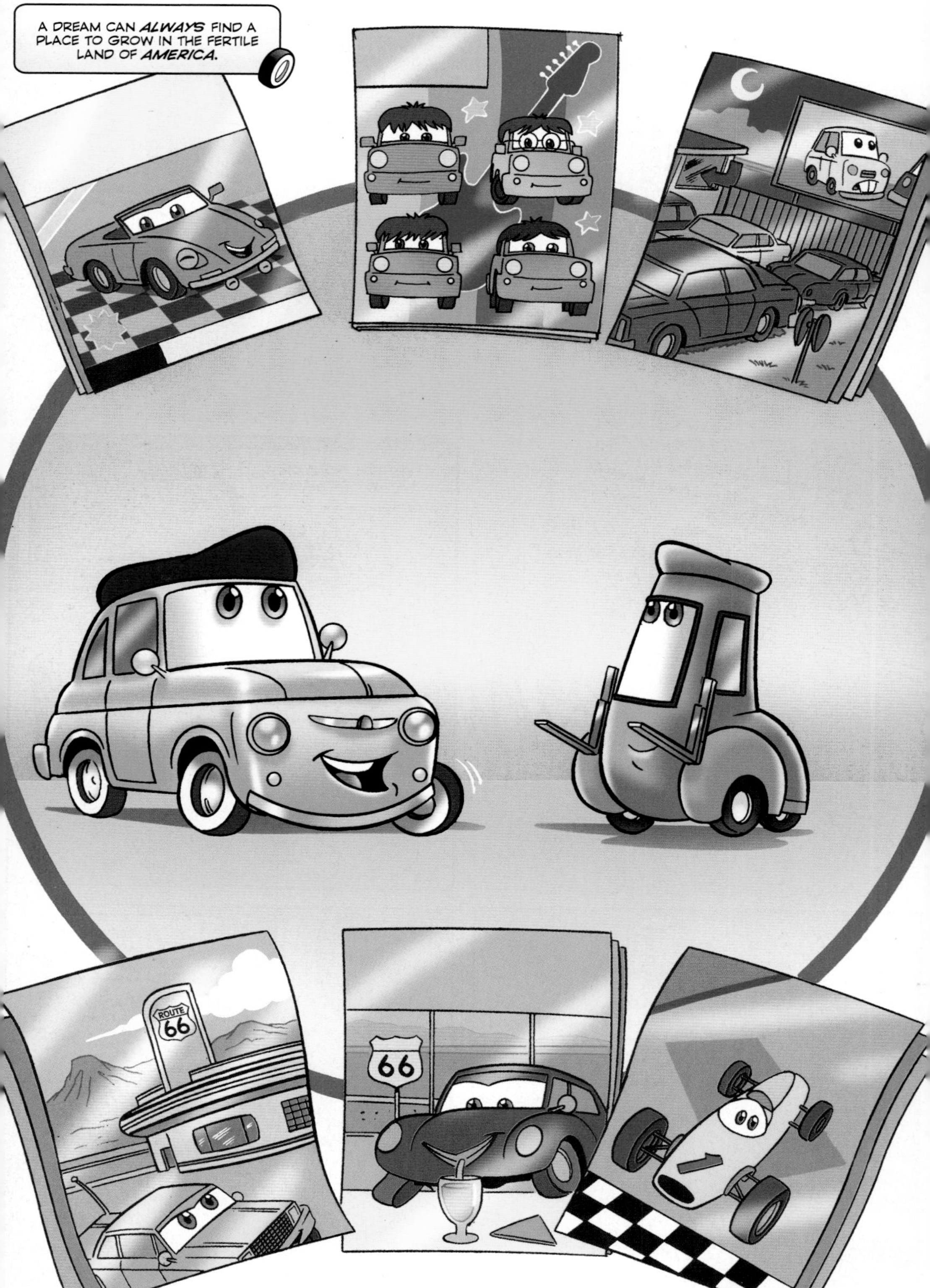
A DREAM CAN *ALWAYS* FIND A PLACE TO GROW IN THE FERTILE LAND OF *AMERICA*.
ROUTE 66
66

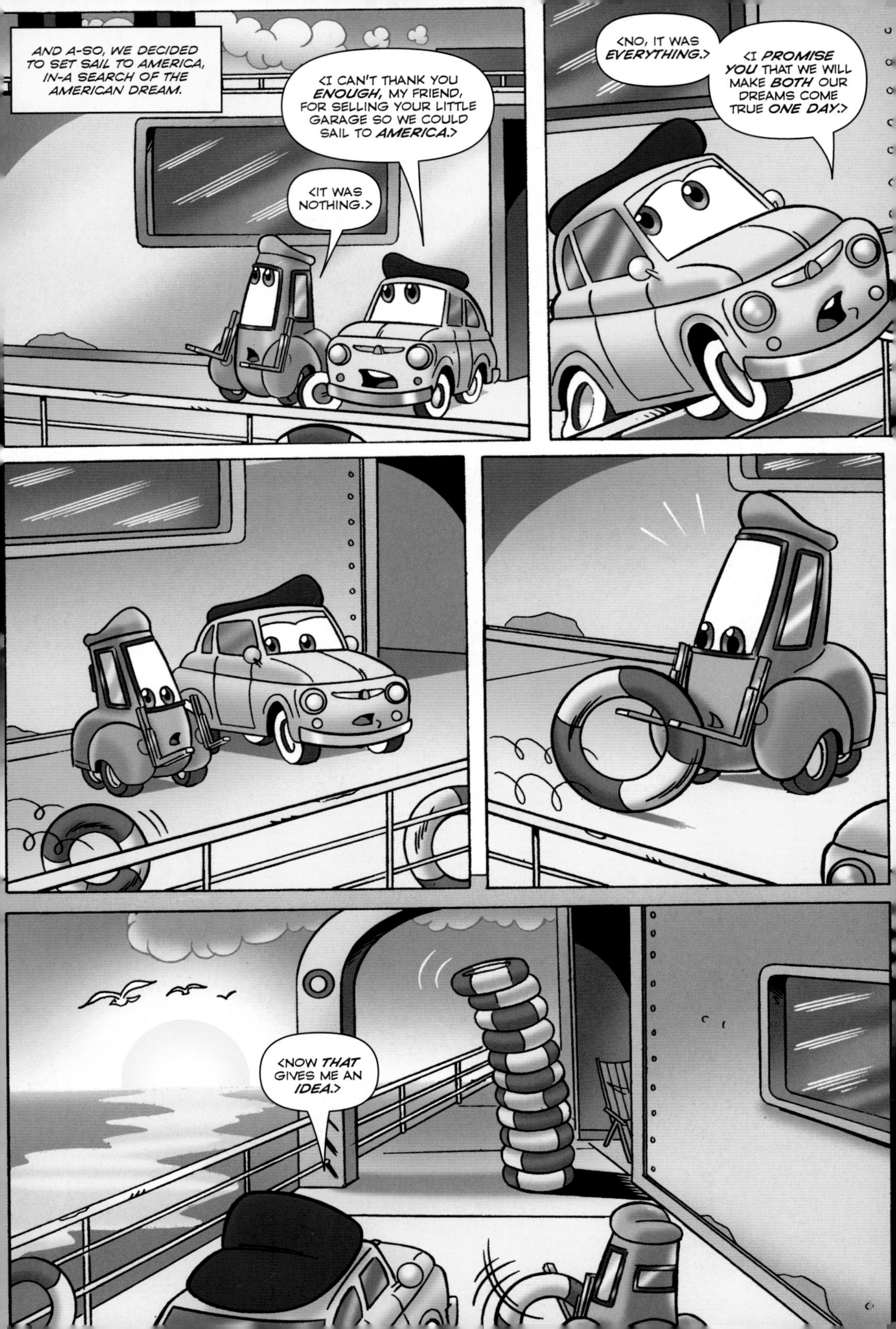
AND A-SO, WE DECIDED TO SET SAIL TO AMERICA, IN-A SEARCH OF THE AMERICAN DREAM.
<I CAN'T THANK YOU ENOUGH, MY FRIEND, FOR SELLING YOUR LITTLE GARAGE SO WE COULD SAIL TO AMERICA.>
<IT WAS NOTHING.>
<NO, IT WAS EVERYTHING.>
<I PROMISE YOU THAT WE WILL MAKE BOTH OUR DREAMS COME TRUE ONE DAY.>
<NOW THAT GIVES ME AN IDEA.>

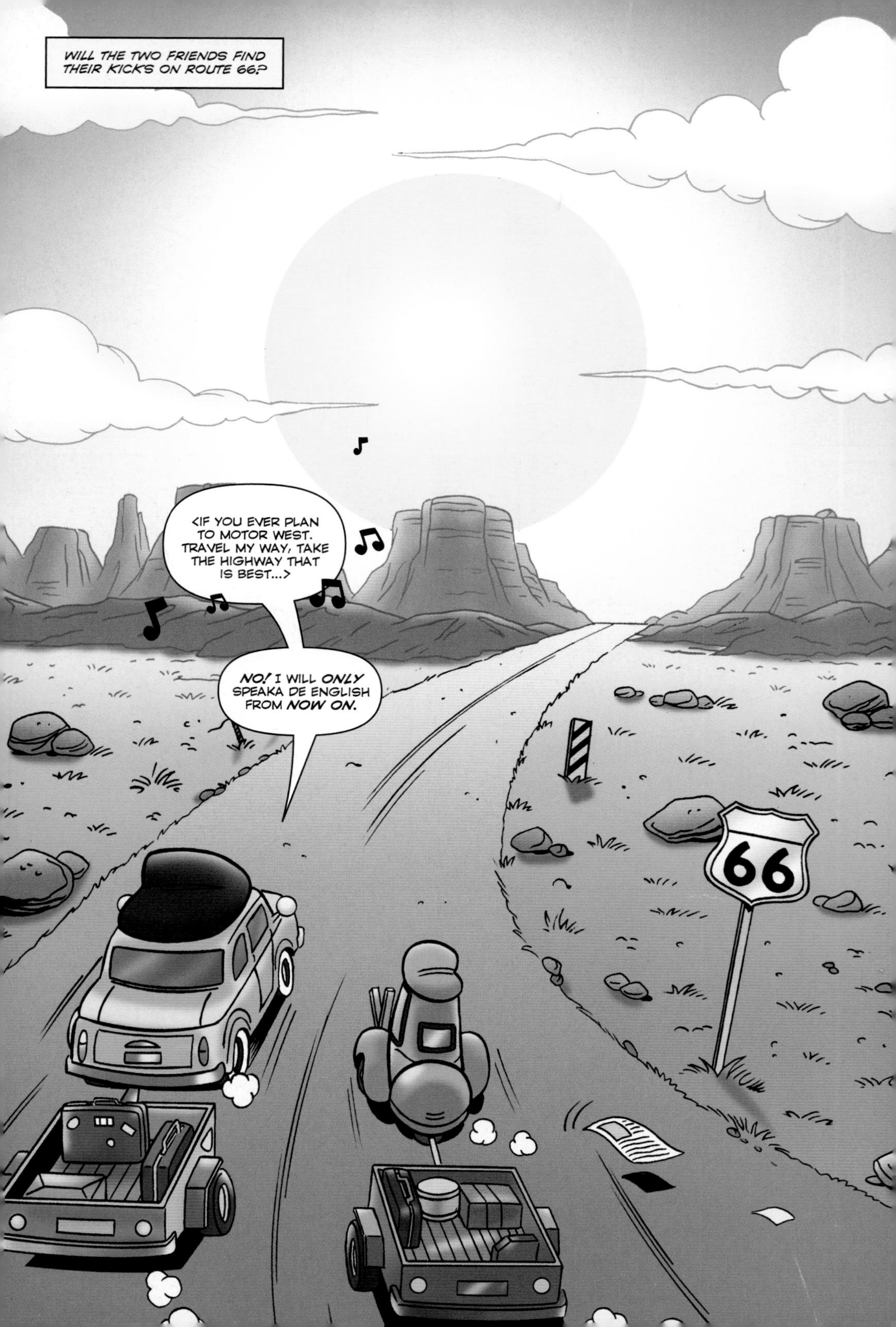
WILL THE TWO FRIENDS FIND THEIR KICKS ON ROUTE 66?
<IF YOU EVER PLAN TO MOTOR WEST. TRAVEL MY WAY, TAKE THE HIGHWAY THAT IS BEST...>
NO! I WILL ONLY SPEAKA DE ENGLISH FROM NOW ON.
66

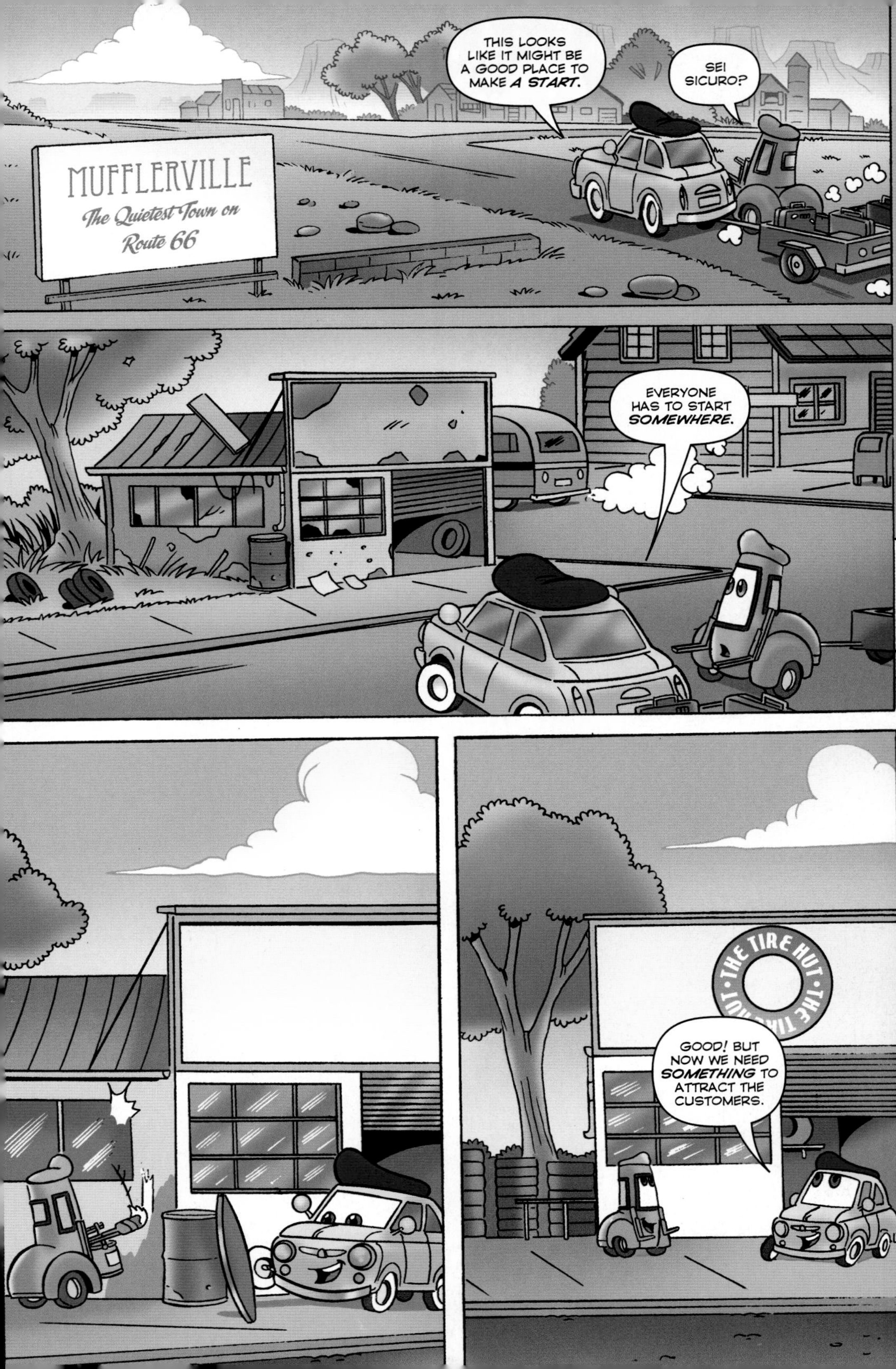
MUFFLERVILLE
The Quietest Town on Route 66
THIS LOOKS LIKE IT MIGHT BE A GOOD PLACE TO MAKE A START.
SEI SICURO?
EVERYONE HAS TO START SOMEWHERE.
THE TIRE HUT · THE TIRE HUT
GOOD! BUT NOW WE NEED SOMETHING TO ATTRACT THE CUSTOMERS.

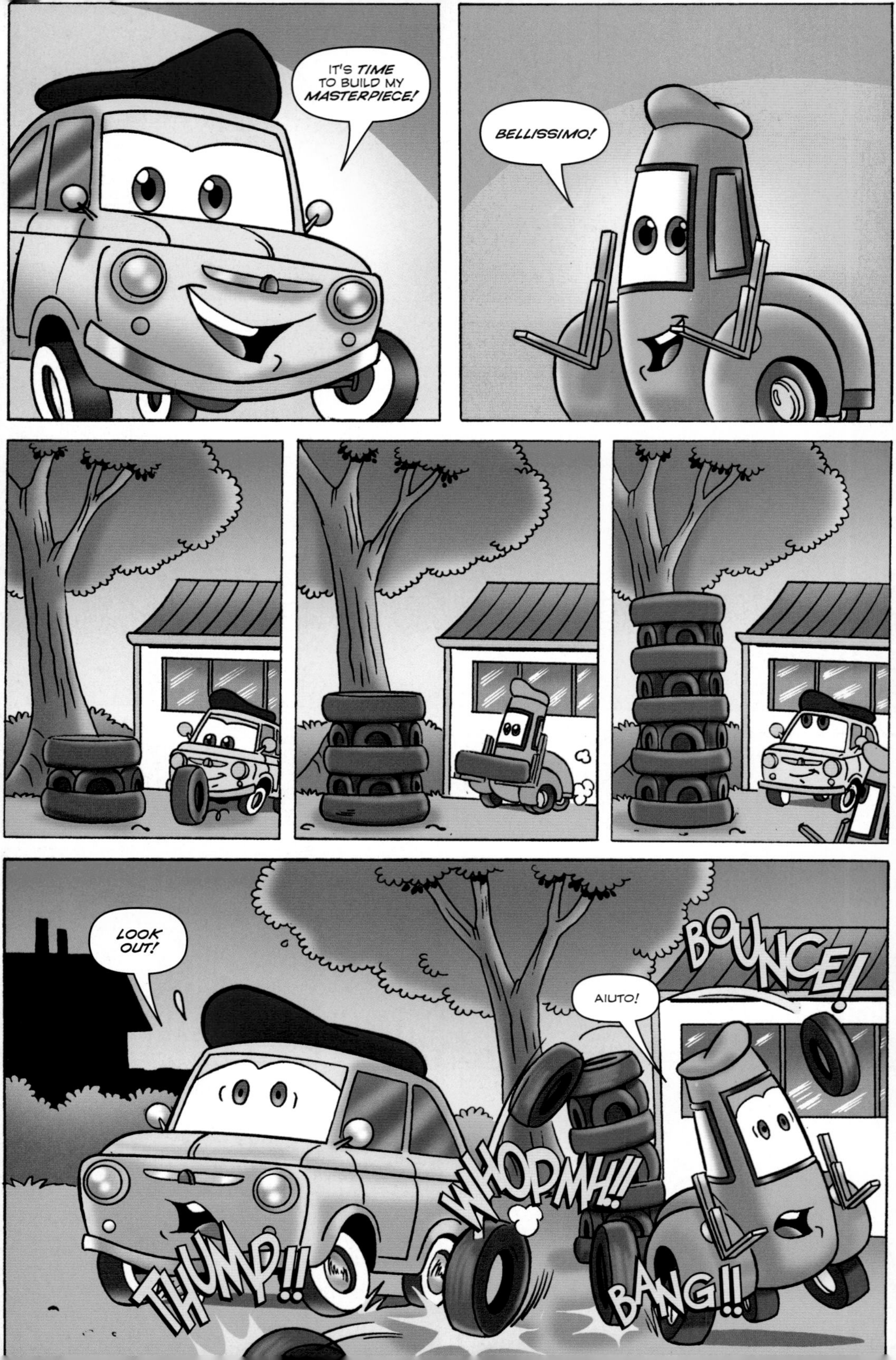
IT'S *TIME* TO BUILD MY *MASTERPIECE!*
BELLISSIMO!
LOOK OUT!
AIUTO!
BOUNCE!
WHOPMH!!
THUMP!!
BANG!!

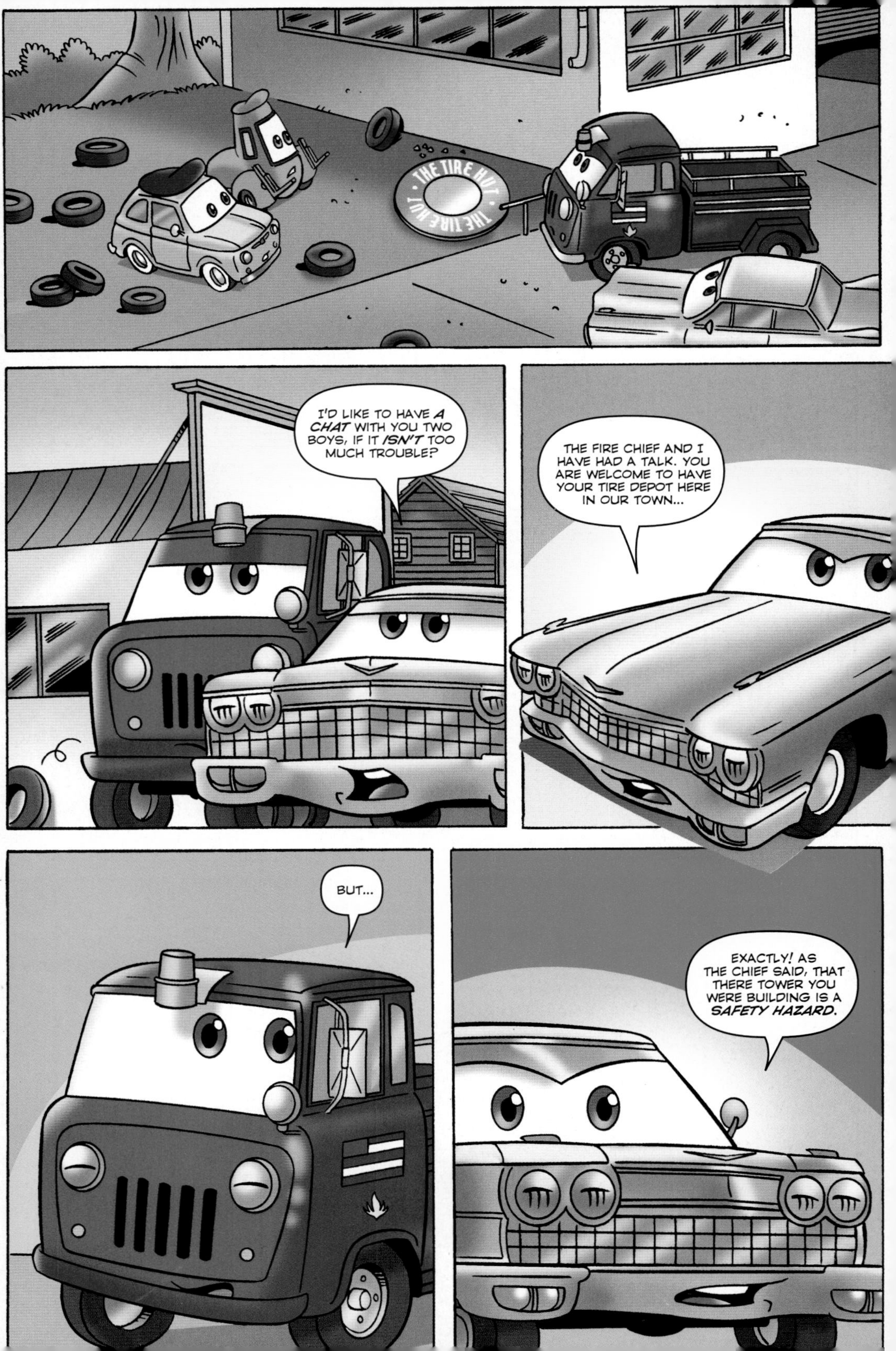
THE TIRE HUT THE TIRE HUT
I'D LIKE TO HAVE *A CHAT* WITH YOU TWO BOYS, IF IT *ISN'T* TOO MUCH TROUBLE?
THE FIRE CHIEF AND I HAVE HAD A TALK. YOU ARE WELCOME TO HAVE YOUR TIRE DEPOT HERE IN OUR TOWN...
BUT...
EXACTLY! AS THE CHIEF SAID, THAT THERE TOWER YOU WERE BUILDING IS A *SAFETY HAZARD*.

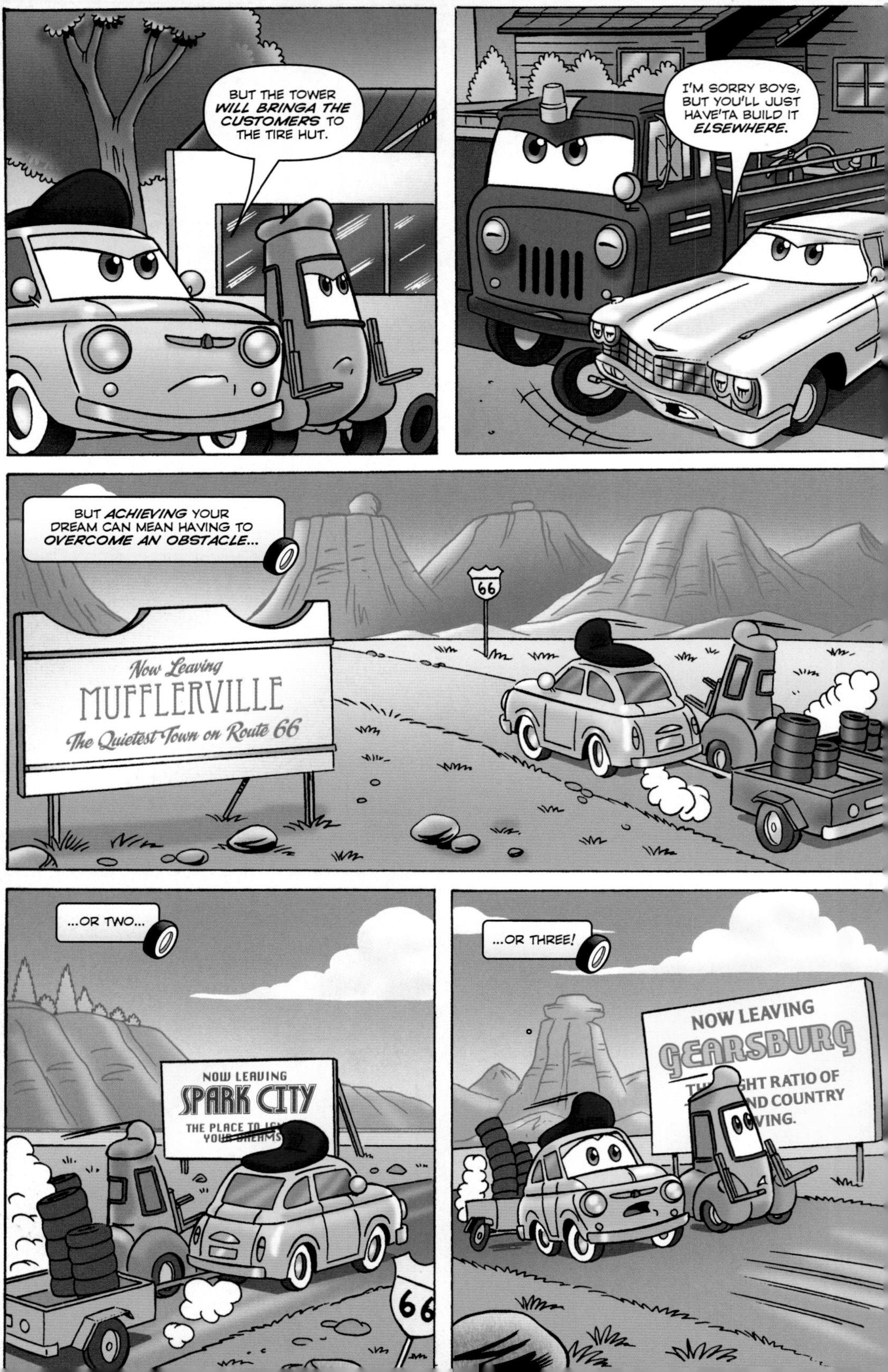
BUT THE TOWER *WILL BRINGA THE CUSTOMERS* TO THE TIRE HUT.
I'M SORRY BOYS, BUT YOU'LL JUST HAVE'TA BUILD IT *ELSEWHERE*.
BUT *ACHIEVING* YOUR DREAM CAN MEAN HAVING TO *OVERCOME AN OBSTACLE*...
66
Now Leaving
MUFFLERVILLE
The Quietest Town on Route 66
...OR TWO...
NOW LEAVING
SPARK CITY
66
...OR THREE!
NOW LEAVING
GEARSBURG

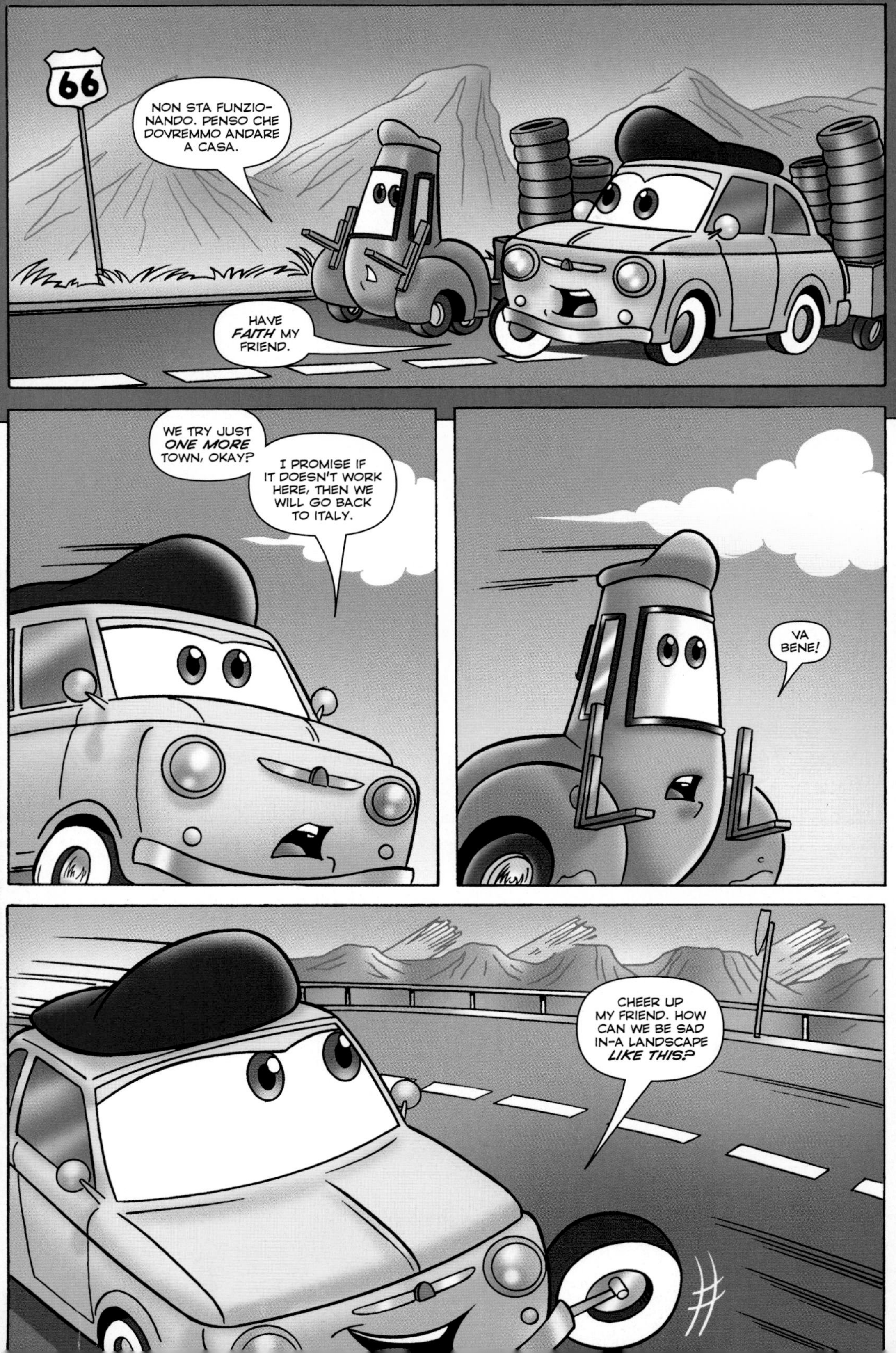
66
NON STA FUNZIONANDO. PENSO CHE DOVREMMO ANDARE A CASA.
HAVE *FAITH* MY FRIEND.
WE TRY JUST *ONE MORE* TOWN, OKAY?
I PROMISE IF IT DOESN'T WORK HERE, THEN WE WILL GO BACK TO ITALY.
VA BENE!
CHEER UP MY FRIEND. HOW CAN WE BE SAD IN-A LANDSCAPE *LIKE THIS?*

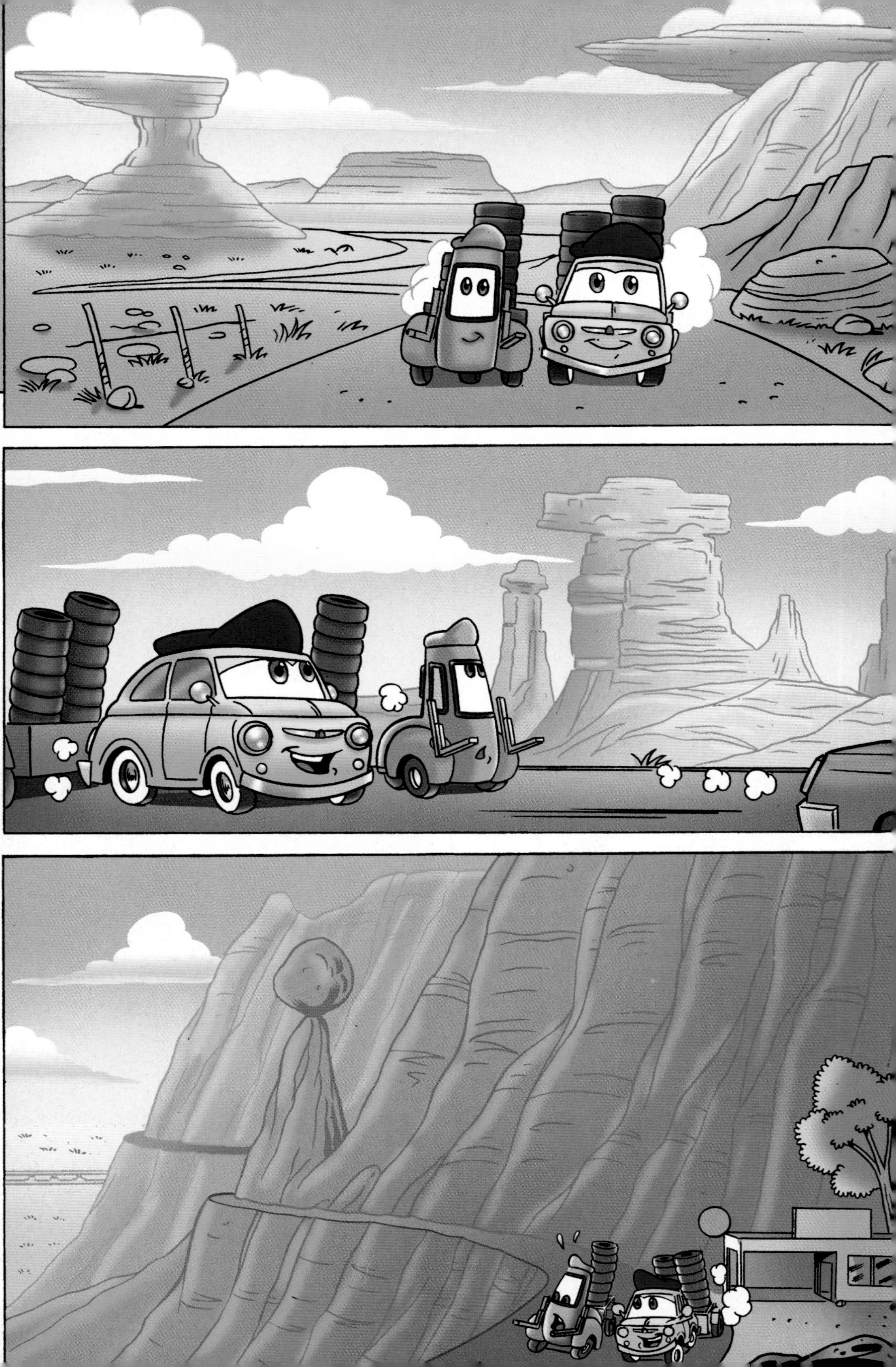

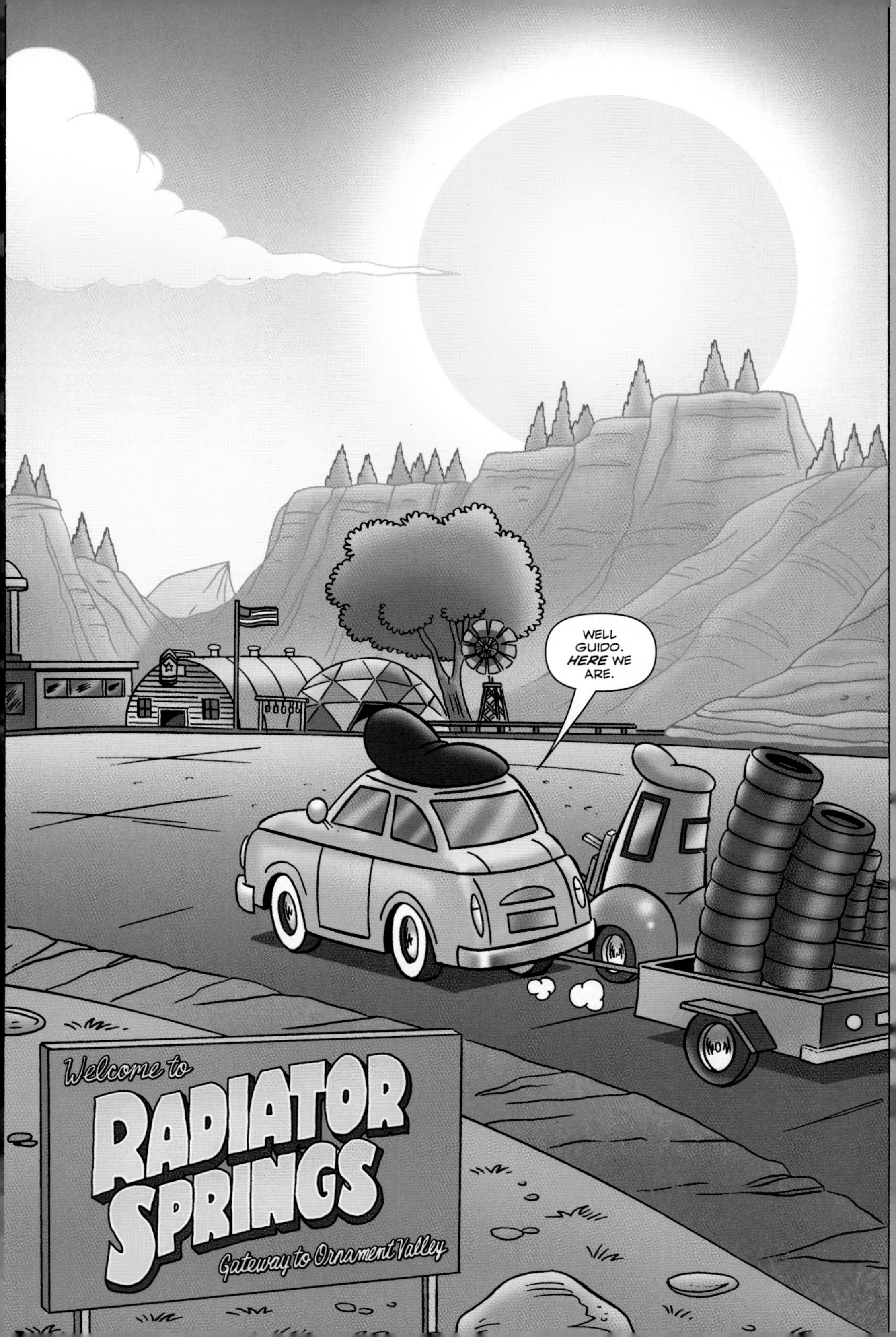
WELL GUIDO. *HERE* WE ARE.
Welcome to
RADIATOR SPRINGS
Gateway to Ornament Valley

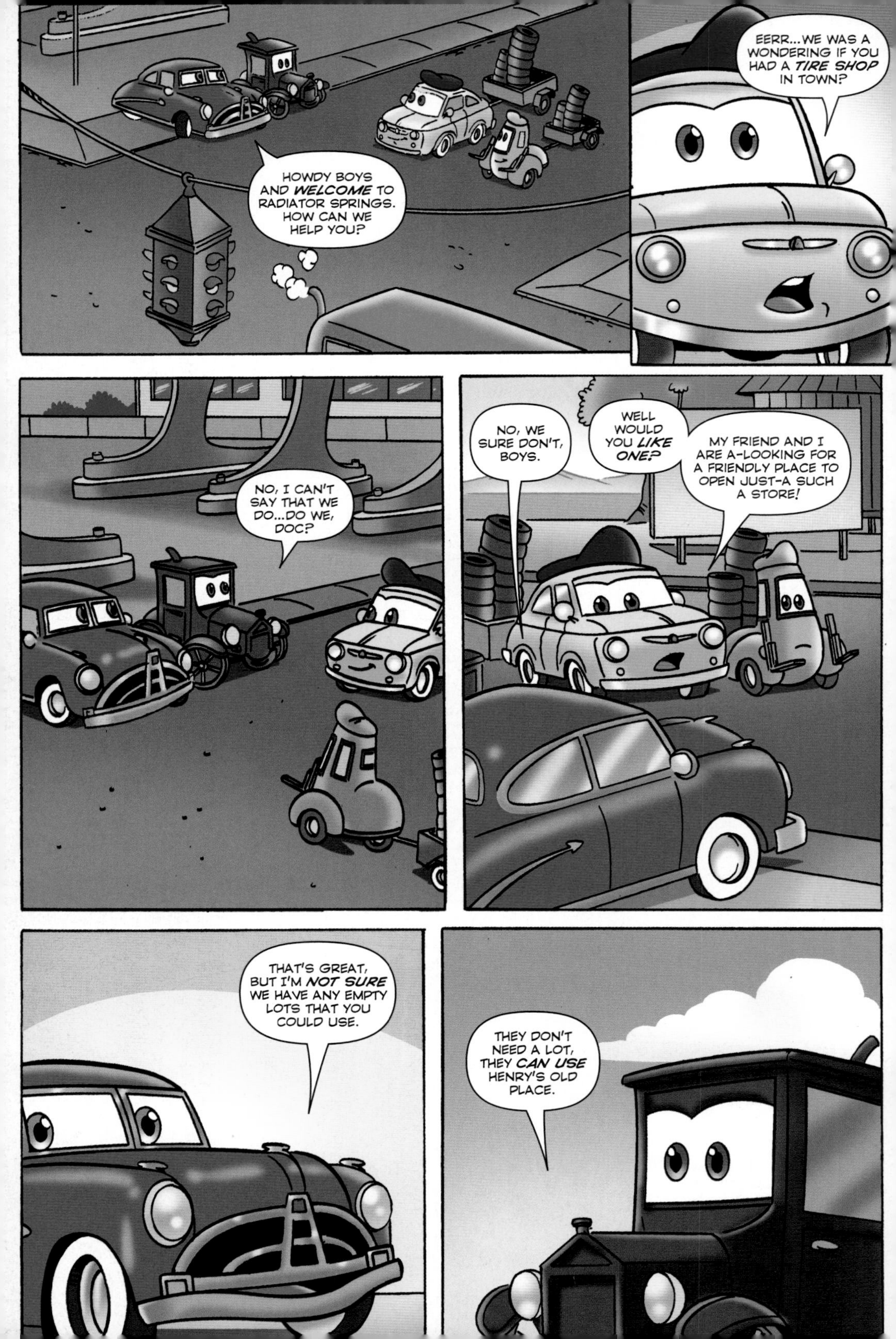
HOWDY BOYS AND WELCOME TO RADIATOR SPRINGS. HOW CAN WE HELP YOU?
EERR...WE WAS A WONDERING IF YOU HAD A TIRE SHOP IN TOWN?
NO, I CAN'T SAY THAT WE DO...DO WE, DOC?
NO, WE SURE DON'T, BOYS.
WELL WOULD YOU LIKE ONE?
MY FRIEND AND I ARE A-LOOKING FOR A FRIENDLY PLACE TO OPEN JUST-A SUCH A STORE!
THAT'S GREAT, BUT I'M NOT SURE WE HAVE ANY EMPTY LOTS THAT YOU COULD USE.
THEY DON'T NEED A LOT, THEY CAN USE HENRY'S OLD PLACE.

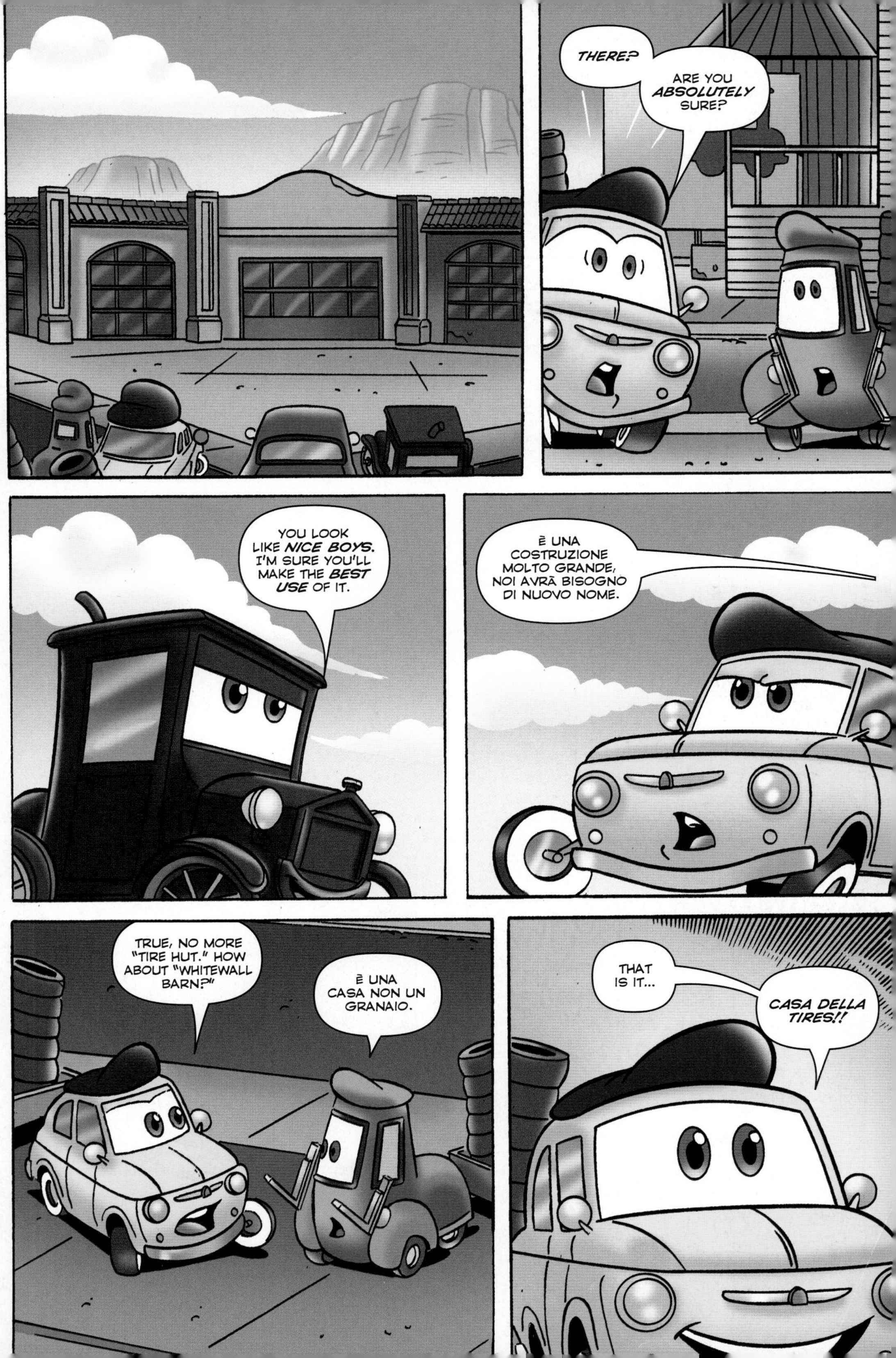
THERE?
ARE YOU ABSOLUTELY SURE?
YOU LOOK LIKE NICE BOYS. I'M SURE YOU'LL MAKE THE BEST USE OF IT.
È UNA COSTRUZIONE MOLTO GRANDE, NOI AVRÀ BISOGNO DI NUOVO NOME.
TRUE, NO MORE "TIRE HUT." HOW ABOUT "WHITEWALL BARN?"
È UNA CASA NON UN GRANAIO.
THAT IS IT...
CASA DELLA TIRES!!

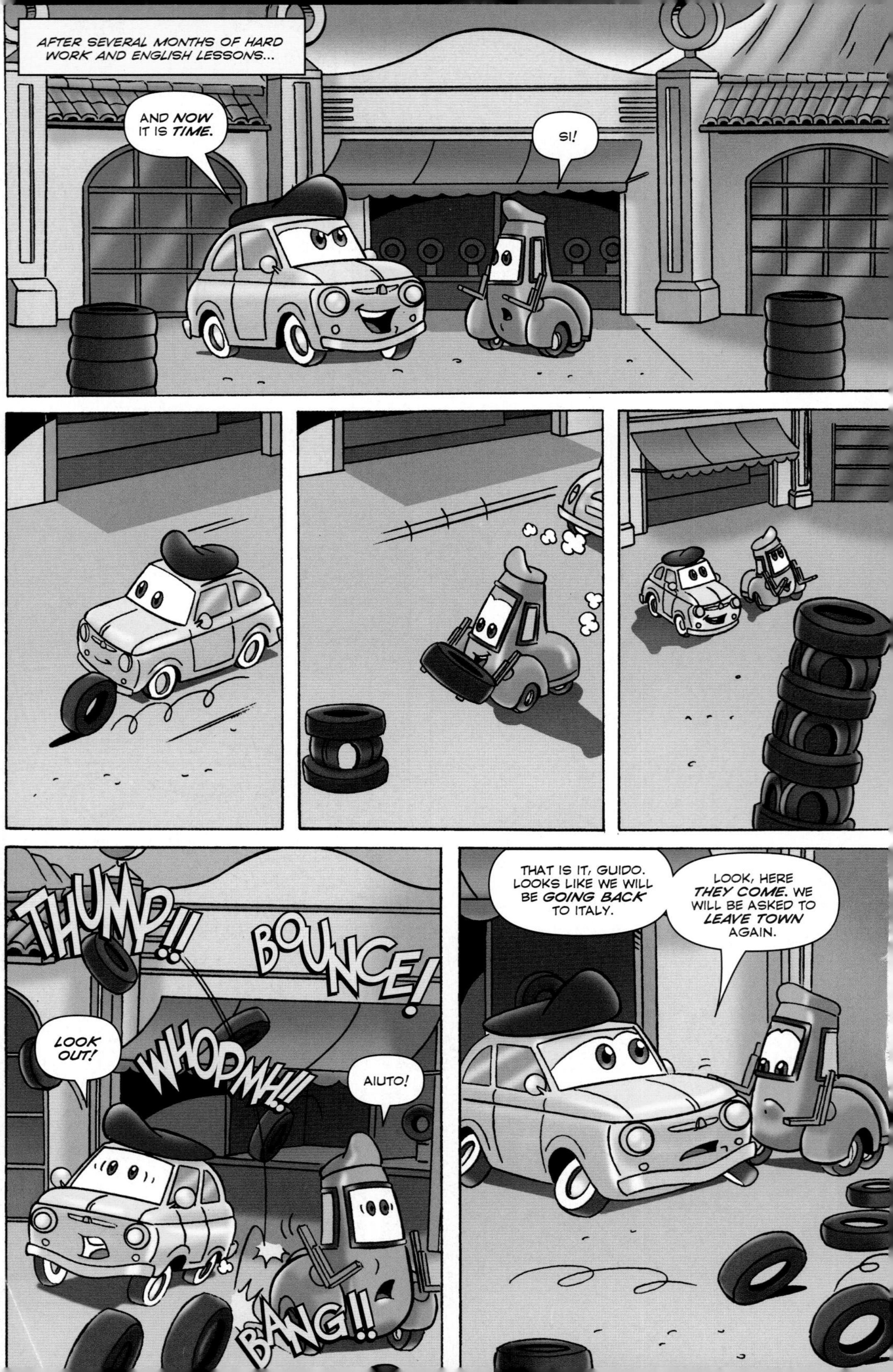
AFTER SEVERAL MONTHS OF HARD WORK AND ENGLISH LESSONS...
AND *NOW* IT IS *TIME.*
SI!
THUMP!!
BOUNCE!
LOOK OUT!
WHOPMH!!
AIUTO!
BANG!!
THAT IS IT, GUIDO. LOOKS LIKE WE WILL BE *GOING BACK* TO ITALY.
LOOK, HERE *THEY COME.* WE WILL BE ASKED TO *LEAVE TOWN* AGAIN.

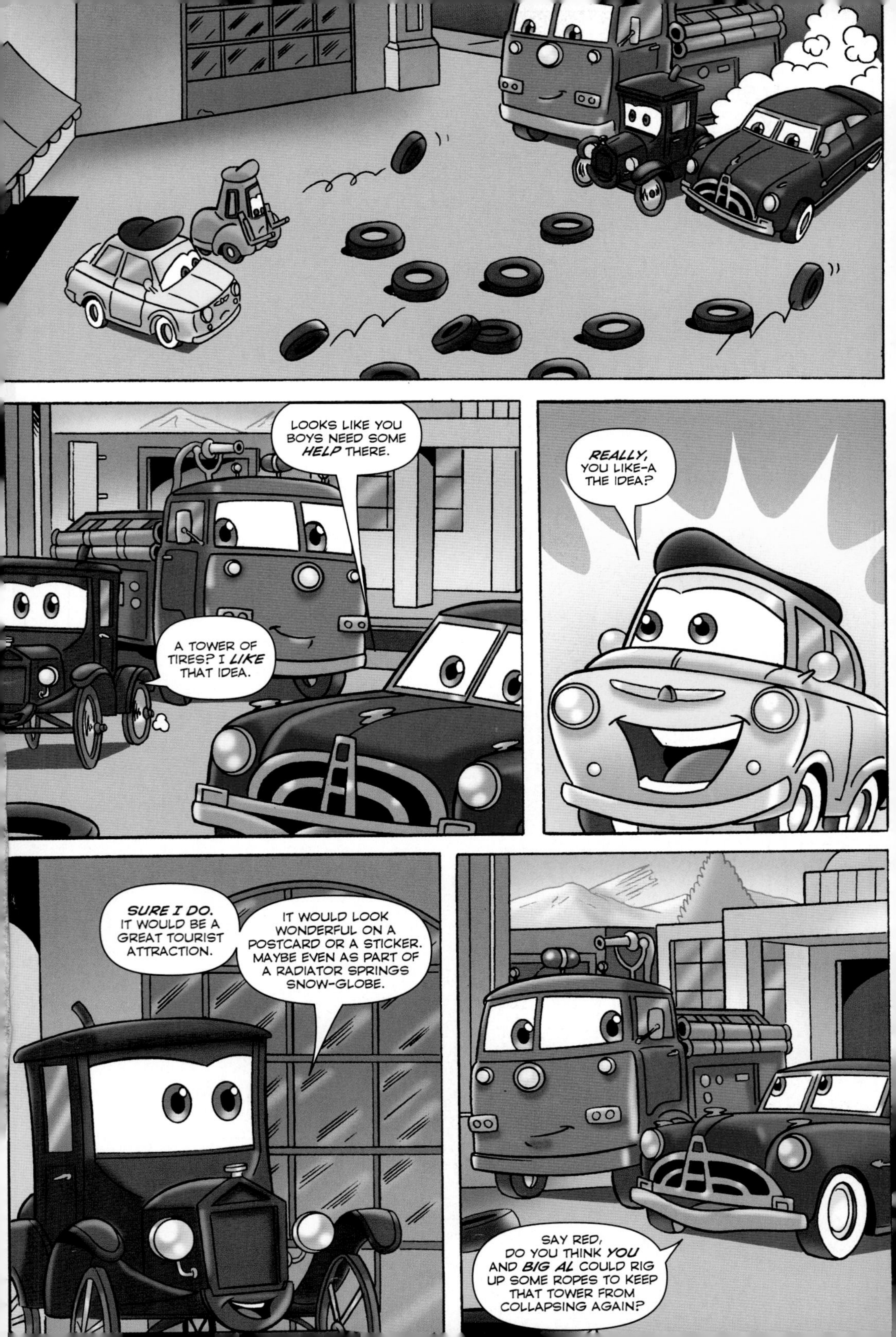
LOOKS LIKE YOU BOYS NEED SOME HELP THERE.
A TOWER OF TIRES? I LIKE THAT IDEA.
REALLY, YOU LIKE-A THE IDEA?
SURE I DO. IT WOULD BE A GREAT TOURIST ATTRACTION.
IT WOULD LOOK WONDERFUL ON A POSTCARD OR A STICKER. MAYBE EVEN AS PART OF A RADIATOR SPRINGS SNOW-GLOBE.
SAY RED, DO YOU THINK YOU AND BIG AL COULD RIG UP SOME ROPES TO KEEP THAT TOWER FROM COLLAPSING AGAIN?

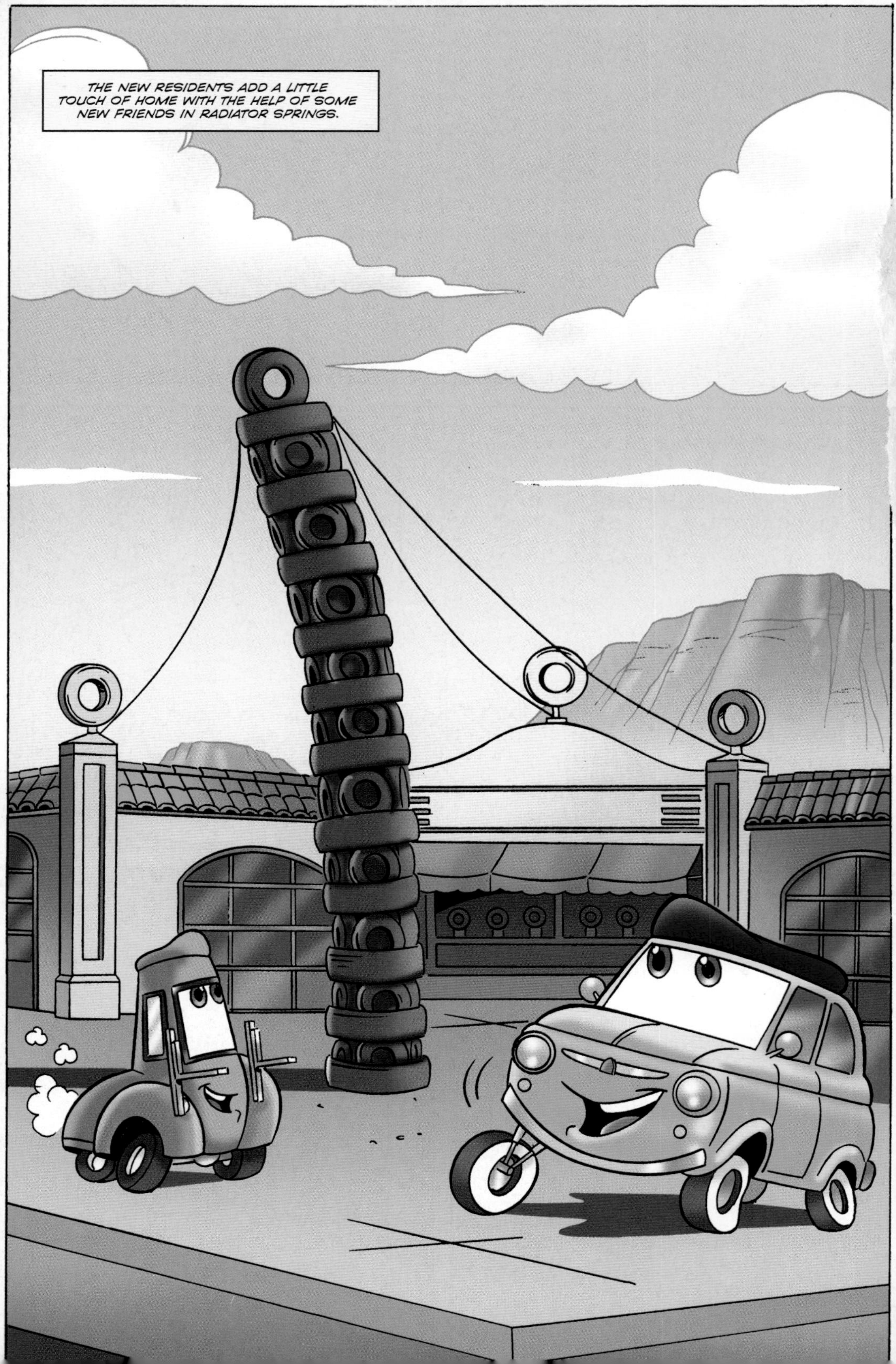
THE NEW RESIDENTS ADD A LITTLE TOUCH OF HOME WITH THE HELP OF SOME NEW FRIENDS IN RADIATOR SPRINGS.

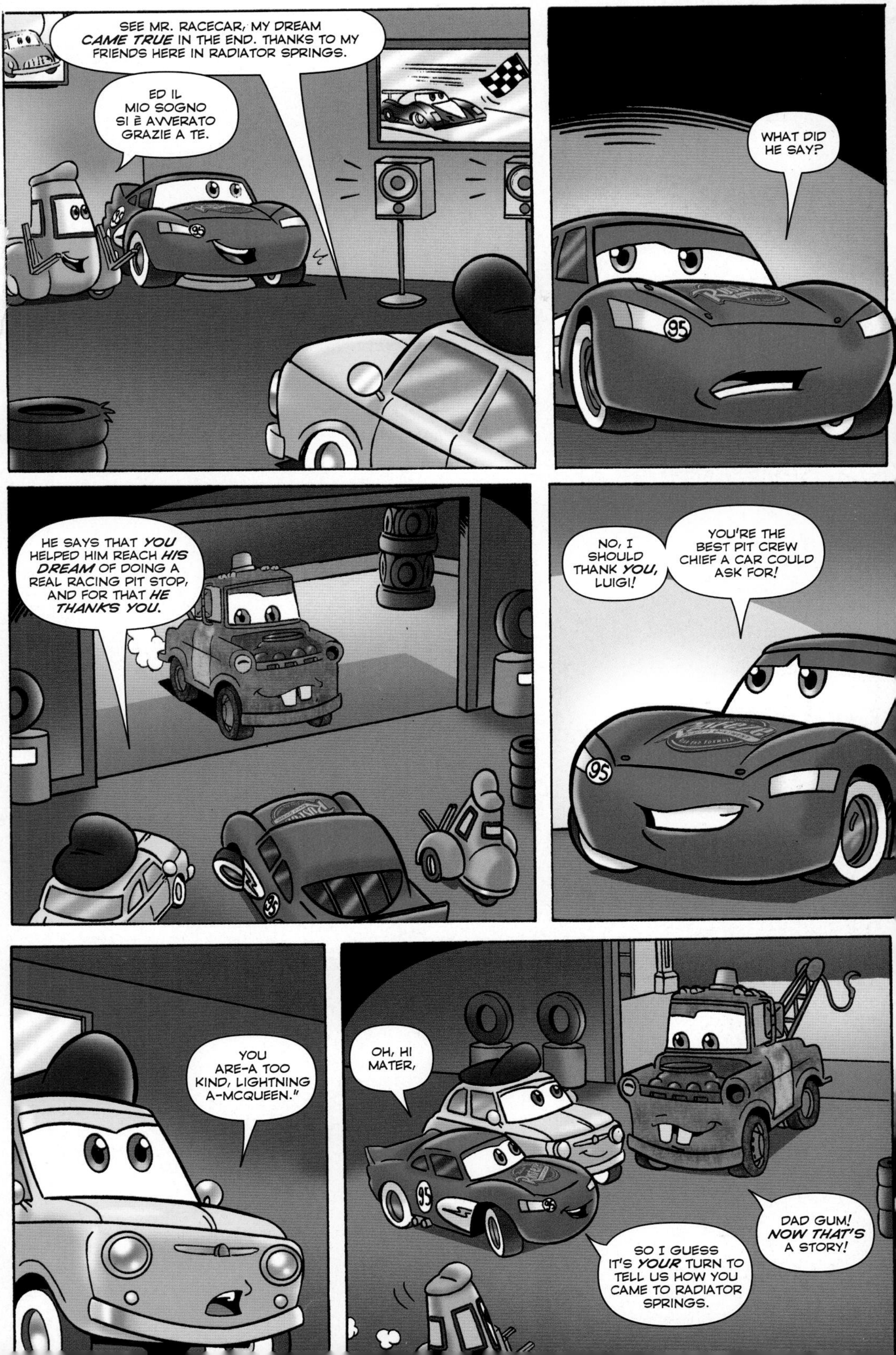
SEE MR. RACECAR, MY DREAM CAME TRUE IN THE END. THANKS TO MY FRIENDS HERE IN RADIATOR SPRINGS.
ED IL MIO SOGNO SI È AVVERATO GRAZIE A TE.
WHAT DID HE SAY?
HE SAYS THAT YOU HELPED HIM REACH HIS DREAM OF DOING A REAL RACING PIT STOP, AND FOR THAT HE THANKS YOU.
NO, I SHOULD THANK YOU, LUIGI!
YOU'RE THE BEST PIT CREW CHIEF A CAR COULD ASK FOR!
YOU ARE-A TOO KIND, LIGHTNING A-MCQUEEN."
OH, HI MATER,
SO I GUESS IT'S YOUR TURN TO TELL US HOW YOU CAME TO RADIATOR SPRINGS.
DAD GUM! NOW THAT'S A STORY!

Chapter Four

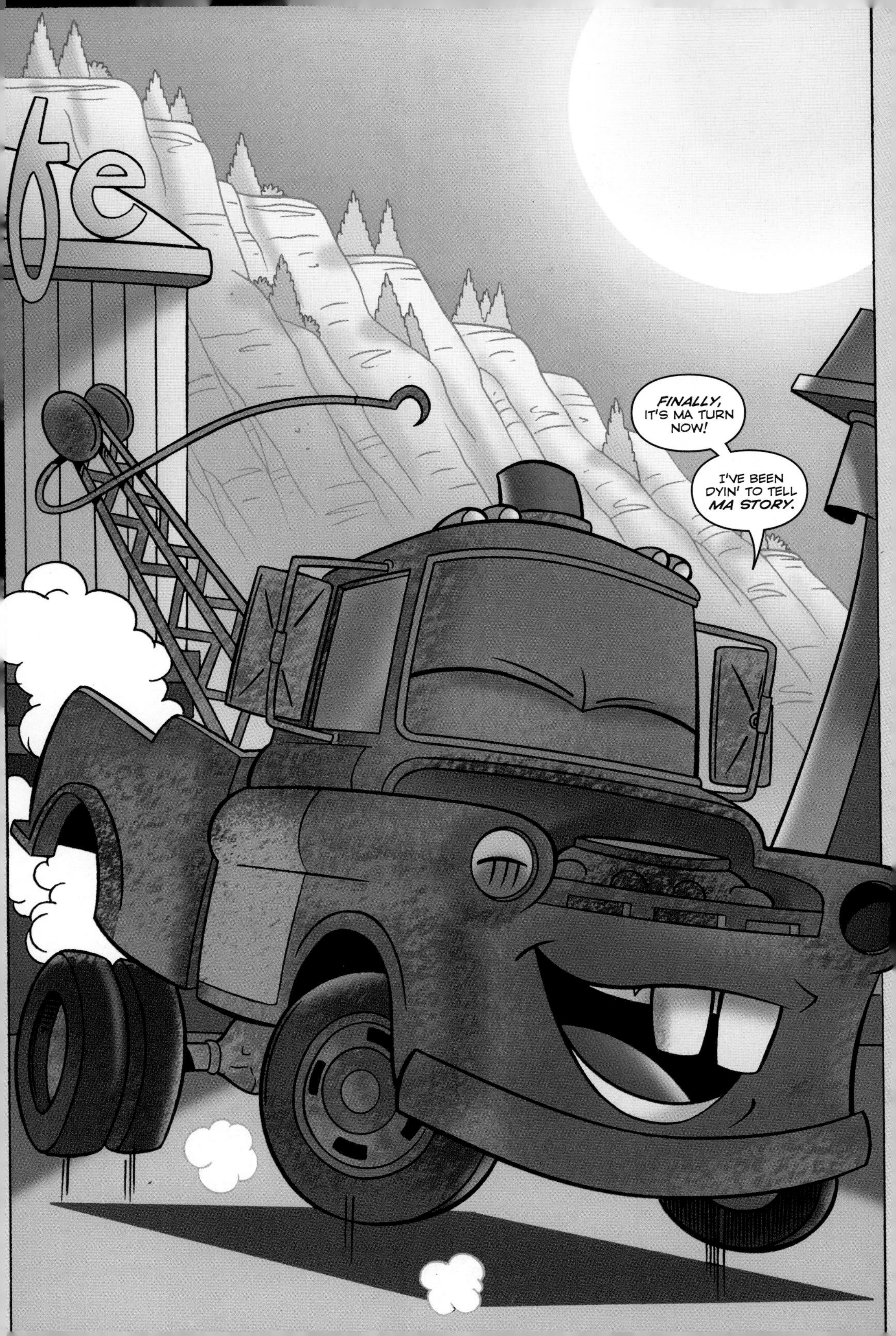
FINALLY, IT'S MA TURN NOW!
I'VE BEEN DYIN' TO TELL MA STORY.

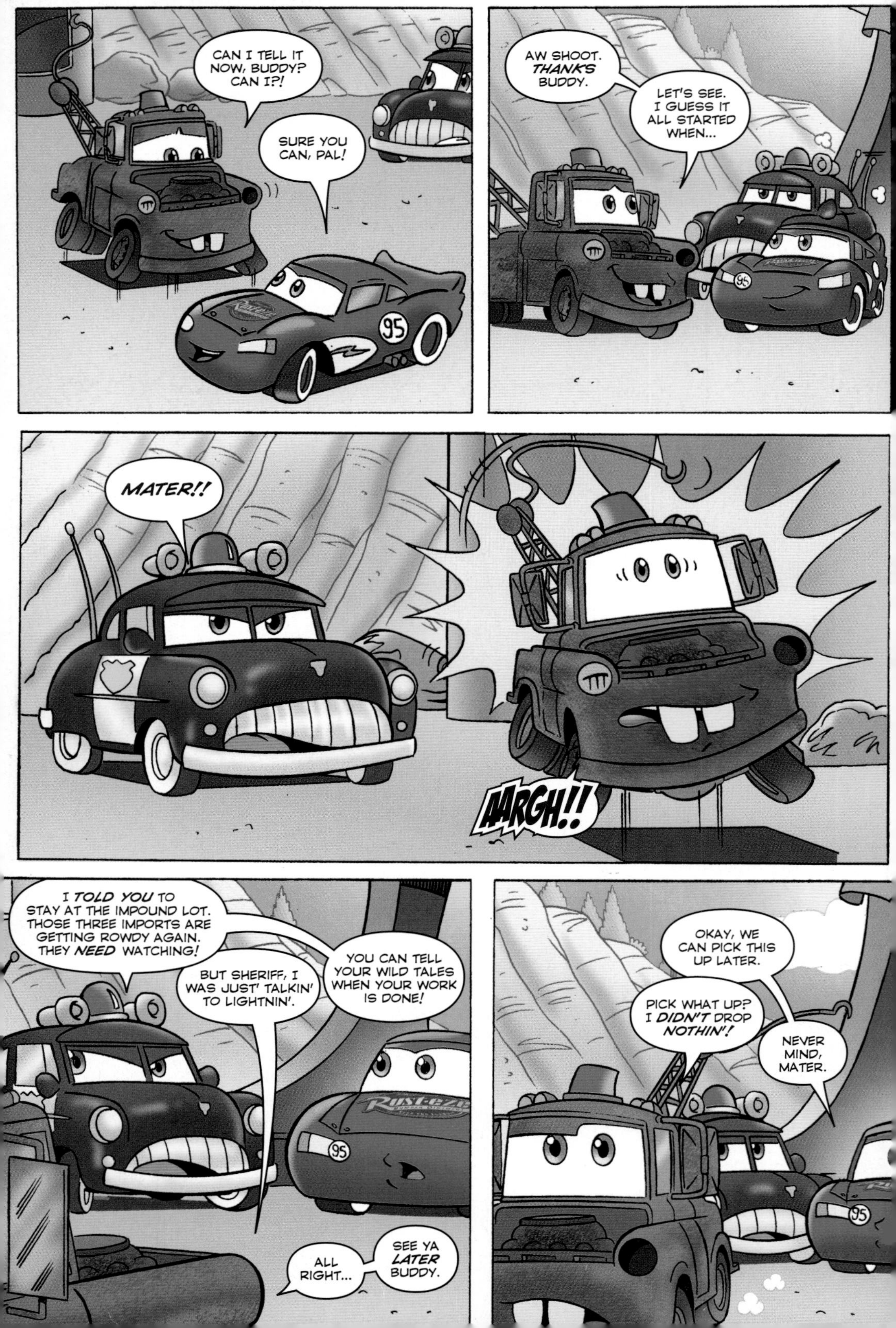
CAN I TELL IT NOW, BUDDY? CAN I?!
SURE YOU CAN, PAL!
AW SHOOT. THANKS BUDDY.
LET'S SEE. I GUESS IT ALL STARTED WHEN...
MATER!!
AARGH!!
I TOLD YOU TO STAY AT THE IMPOUND LOT. THOSE THREE IMPORTS ARE GETTING ROWDY AGAIN. THEY NEED WATCHING!
BUT SHERIFF, I WAS JUST' TALKIN' TO LIGHTNIN'.
YOU CAN TELL YOUR WILD TALES WHEN YOUR WORK IS DONE!
ALL RIGHT...
SEE YA LATER BUDDY.
OKAY, WE CAN PICK THIS UP LATER.
PICK WHAT UP? I DIDN'T DROP NOTHIN'!
NEVER MIND, MATER.

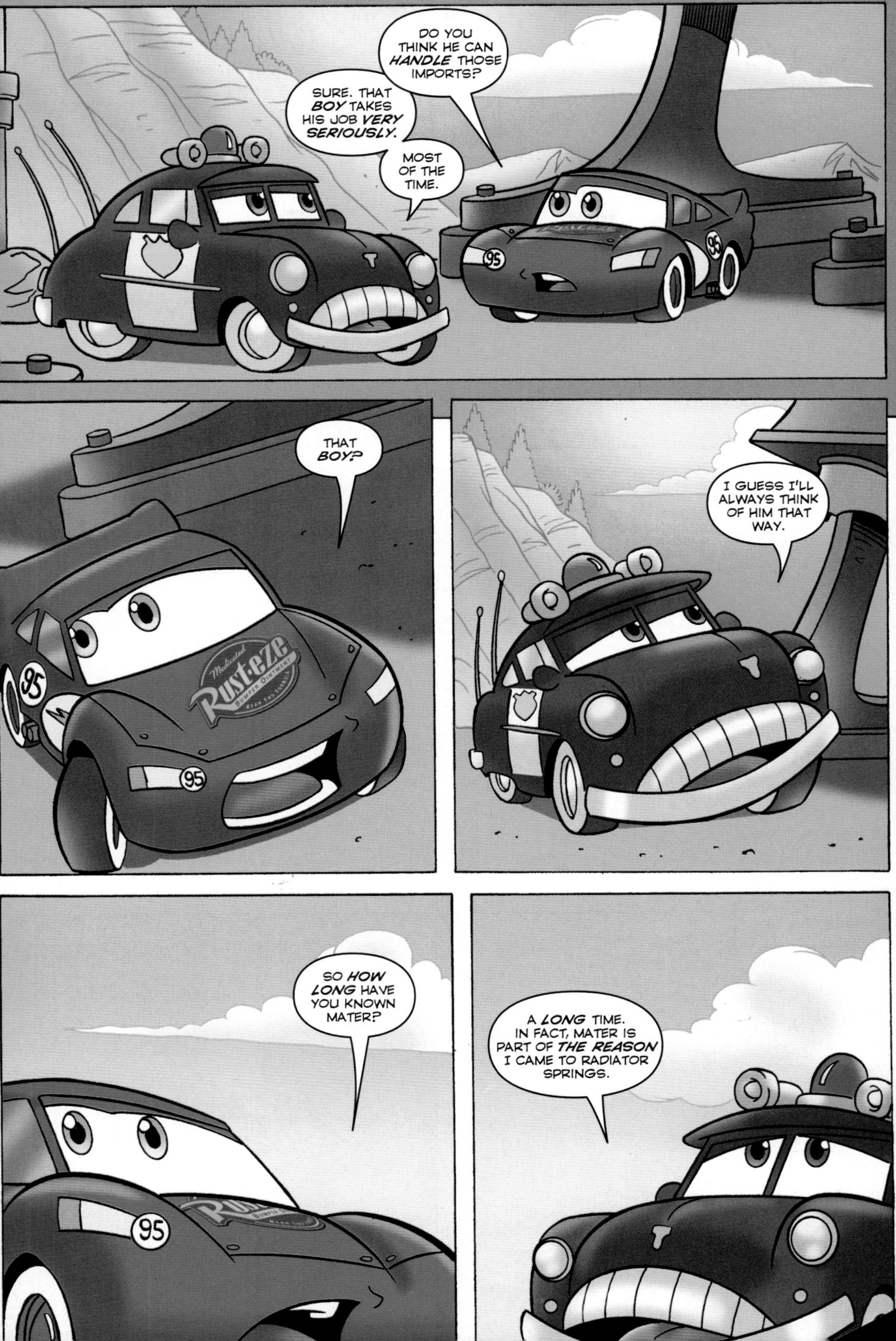
DO YOU THINK HE CAN HANDLE THOSE IMPORTS?
SURE. THAT BOY TAKES HIS JOB VERY SERIOUSLY.
MOST OF THE TIME.
THAT BOY?
I GUESS I'LL ALWAYS THINK OF HIM THAT WAY.
SO HOW LONG HAVE YOU KNOWN MATER?
A LONG TIME. IN FACT, MATER IS PART OF THE REASON I CAME TO RADIATOR SPRINGS.
95
Medicated Rust-eze BUMPER OINTMENT

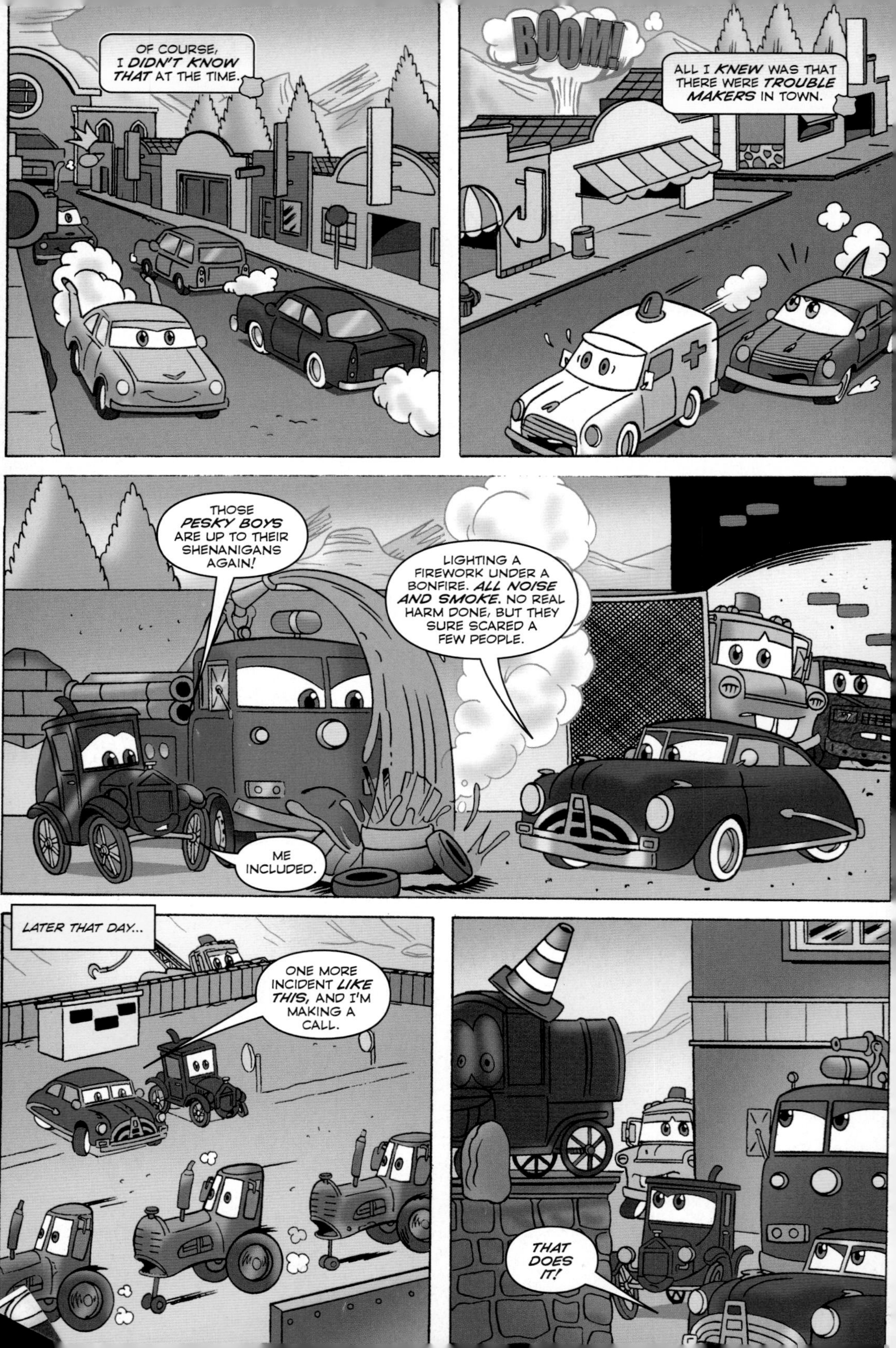
OF COURSE, I DIDN'T KNOW THAT AT THE TIME.
BOOM!
ALL I KNEW WAS THAT THERE WERE TROUBLE MAKERS IN TOWN.
THOSE PESKY BOYS ARE UP TO THEIR SHENANIGANS AGAIN!
LIGHTING A FIREWORK UNDER A BONFIRE. ALL NOISE AND SMOKE. NO REAL HARM DONE, BUT THEY SURE SCARED A FEW PEOPLE.
ME INCLUDED.
LATER THAT DAY...
ONE MORE INCIDENT LIKE THIS, AND I'M MAKING A CALL.
THAT DOES IT!

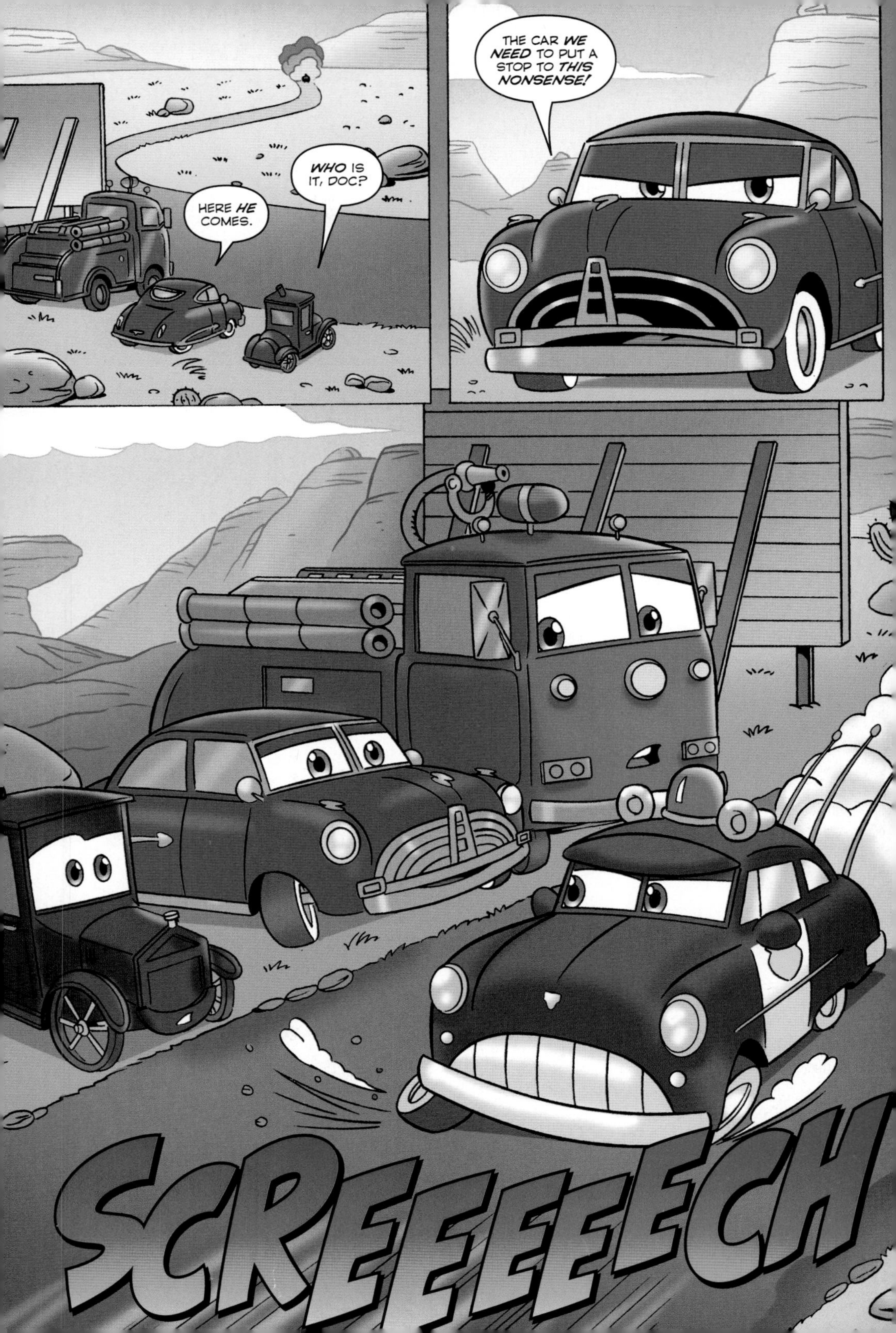
HERE HE COMES.
WHO IS IT, DOC?
THE CAR WE NEED TO PUT A STOP TO THIS NONSENSE!
SCREEEEECH

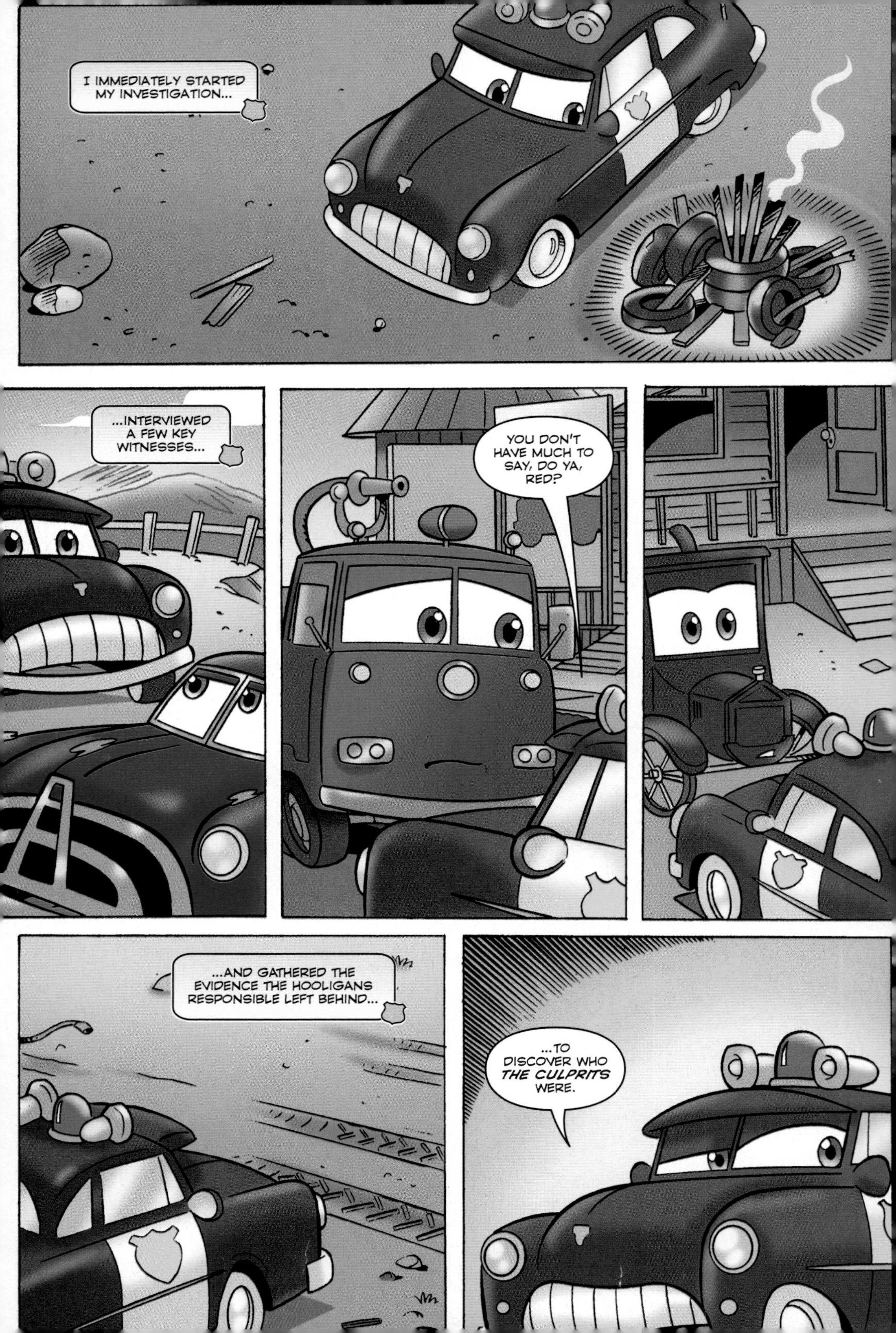
I IMMEDIATELY STARTED MY INVESTIGATION...
...INTERVIEWED A FEW KEY WITNESSES...
YOU DON'T HAVE MUCH TO SAY, DO YA, RED?
...AND GATHERED THE EVIDENCE THE HOOLIGANS RESPONSIBLE LEFT BEHIND...
...TO DISCOVER WHO *THE CULPRITS* WERE.

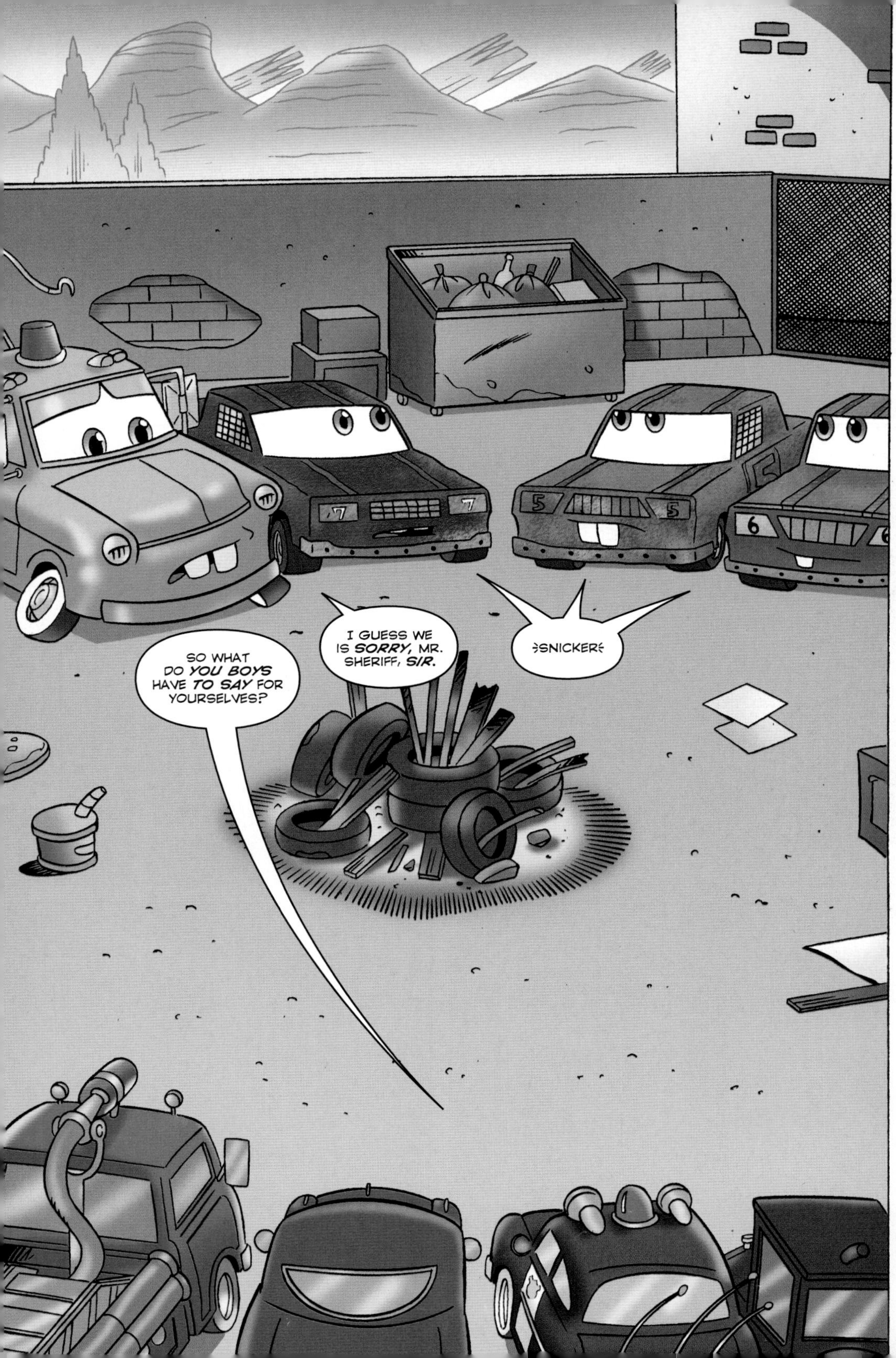
SO WHAT DO YOU BOYS HAVE TO SAY FOR YOURSELVES?
I GUESS WE IS SORRY, MR. SHERIFF, SIR.
SNICKER

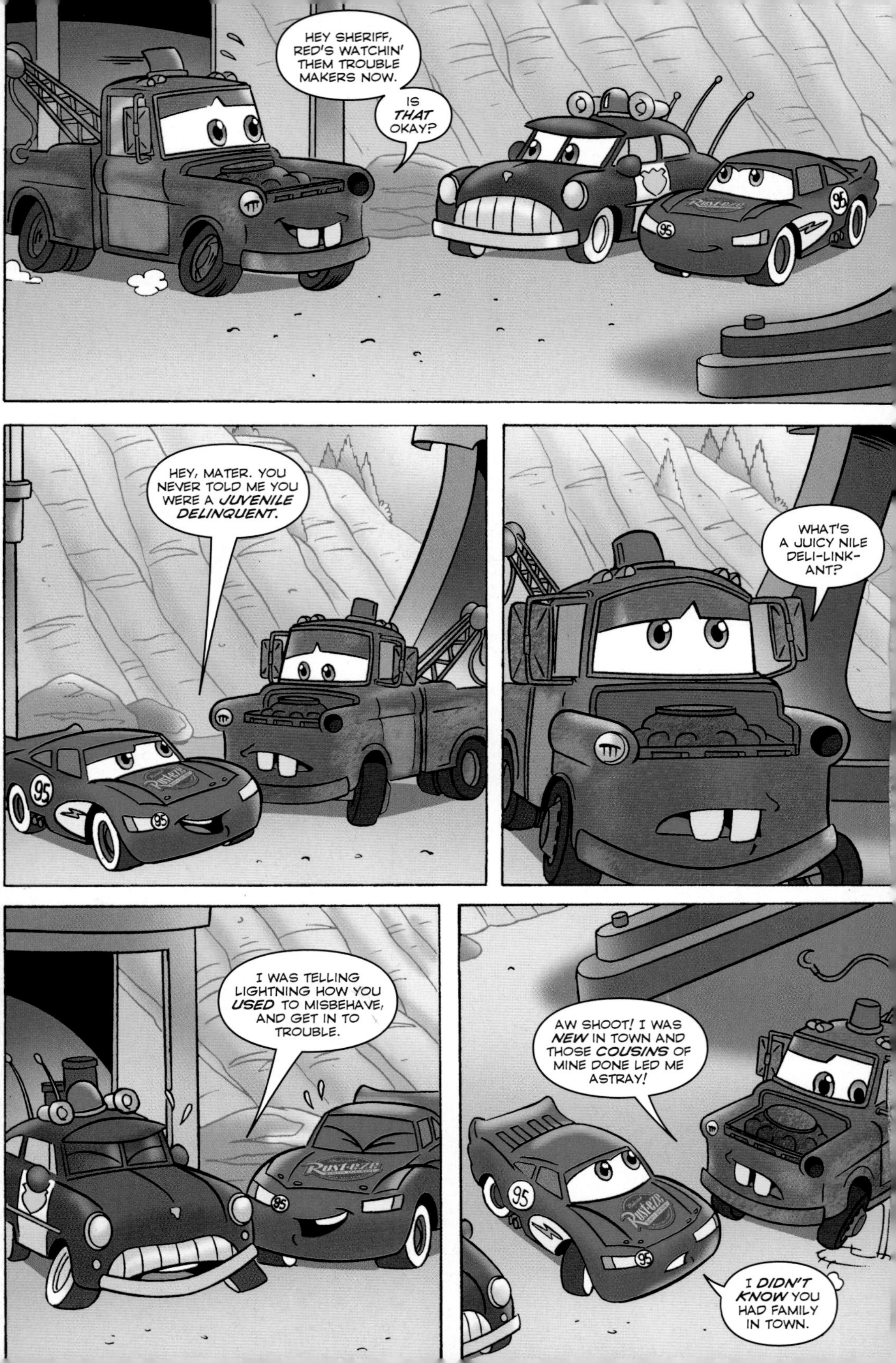
HEY SHERIFF, RED'S WATCHIN' THEM TROUBLE MAKERS NOW.
IS *THAT* OKAY?
HEY, MATER. YOU NEVER TOLD ME YOU WERE A *JUVENILE DELINQUENT*.
WHAT'S A JUICY NILE DELI-LINK-ANT?
I WAS TELLING LIGHTNING HOW YOU *USED* TO MISBEHAVE, AND GET IN TO TROUBLE.
AW SHOOT! I WAS *NEW* IN TOWN AND THOSE *COUSINS* OF MINE DONE LED ME ASTRAY!
I *DIDN'T KNOW* YOU HAD FAMILY IN TOWN.

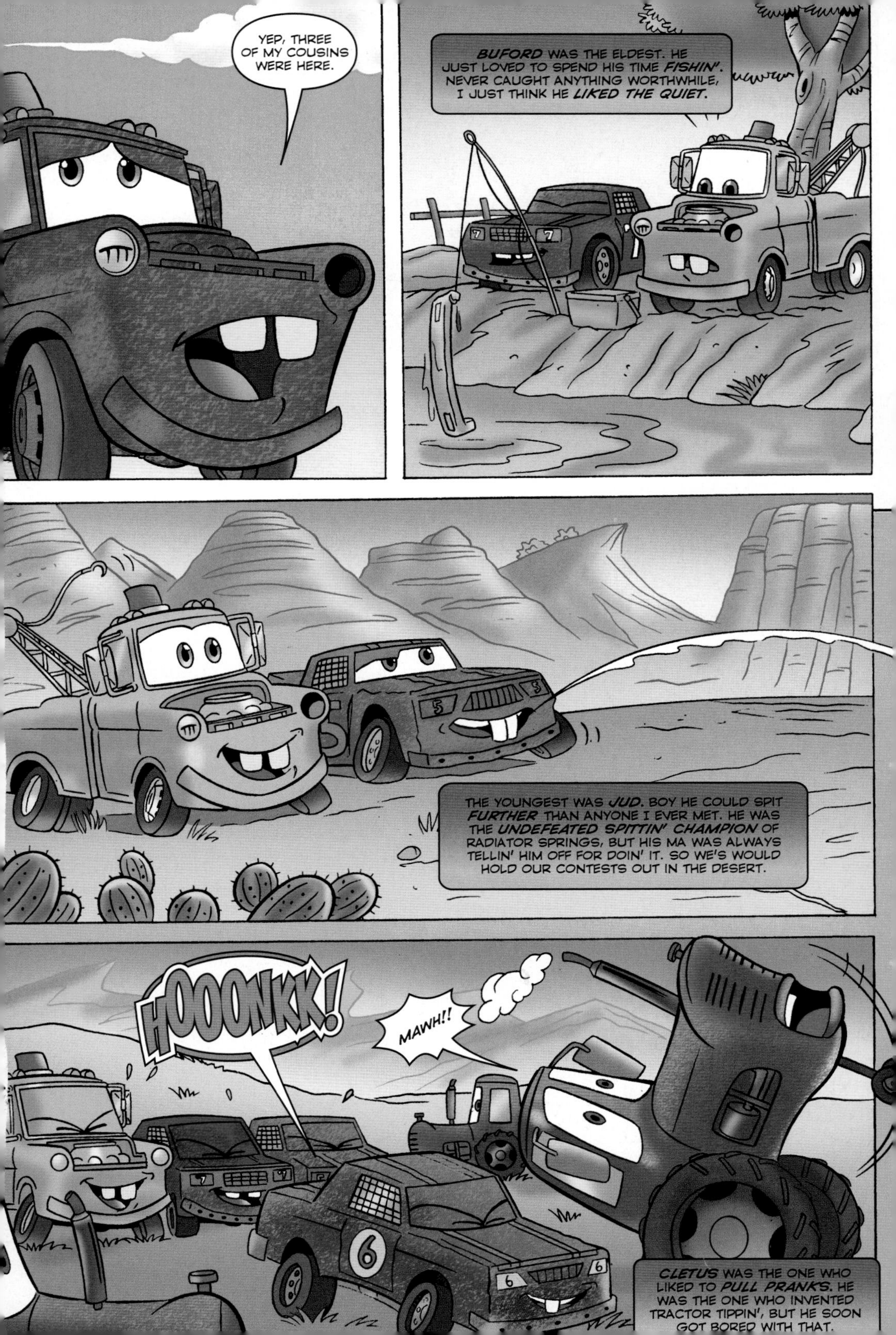
YEP, THREE OF MY COUSINS WERE HERE.
BUFORD WAS THE ELDEST. HE JUST LOVED TO SPEND HIS TIME FISHIN'. NEVER CAUGHT ANYTHING WORTHWHILE, I JUST THINK HE LIKED THE QUIET.
THE YOUNGEST WAS JUD. BOY HE COULD SPIT FURTHER THAN ANYONE I EVER MET. HE WAS THE UNDEFEATED SPITTIN' CHAMPION OF RADIATOR SPRINGS, BUT HIS MA WAS ALWAYS TELLIN' HIM OFF FOR DOIN' IT. SO WE'S WOULD HOLD OUR CONTESTS OUT IN THE DESERT.
HOOONKK!
MAWH!!
CLETUS WAS THE ONE WHO LIKED TO PULL PRANKS. HE WAS THE ONE WHO INVENTED TRACTOR TIPPIN', BUT HE SOON GOT BORED WITH THAT.

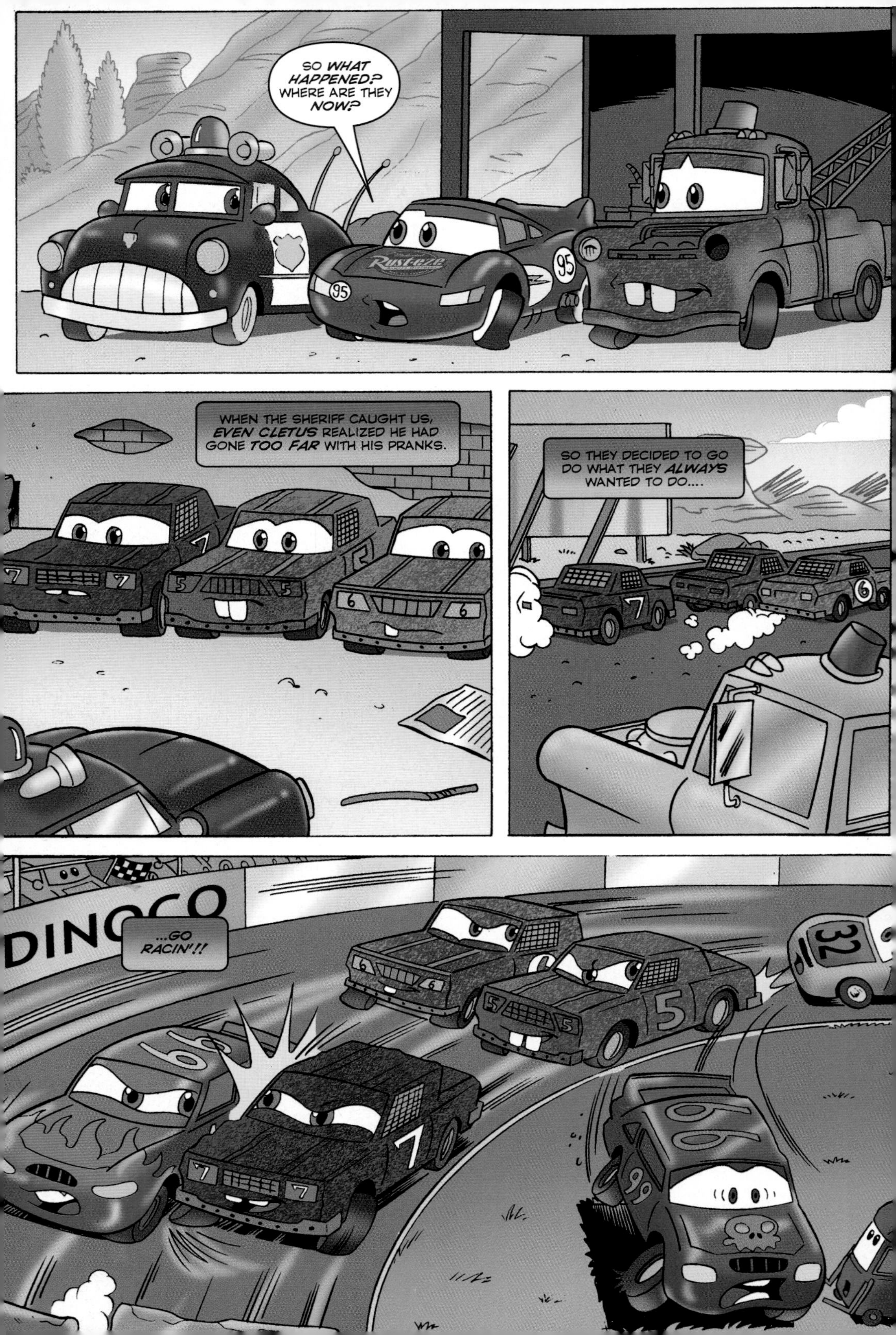
SO WHAT HAPPENED? WHERE ARE THEY NOW?
WHEN THE SHERIFF CAUGHT US, EVEN CLETUS REALIZED HE HAD GONE TOO FAR WITH HIS PRANKS.
SO THEY DECIDED TO GO DO WHAT THEY ALWAYS WANTED TO DO....
...GO RACIN'!!

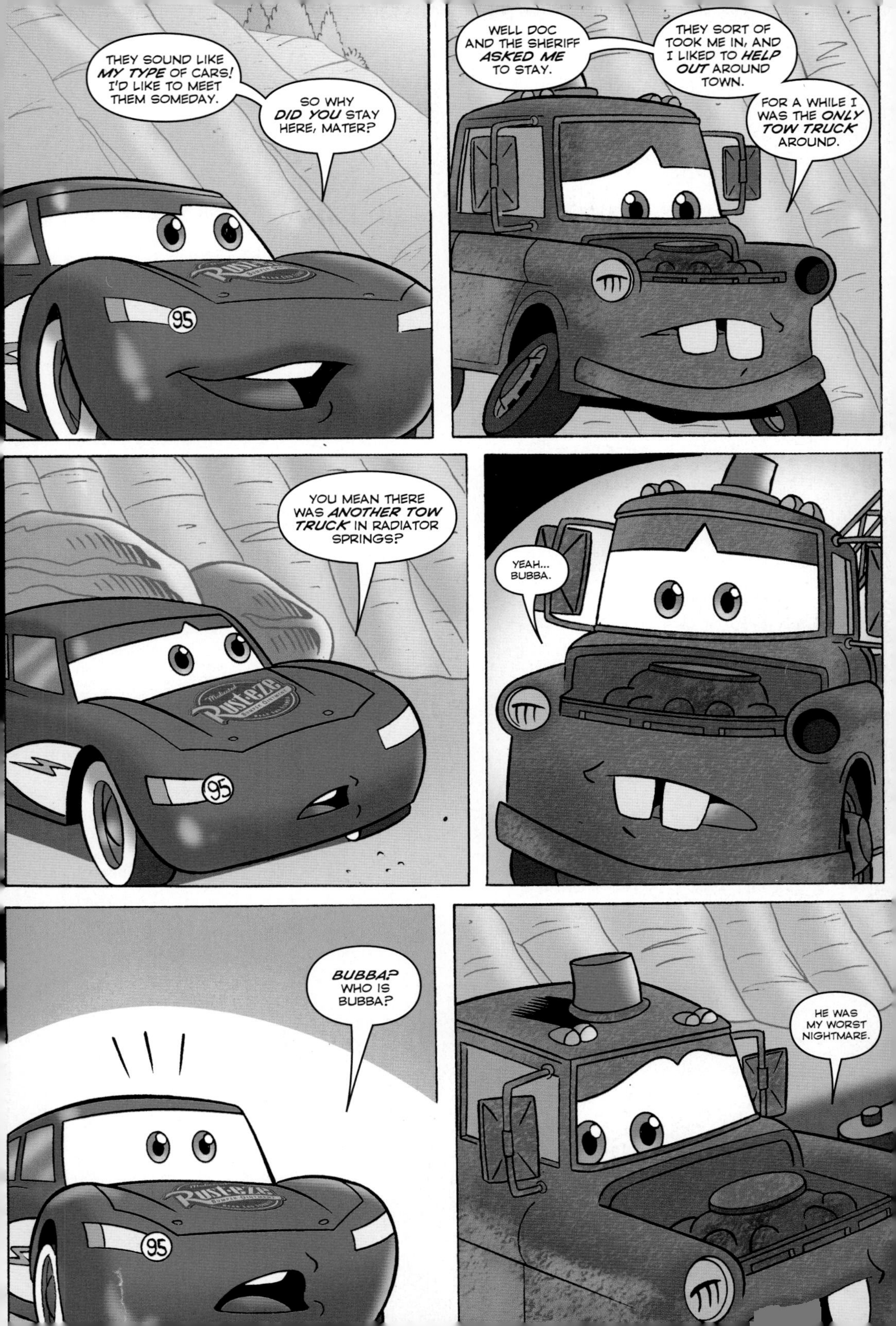
THEY SOUND LIKE MY TYPE OF CARS! I'D LIKE TO MEET THEM SOMEDAY.
SO WHY DID YOU STAY HERE, MATER?
WELL DOC AND THE SHERIFF ASKED ME TO STAY.
THEY SORT OF TOOK ME IN, AND I LIKED TO HELP OUT AROUND TOWN.
FOR A WHILE I WAS THE ONLY TOW TRUCK AROUND.
YOU MEAN THERE WAS ANOTHER TOW TRUCK IN RADIATOR SPRINGS?
YEAH... BUBBA.
BUBBA? WHO IS BUBBA?
HE WAS MY WORST NIGHTMARE.

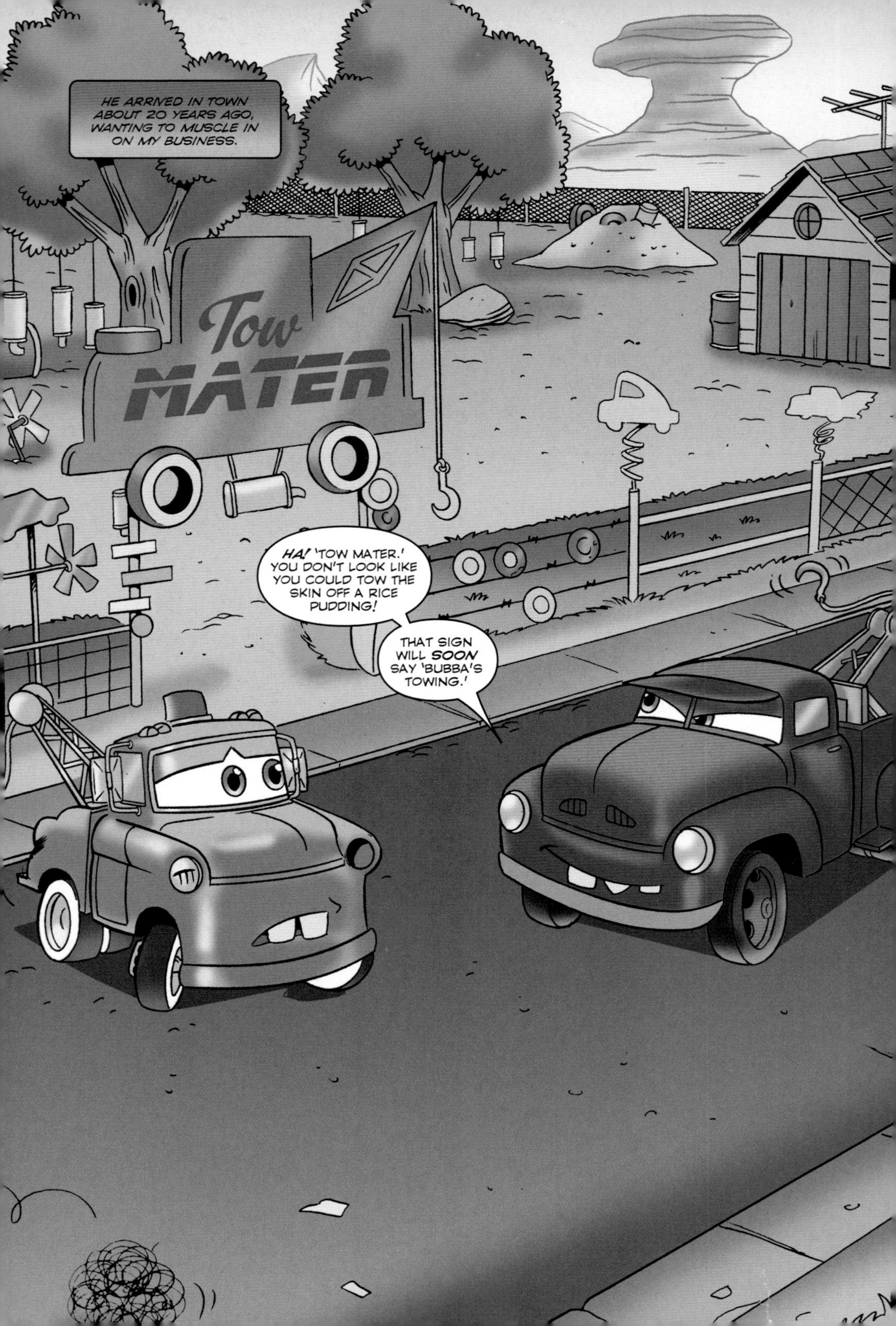
HE ARRIVED IN TOWN ABOUT 20 YEARS AGO, WANTING TO MUSCLE IN ON MY BUSINESS.
Tow MATER
HA! 'TOW MATER.' YOU DON'T LOOK LIKE YOU COULD TOW THE SKIN OFF A RICE PUDDING!
THAT SIGN WILL SOON SAY 'BUBBA'S TOWING.'

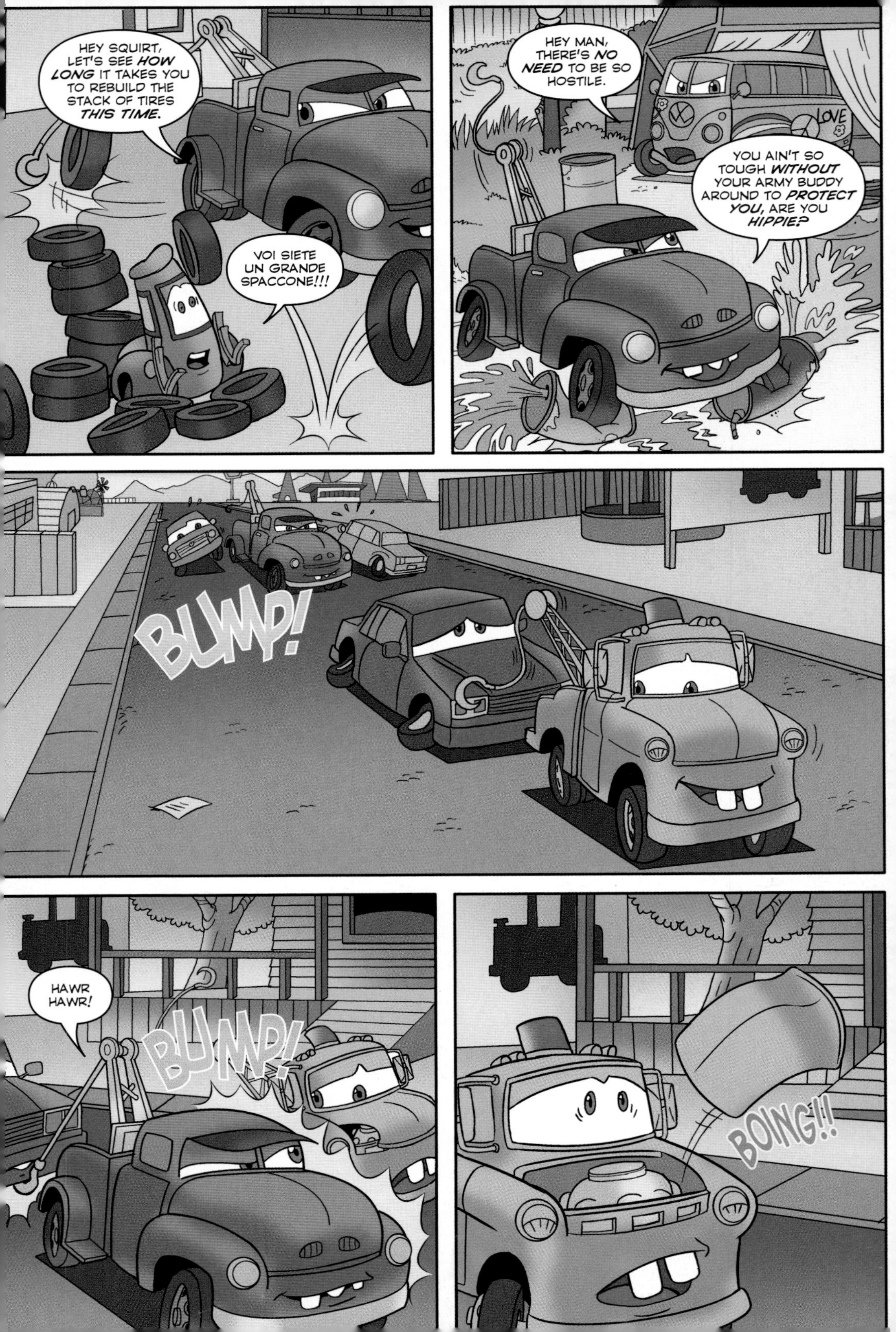
HEY SQUIRT, LET'S SEE HOW LONG IT TAKES YOU TO REBUILD THE STACK OF TIRES THIS TIME.
VOI SIETE UN GRANDE SPACCONE!!!
HEY MAN, THERE'S NO NEED TO BE SO HOSTILE.
LOVE
YOU AIN'T SO TOUGH WITHOUT YOUR ARMY BUDDY AROUND TO PROTECT YOU, ARE YOU HIPPIE?
BUMP!
HAWR HAWR!
BUMP!
BOING!!

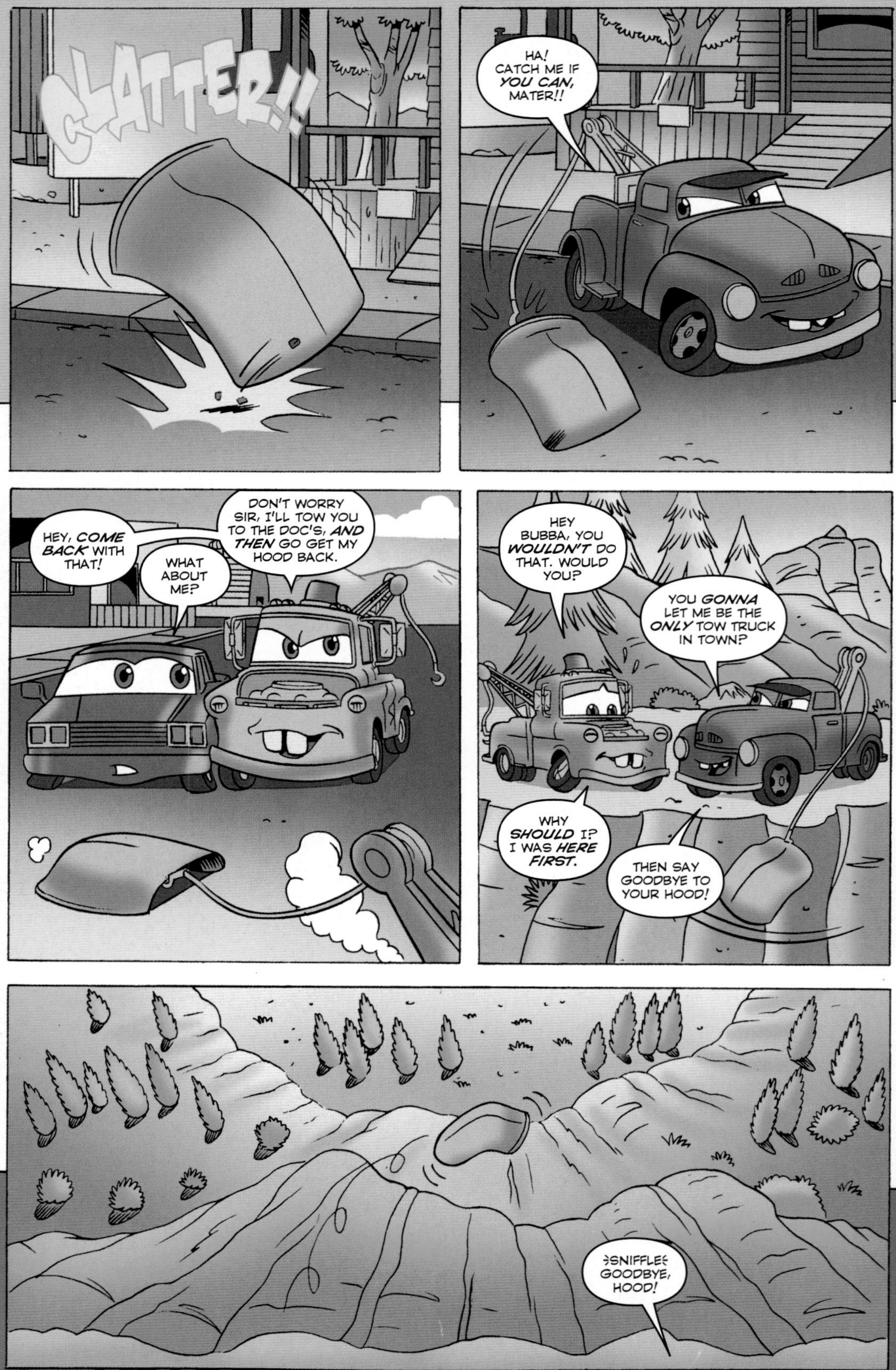
CLATTER!!
HA! CATCH ME IF YOU CAN, MATER!!
HEY, COME BACK WITH THAT!
DON'T WORRY SIR, I'LL TOW YOU TO THE DOC'S, AND THEN GO GET MY HOOD BACK.
WHAT ABOUT ME?
HEY BUBBA, YOU WOULDN'T DO THAT. WOULD YOU?
YOU GONNA LET ME BE THE ONLY TOW TRUCK IN TOWN?
WHY SHOULD I? I WAS HERE FIRST.
THEN SAY GOODBYE TO YOUR HOOD!
SNIFFLE GOODBYE, HOOD!

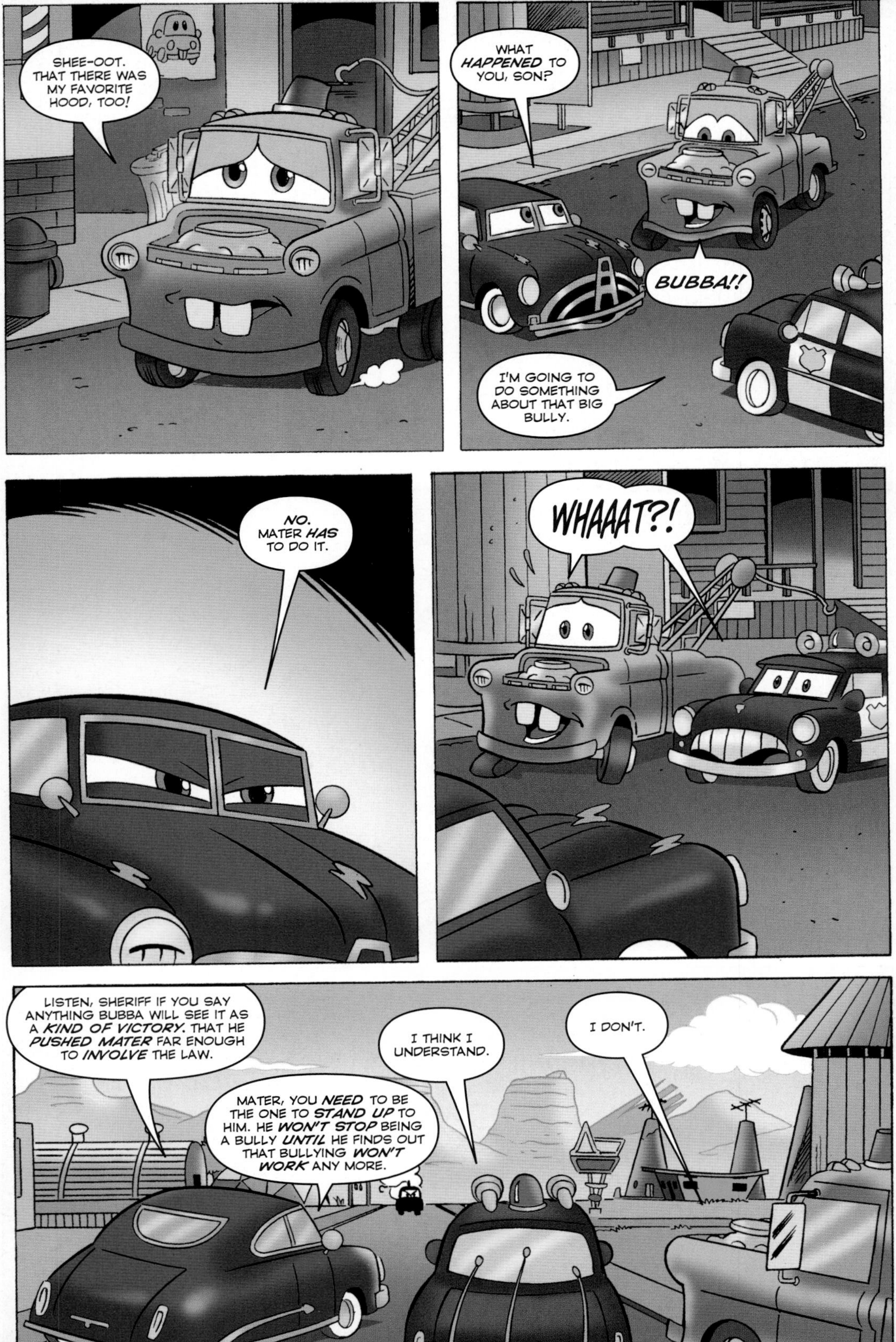
SHEE-OOT. THAT THERE WAS MY FAVORITE HOOD, TOO!
WHAT HAPPENED TO YOU, SON?
BUBBA!!
I'M GOING TO DO SOMETHING ABOUT THAT BIG BULLY.
NO. MATER HAS TO DO IT.
WHAAAT?!
LISTEN, SHERIFF IF YOU SAY ANYTHING BUBBA WILL SEE IT AS A KIND OF VICTORY. THAT HE PUSHED MATER FAR ENOUGH TO INVOLVE THE LAW.
MATER, YOU NEED TO BE THE ONE TO STAND UP TO HIM. HE WON'T STOP BEING A BULLY UNTIL HE FINDS OUT THAT BULLYING WON'T WORK ANY MORE.
I THINK I UNDERSTAND.
I DON'T.

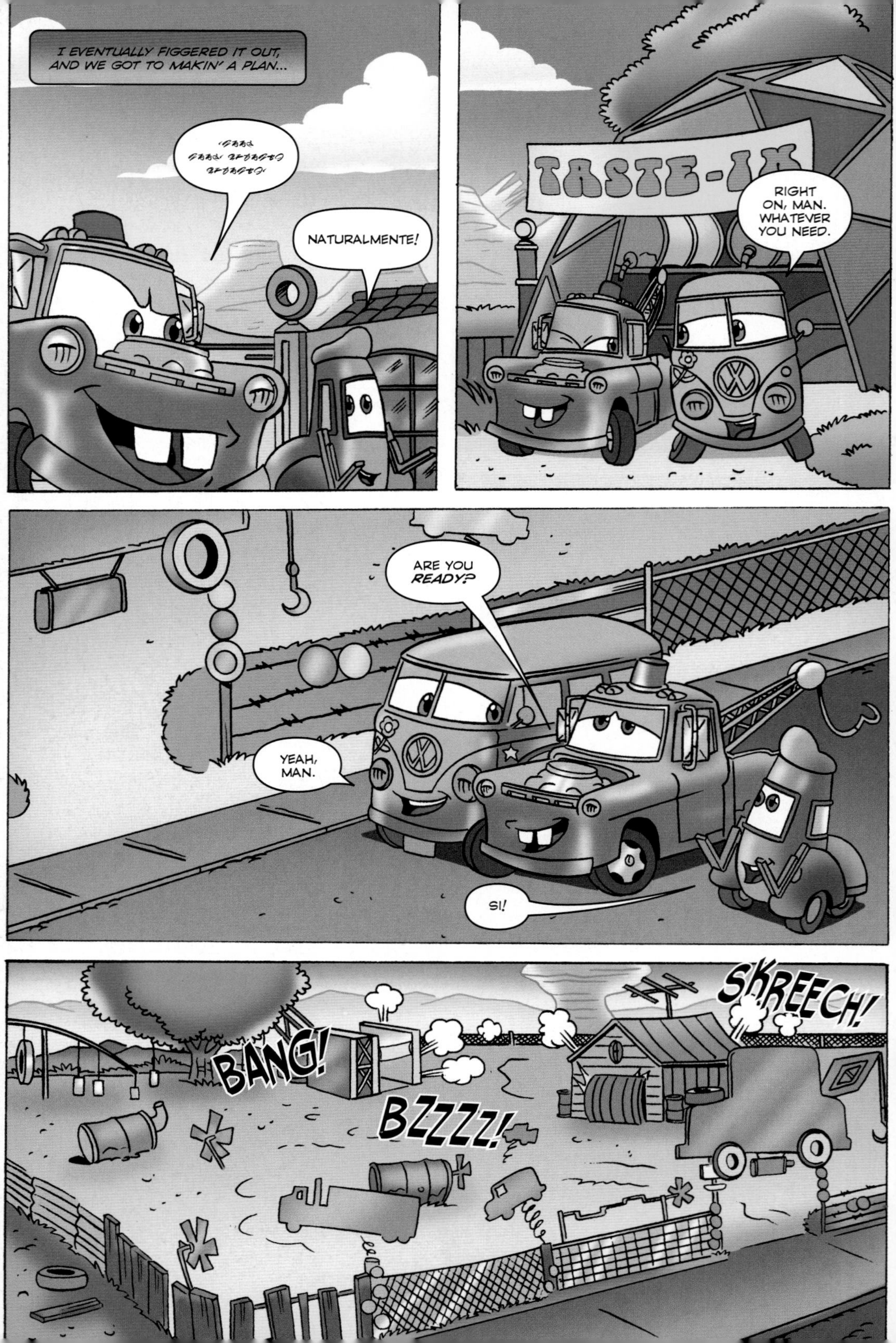
I EVENTUALLY FIGGERED IT OUT, AND WE GOT TO MAKIN' A PLAN...
NATURALMENTE!
TASTE-IN
RIGHT ON, MAN. WHATEVER YOU NEED.
ARE YOU *READY?*
YEAH, MAN.
SI!
BANG!
BZZZZ!
SKREECH!

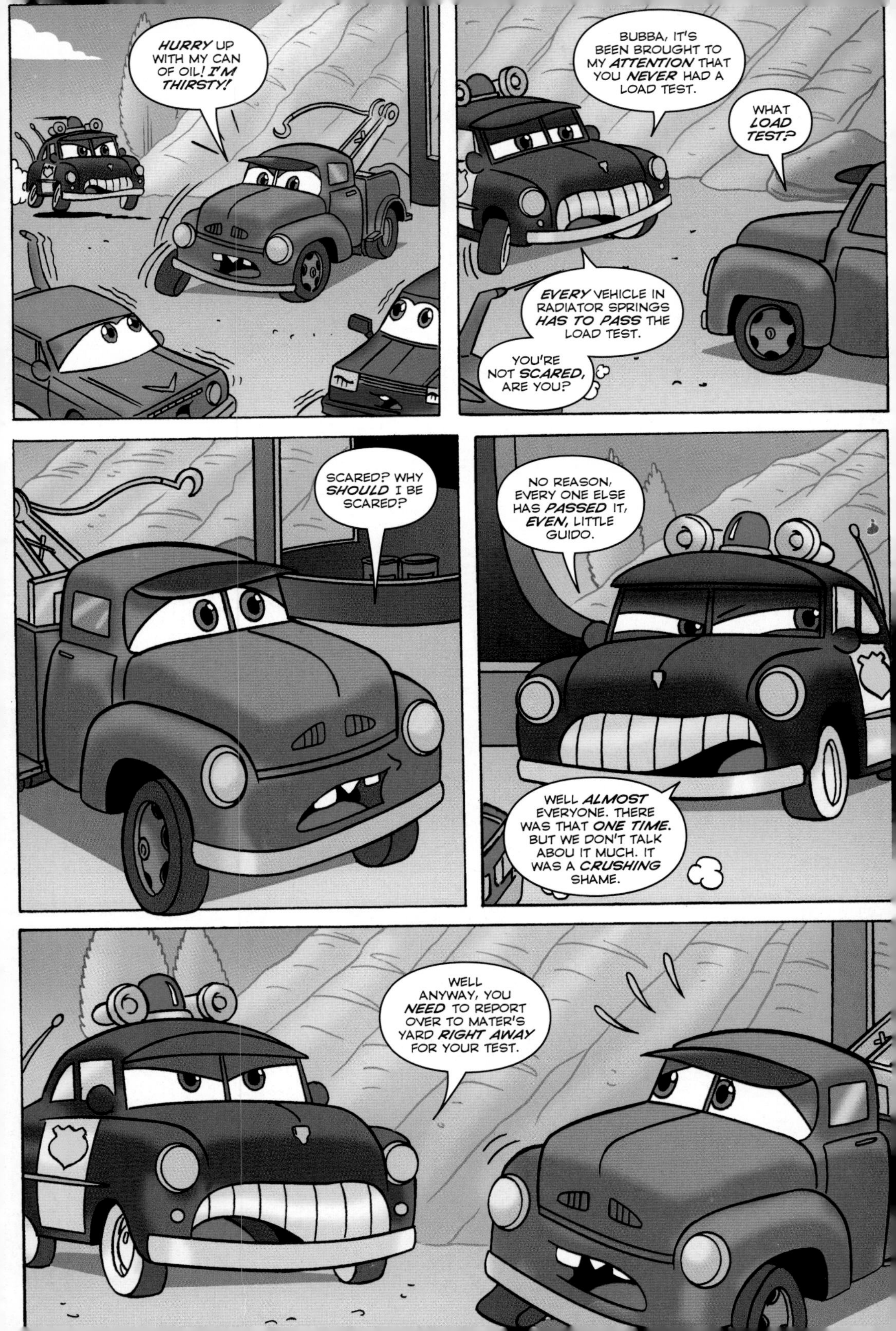

HURRY UP WITH MY CAN OF OIL! I'M THIRSTY!
BUBBA, IT'S BEEN BROUGHT TO MY ATTENTION THAT YOU NEVER HAD A LOAD TEST.
WHAT LOAD TEST?
EVERY VEHICLE IN RADIATOR SPRINGS HAS TO PASS THE LOAD TEST.
YOU'RE NOT SCARED, ARE YOU?
SCARED? WHY SHOULD I BE SCARED?
NO REASON, EVERY ONE ELSE HAS PASSED IT, EVEN, LITTLE GUIDO.
WELL ALMOST EVERYONE. THERE WAS THAT ONE TIME. BUT WE DON'T TALK ABOU IT MUCH. IT WAS A CRUSHING SHAME.
WELL ANYWAY, YOU NEED TO REPORT OVER TO MATER'S YARD RIGHT AWAY FOR YOUR TEST.

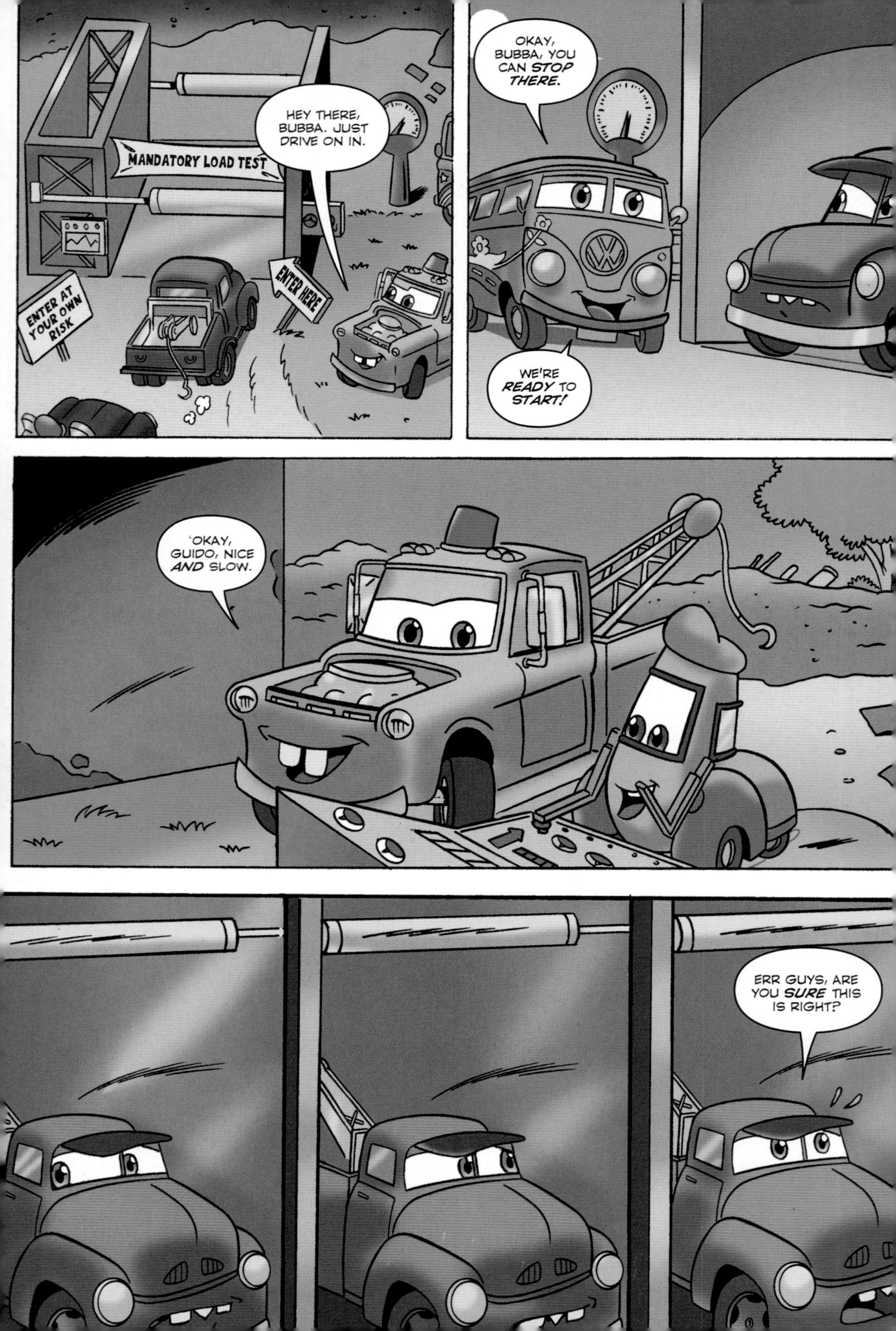
MANDATORY LOAD TEST
ENTER AT YOUR OWN RISK
ENTER HERE
HEY THERE, BUBBA. JUST DRIVE ON IN.
OKAY, BUBBA, YOU CAN *STOP THERE.*
WE'RE *READY* TO *START!*
'OKAY, GUIDO, NICE *AND* SLOW.
ERR GUYS, ARE YOU *SURE* THIS IS RIGHT?

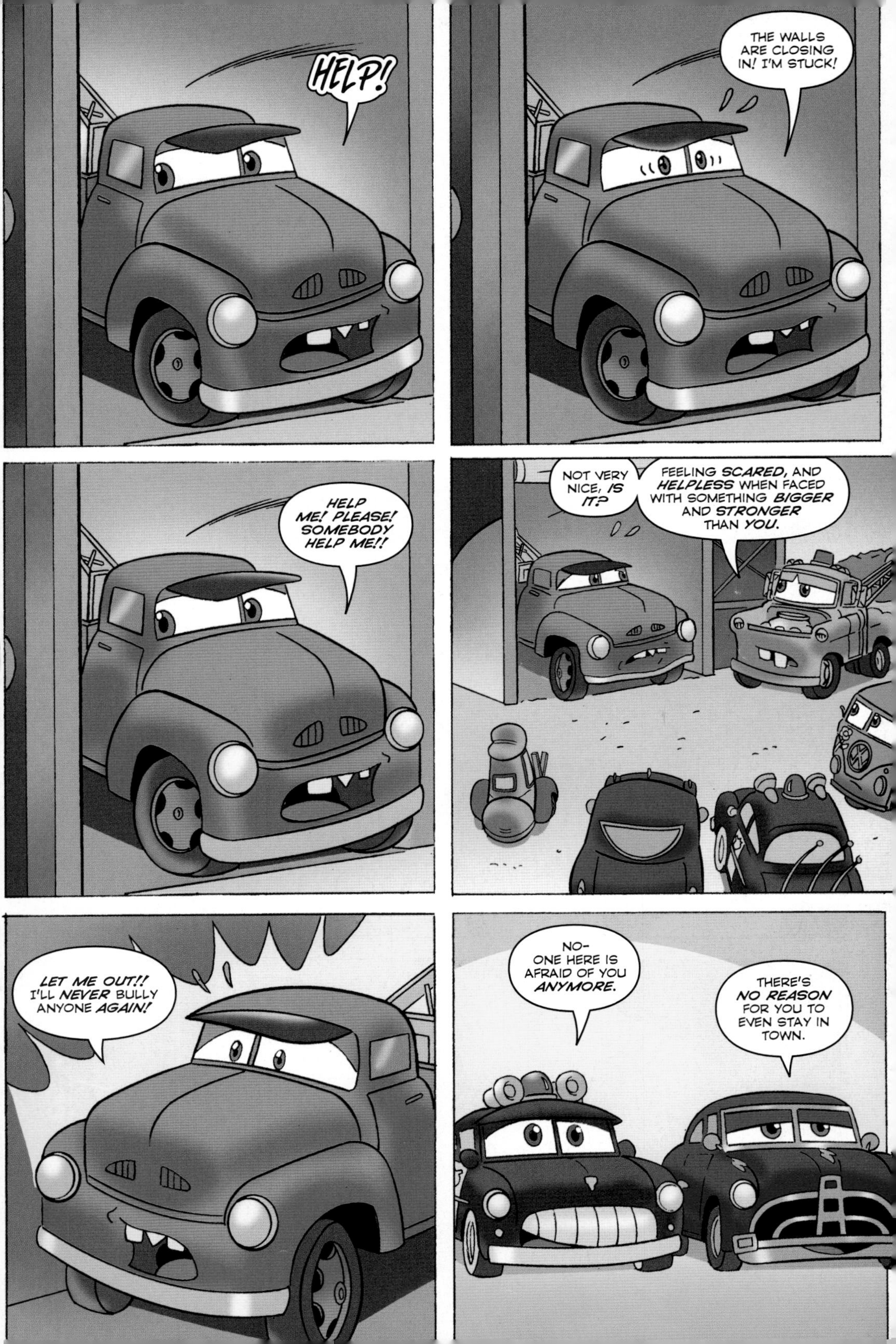
HELP!
THE WALLS ARE CLOSING IN! I'M STUCK!
HELP ME! PLEASE! SOMEBODY HELP ME!!
NOT VERY NICE, IS IT?
FEELING SCARED, AND HELPLESS WHEN FACED WITH SOMETHING BIGGER AND STRONGER THAN YOU.
LET ME OUT!! I'LL NEVER BULLY ANYONE AGAIN!
NO-ONE HERE IS AFRAID OF YOU ANYMORE.
THERE'S NO REASON FOR YOU TO EVEN STAY IN TOWN.

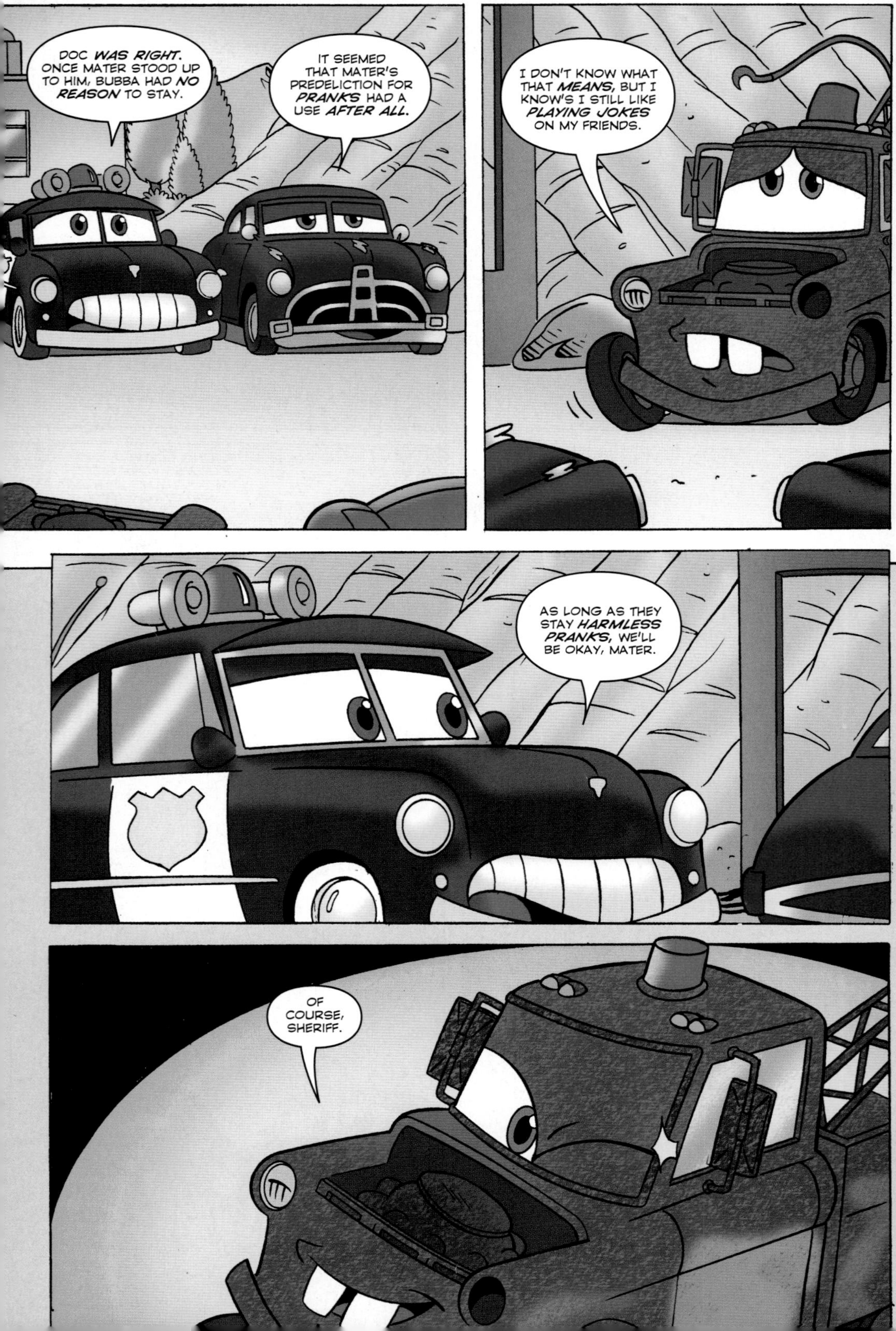
DOC WAS RIGHT. ONCE MATER STOOD UP TO HIM, BUBBA HAD NO REASON TO STAY.
IT SEEMED THAT MATER'S PREDELICTION FOR PRANKS HAD A USE AFTER ALL.
I DON'T KNOW WHAT THAT MEANS, BUT I KNOW'S I STILL LIKE PLAYING JOKES ON MY FRIENDS.
AS LONG AS THEY STAY HARMLESS PRANKS, WE'LL BE OKAY, MATER.
OF COURSE, SHERIFF.

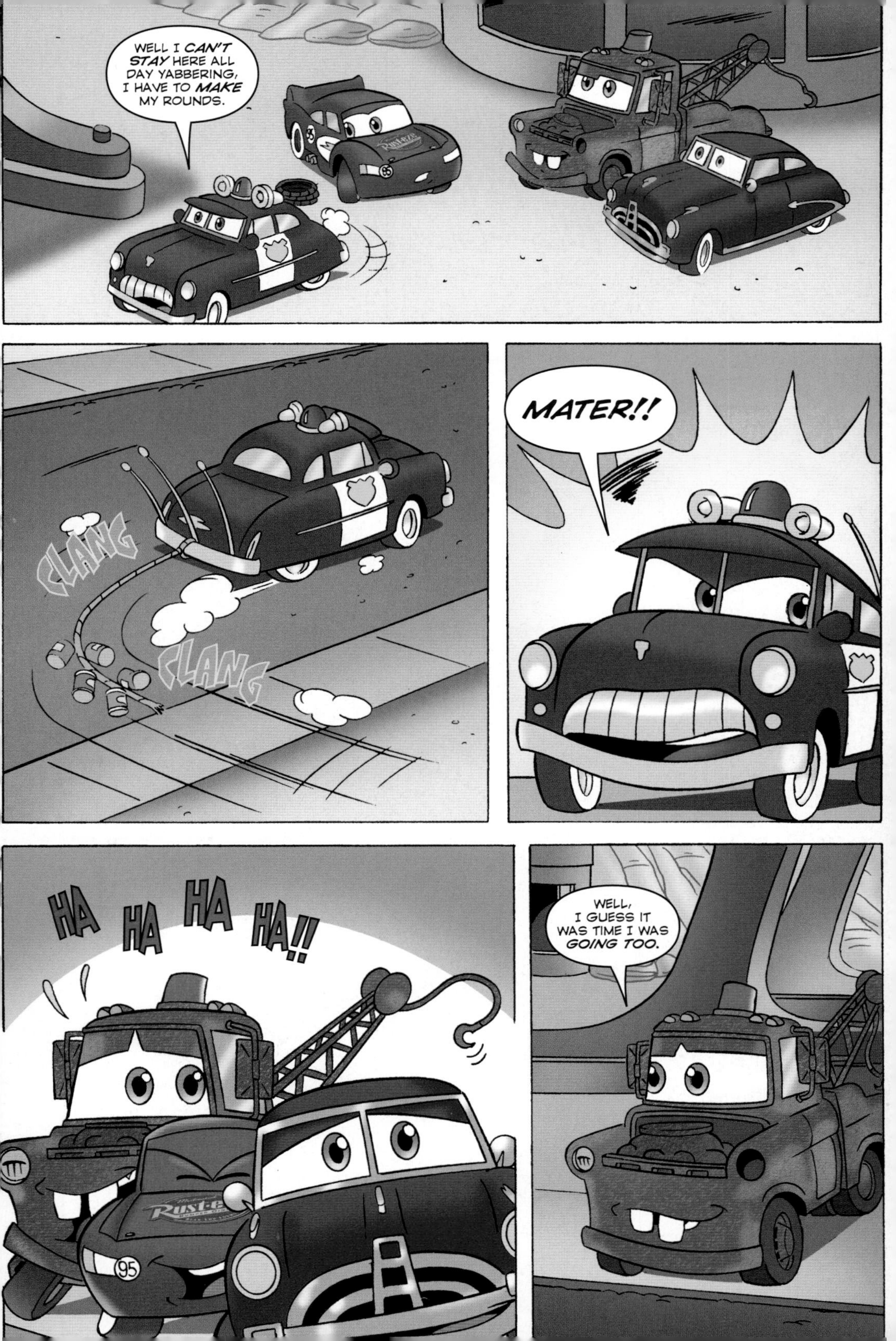
WELL I *CAN'T STAY* HERE ALL DAY YABBERING, I HAVE TO *MAKE* MY ROUNDS.
CLANG
CLANG
MATER!!
HA HA HA HA!!
WELL, I GUESS IT WAS TIME I WAS *GOING TOO.*

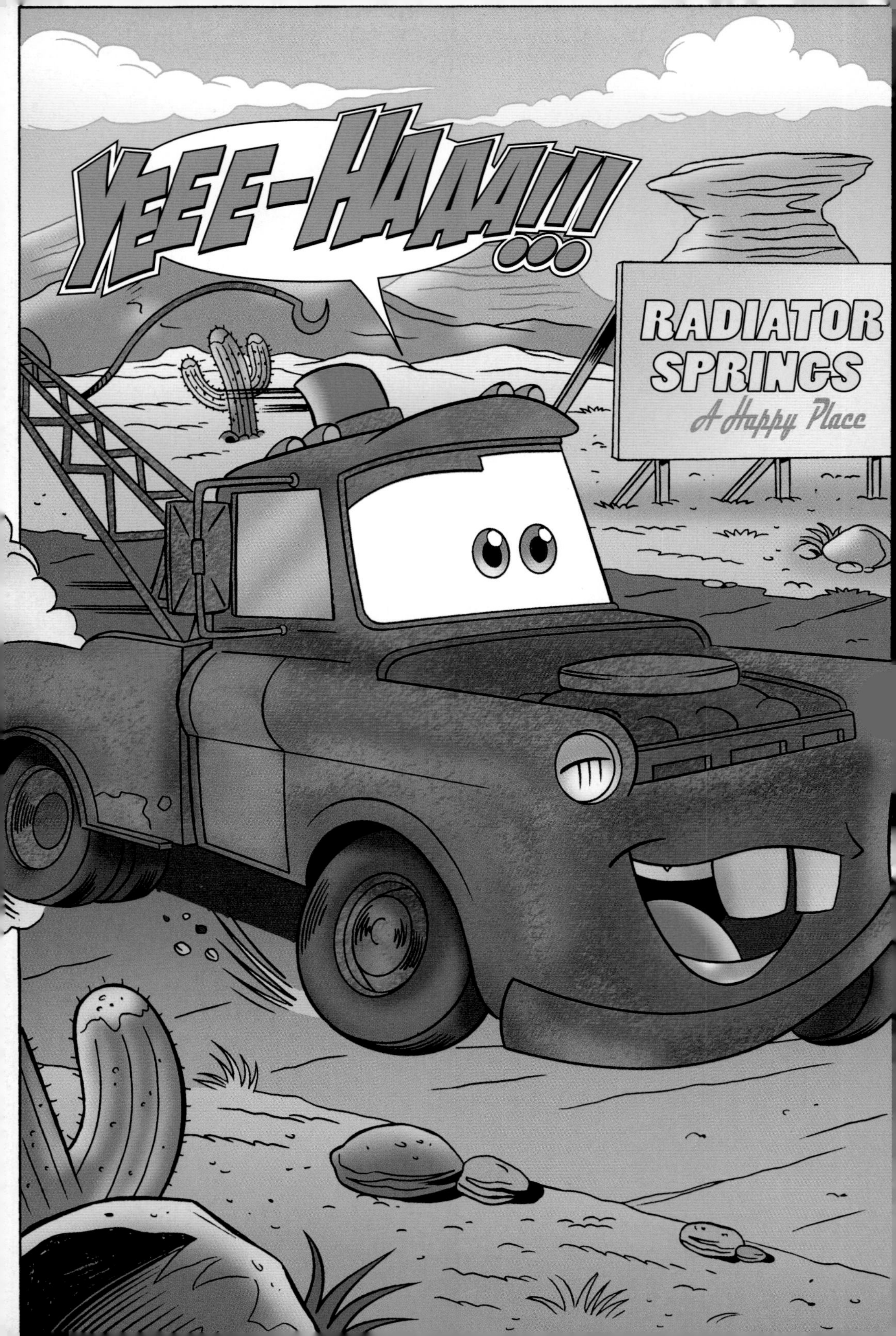
YEEEE-HAAA!!!
RADIATOR SPRINGS
A Happy Place

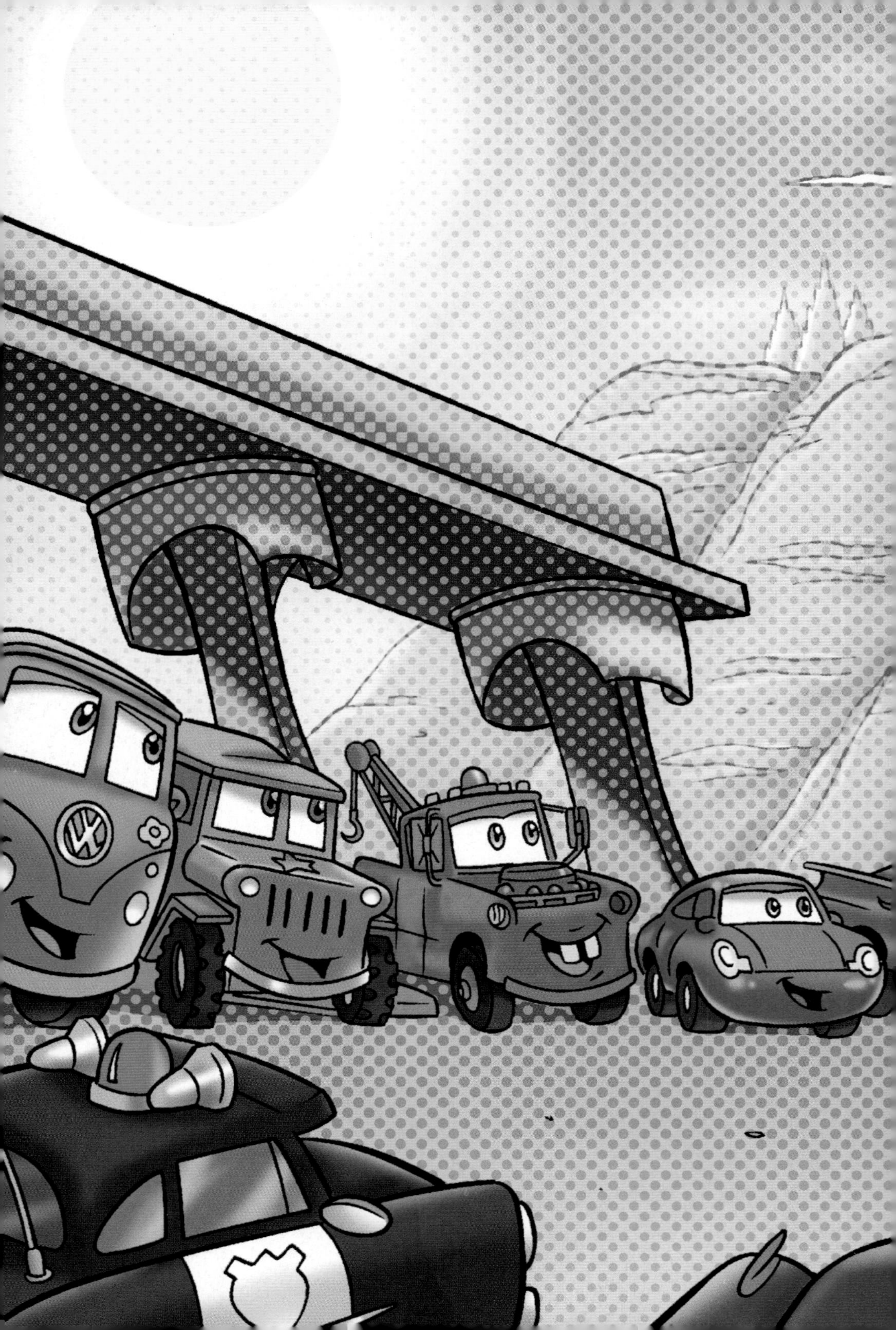

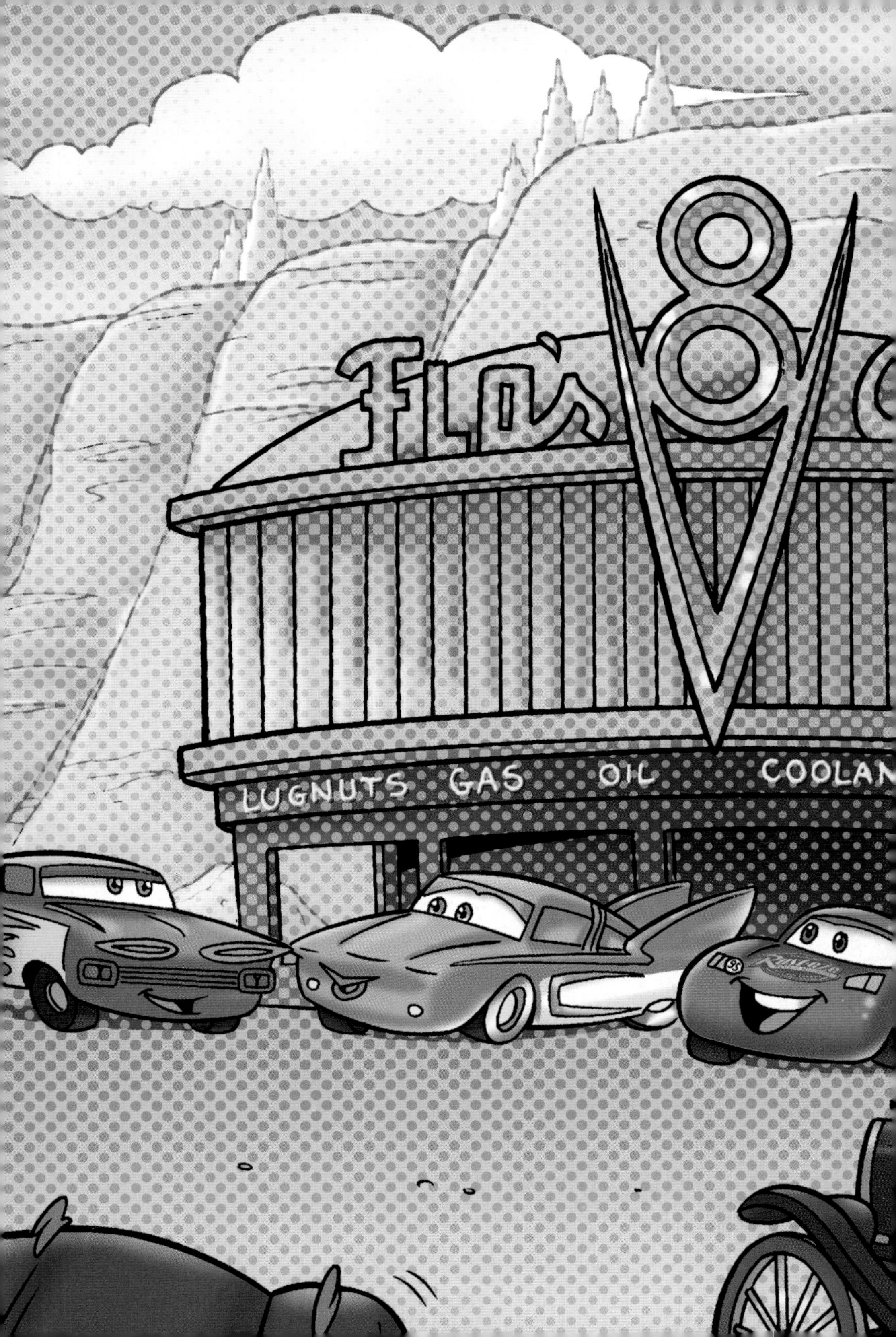
Flo's
LUGNUTS GAS OIL COOLAN

Disney · PIXAR

Cars

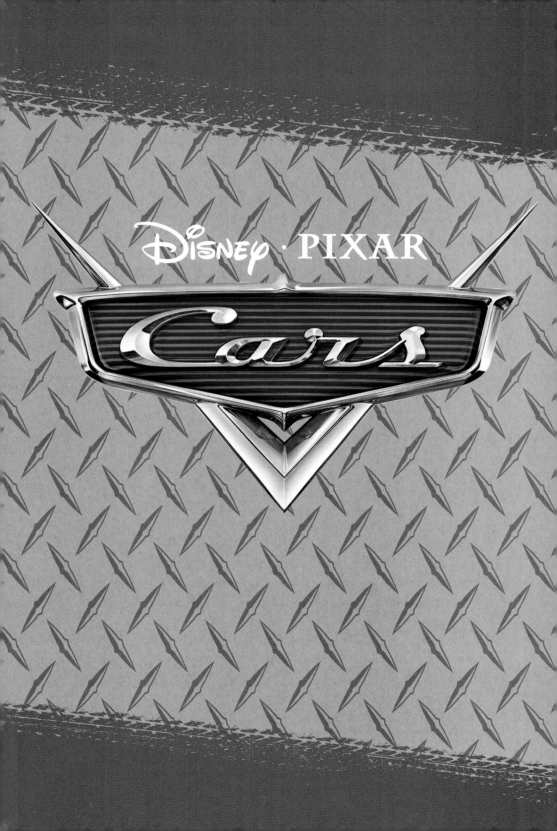

Cover Gallery

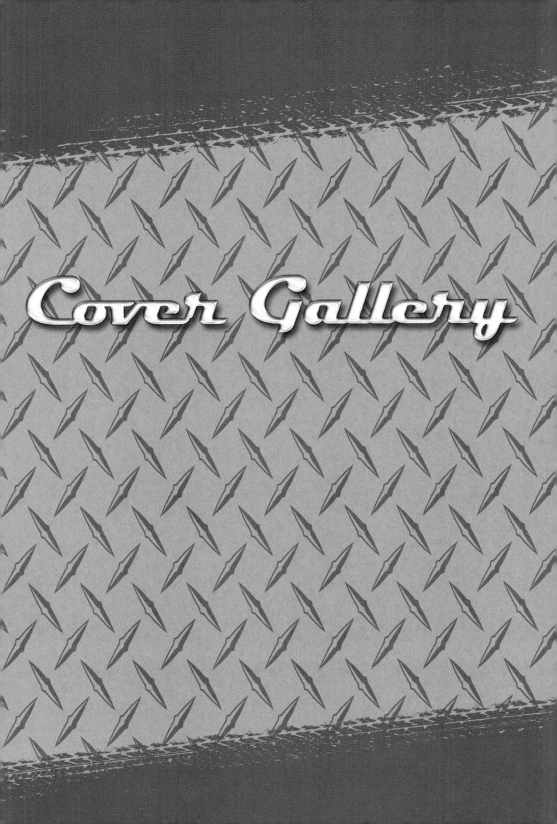

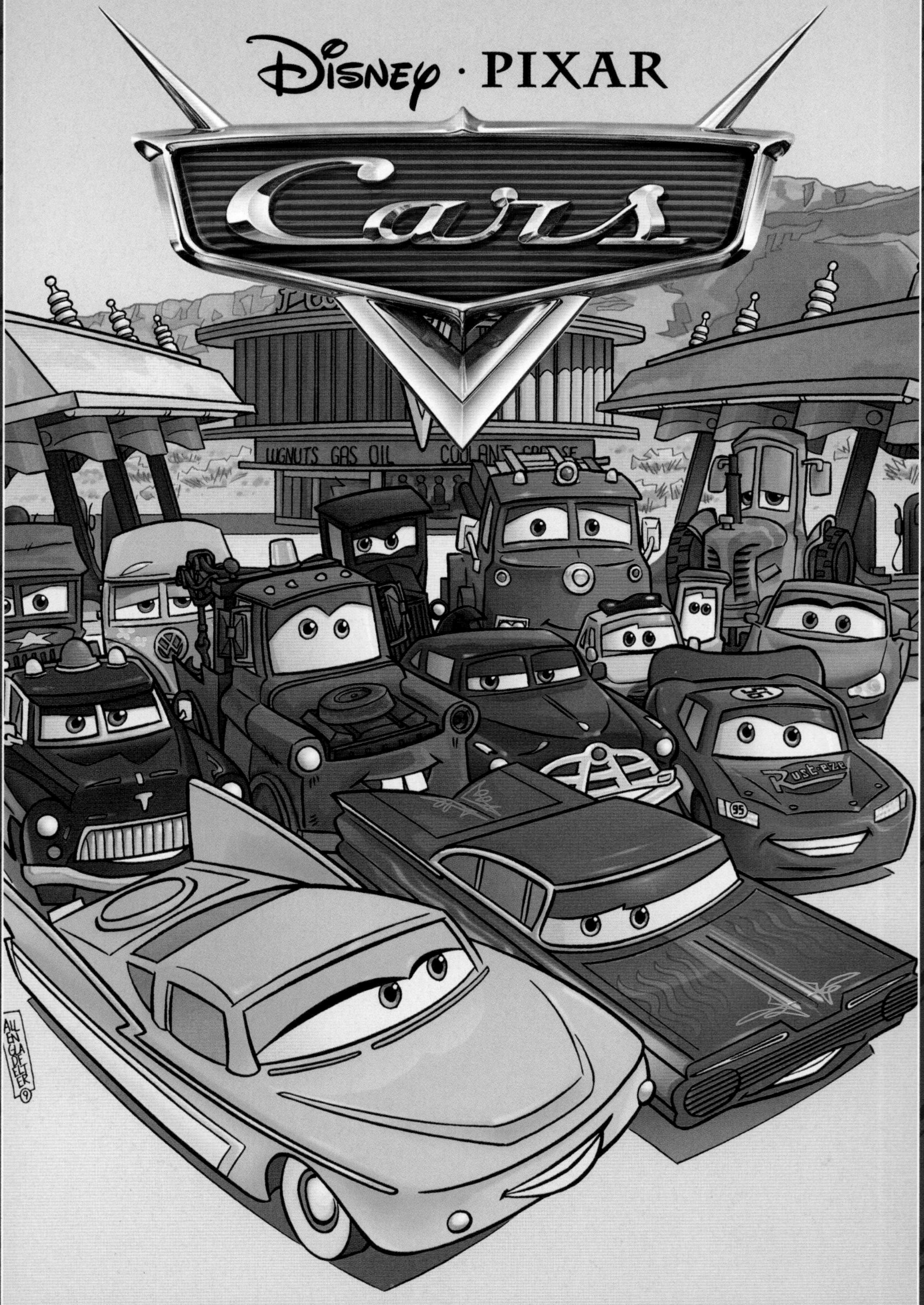
Disney · PIXAR
Cars
LUGNUTS GAS OIL
Rust-eze
95
ALLEN GLADFELTER

COVER 1A
ALLEN GLADFELTER

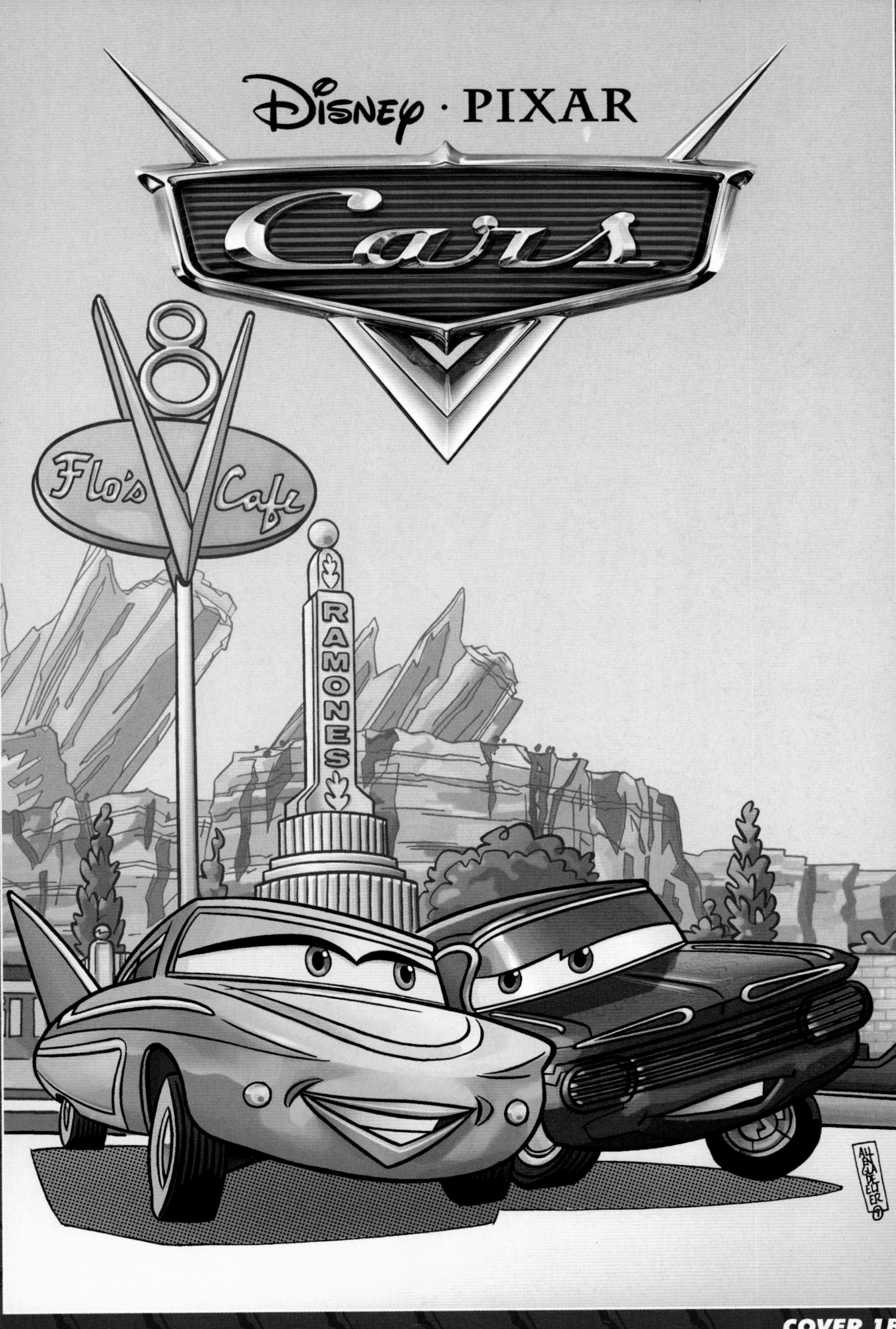
DISNEY · PIXAR
Cars
Flo's Cafe
RAMONES
ALLEN GLADFELTER

COVER 1B
ALLEN GLADFELTER

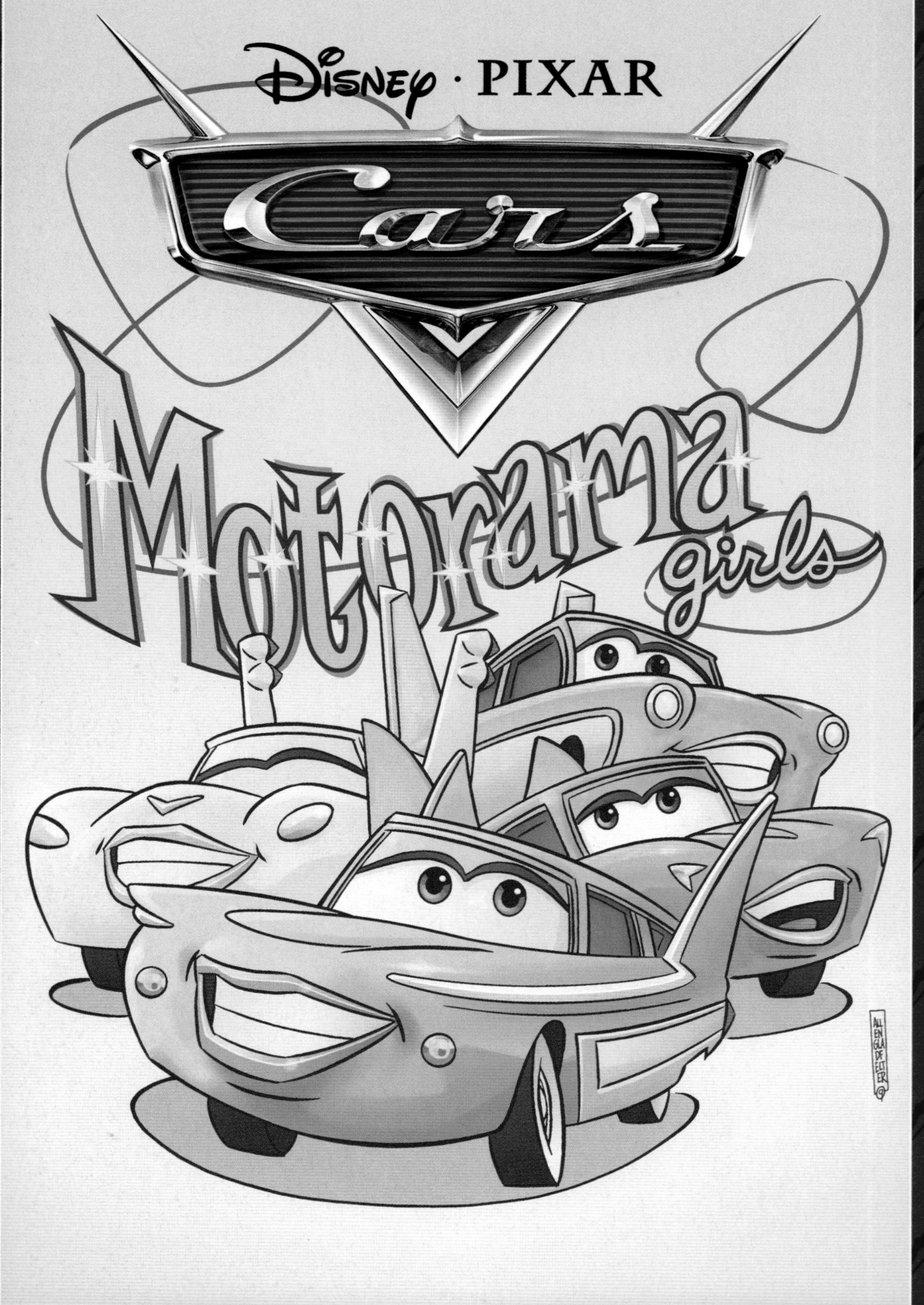
DISNEY · PIXAR
Cars
Motorama
girls
ALLEN GLADFELTER

COVER 1C
ALLEN GLADFELTER

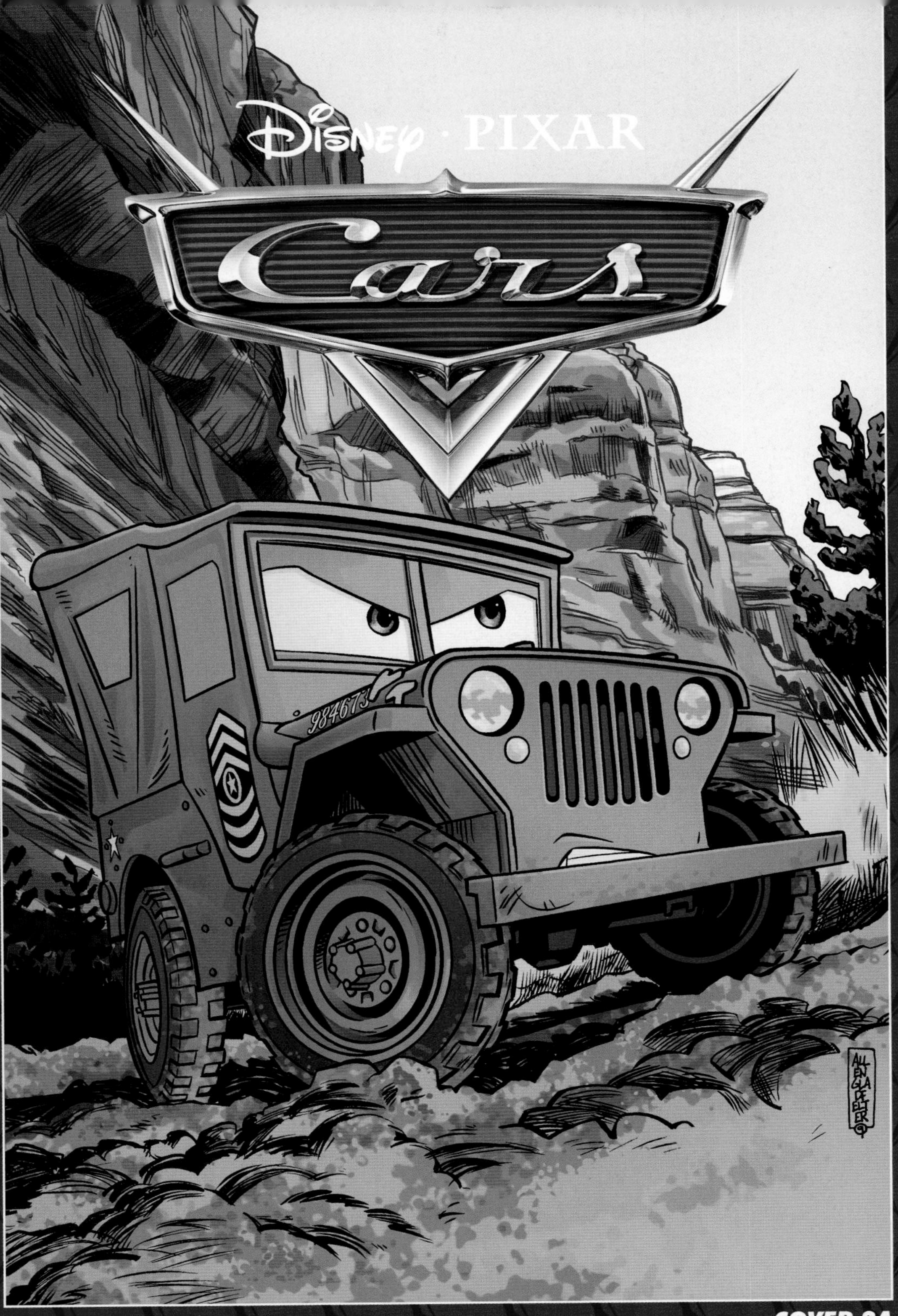
DISNEY · PIXAR
Cars
984673
ALLEN GLADFELTER

COVER 2A
ALLEN GLADFELTER

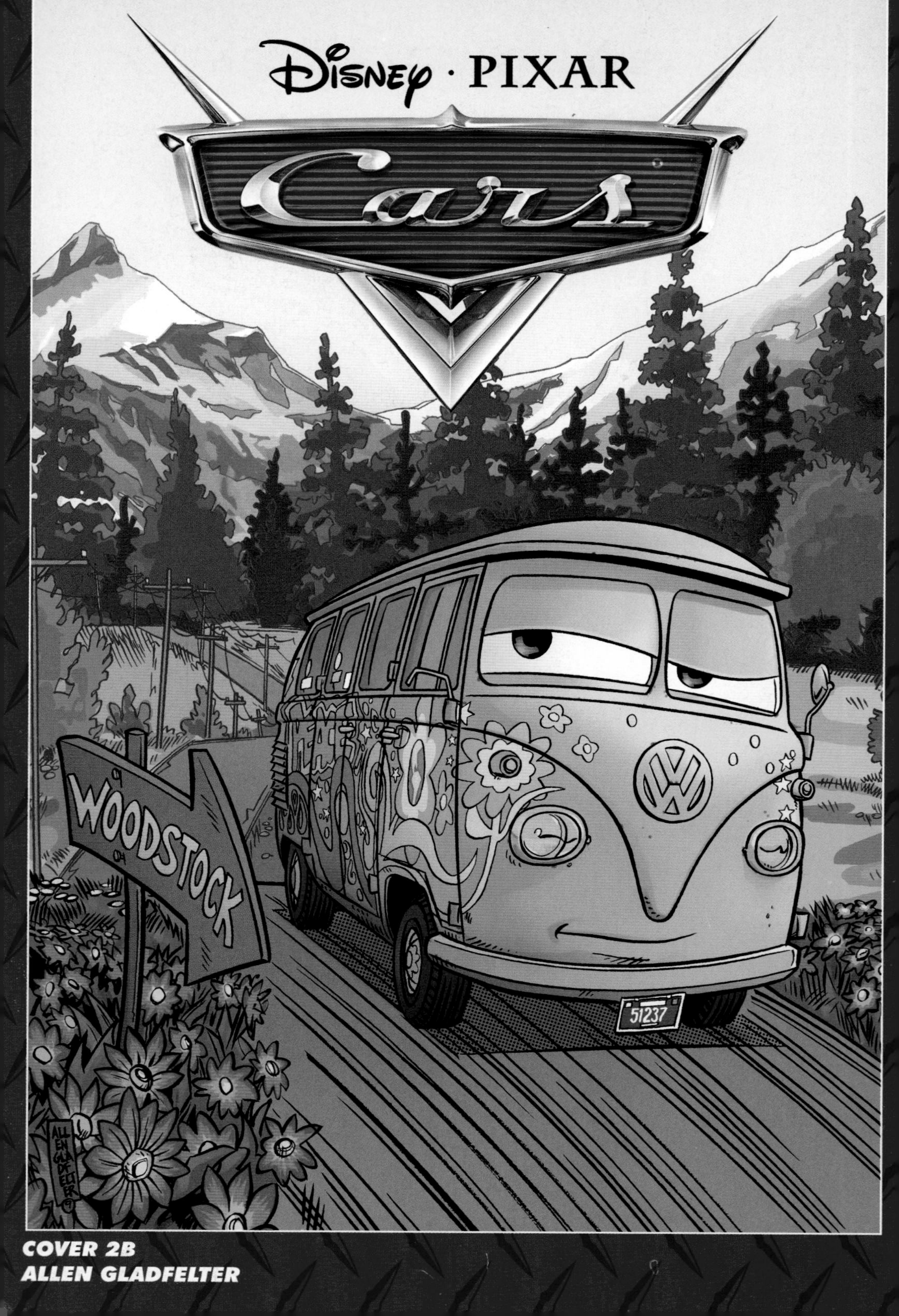
DISNEY · PIXAR
Cars
WOODSTOCK
51237

COVER 2B
ALLEN GLADFELTER

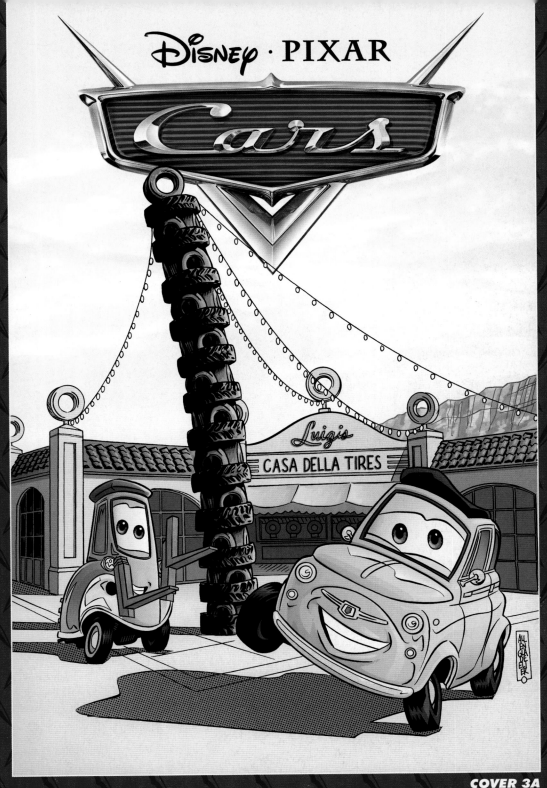

DISNEY · PIXAR

Cars

Luigi's
CASA DELLA TIRES

COVER 3A
ALLEN GLADFELTER

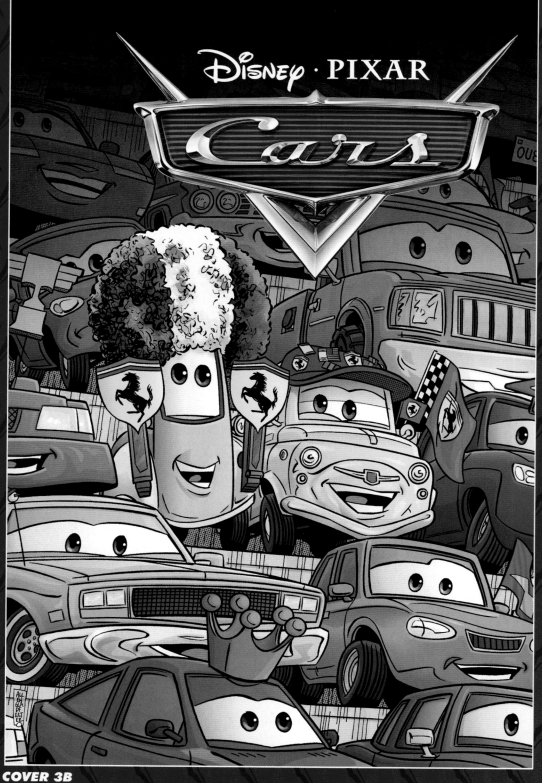

COVER 3B
ALLEN GLADFELTER

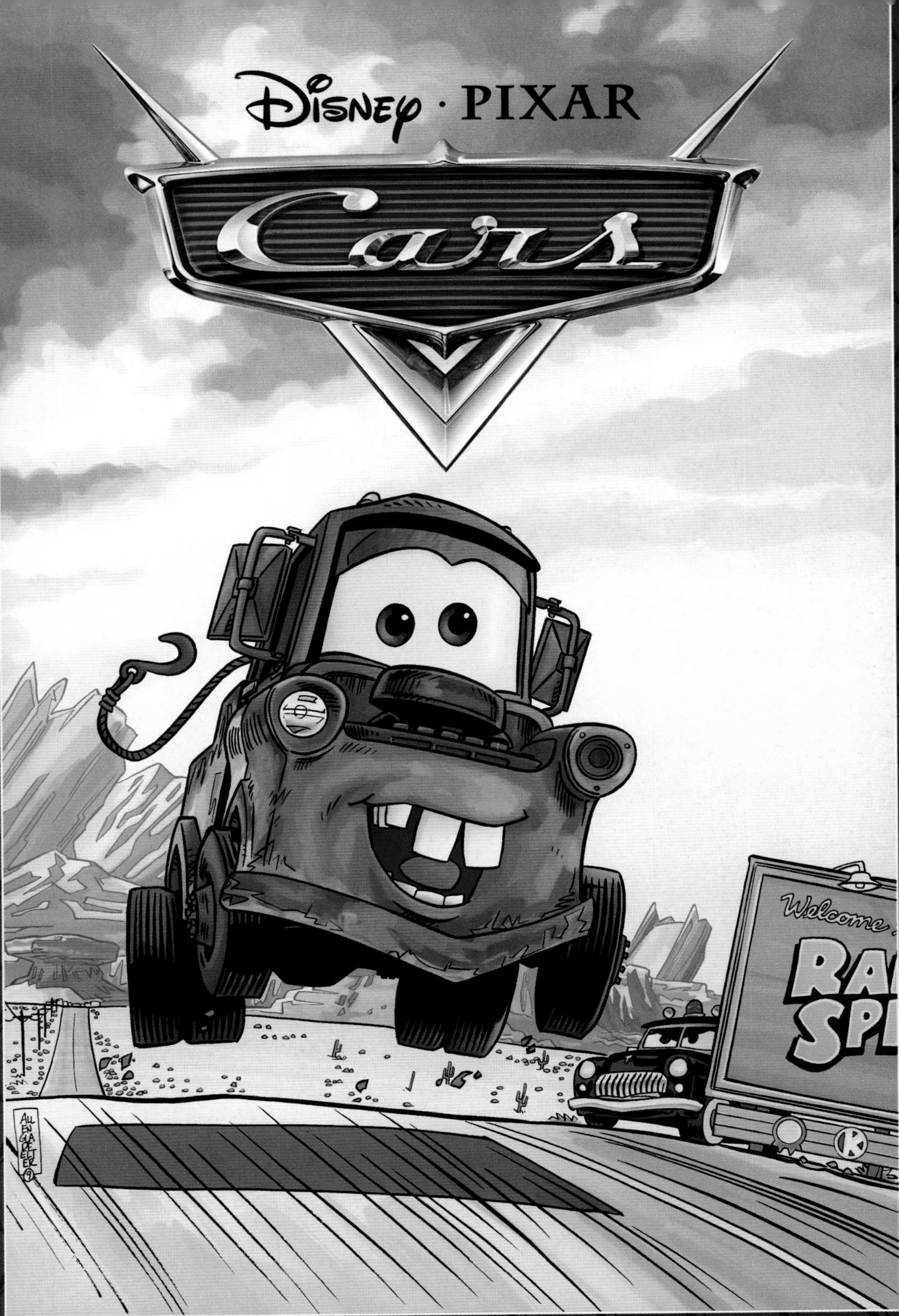
Disney · PIXAR
Cars
Welcome

COVER 4A
ALLEN GLADFELTER

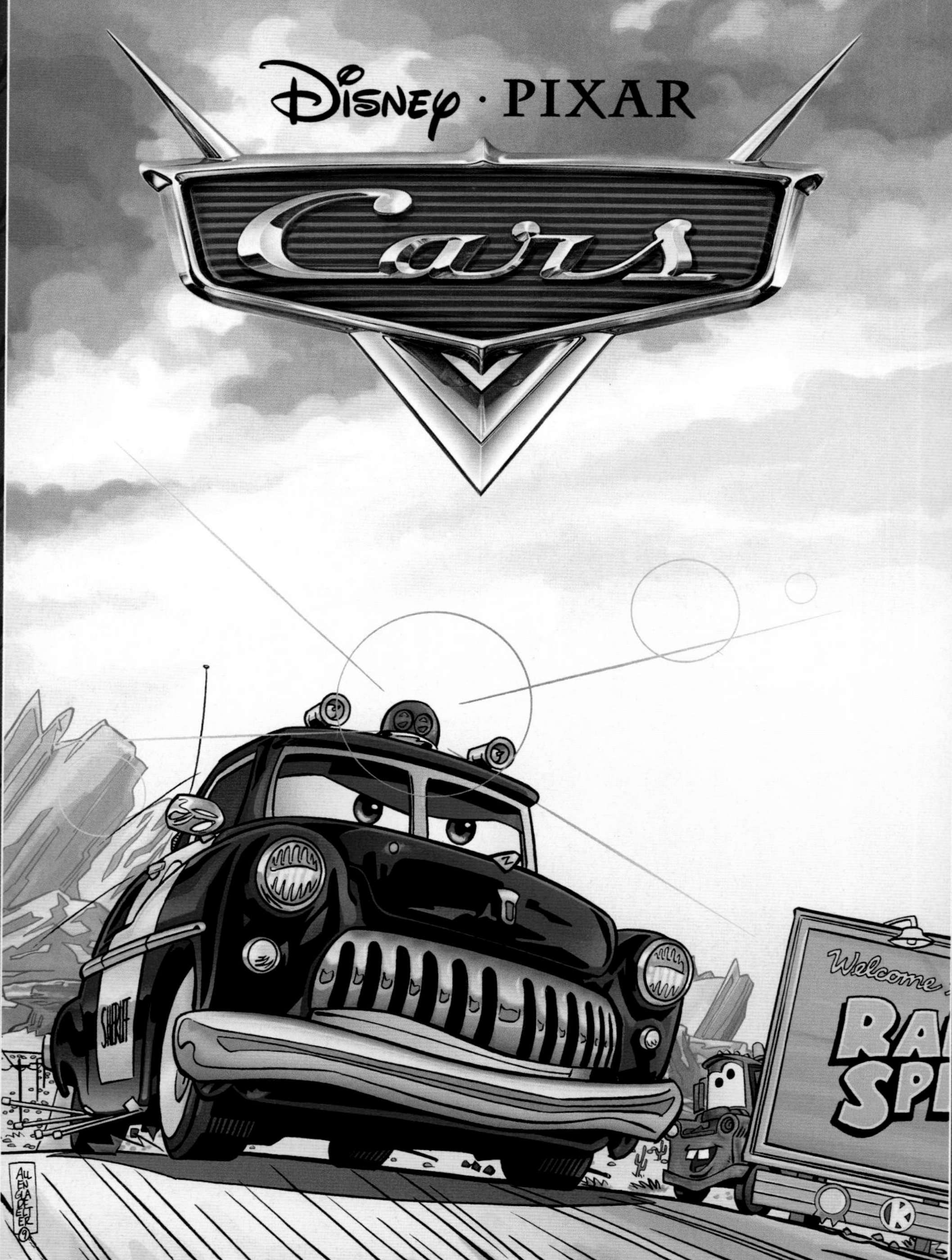
DISNEY · PIXAR
Cars
SHERIFF
Welcome

COVER 4B
ALLEN GLADFELTER

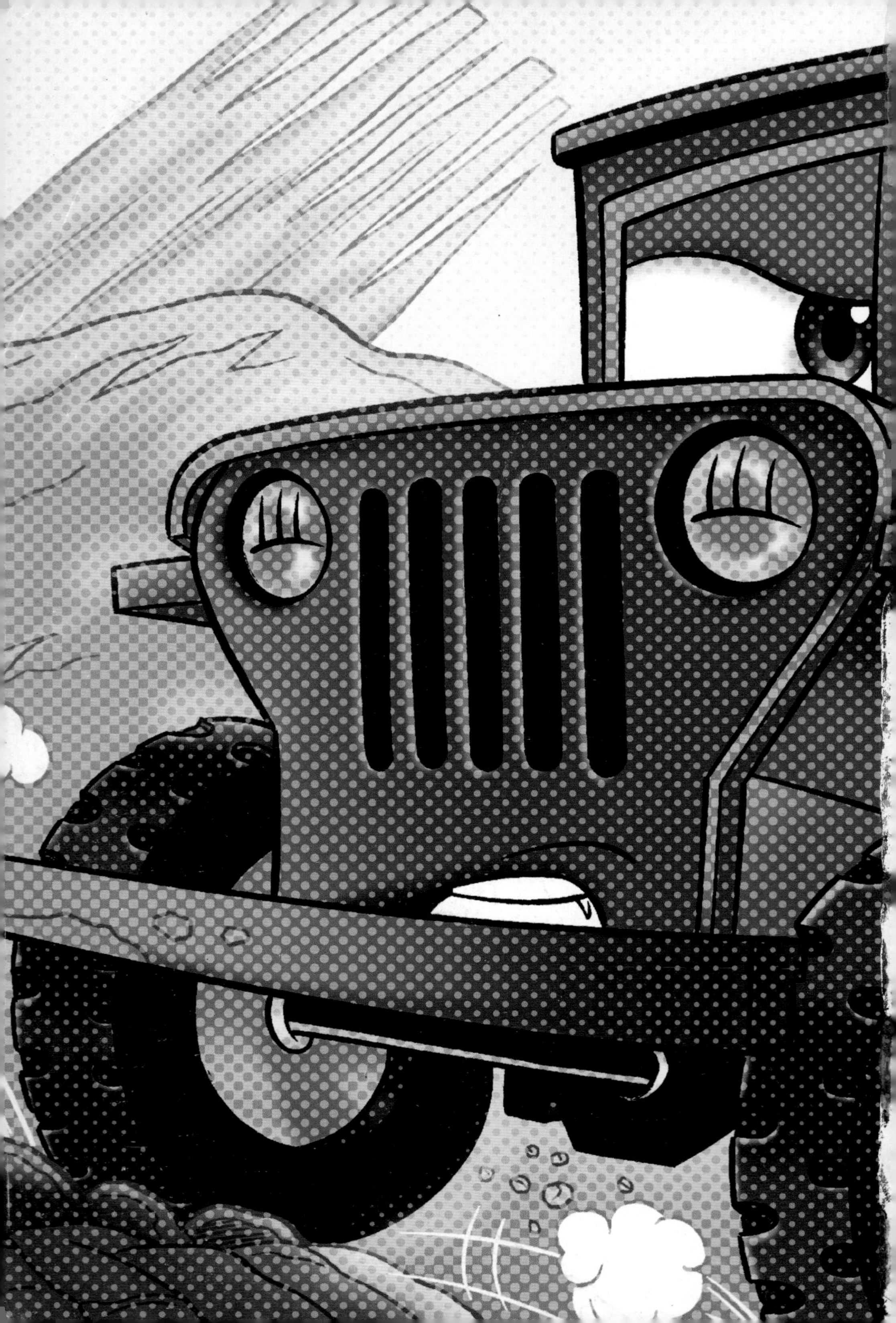